Pieces
of a
life

JEWEL E. ANN

PIECES OF A LIFE

COLTEN & JOSIE: PART ONE

JEWEL E. ANN

This book is a work of fiction. Any resemblances to actual persons, living or dead, events, or locales are purely coincidental.

Cover Designer: Jenn Beach

Photo: © Regina Wamba

Cover Models: Hannah Peltier and Jered Sternaman

Formatting: Jenn Beach

To that disturbing voice in my head ... you win.

Prologue

"MY DAD SAID I need to stay close to you until my mom comes back. He's afraid a bad person will hurt me."

While my mom zips the back of my white gown, I stare at the little girl before me.

So innocent.

So loved.

So beautiful.

Her dad is right. There are bad people who do bad things to children.

However, we are at a private venue surrounded by family and close friends. Whether it's right or not, this is the perfect example of allowing kids to roam freely until corralled at the last possible minute—there's an assumption that *someone* is watching them.

Her dad is feeling extra protective today because Winston Jeffries preyed on little girls running around at family events, like weddings, between 1892 and 1901. Nearly a decade of kidnapping. Nearly a decade of long hair hanging from trees in churchyards. Just the hair.

The bodies were never found.

Jeffries was convicted of thirty-seven counts of first-degree murder and hanged in Owensboro, Kentucky, on February 10, 1902 without a single body discovered.

He took the location of the bodies to his grave.

"A bad person, huh?"

The young girl nods, her long, dark curls and pink ribbons bouncing with each tip of her chin.

Her father's not worried about a mysterious "bad person." He's worried his bride might flee at the last second.

This girl has been sent here to keep an eye on me.

But why scare her? Why not just tell her I need help getting dressed? Why send her to deliver the one message that would make me want to kick off my heels, toss aside my veil, and run until my heart gives out?

"Mom, will you give us a minute?" I ask.

She straightens the skirt of my gown. "Sure. I need to check on your dad anyway."

When it's just the young girl and me, I bend down so we're at eye level. "Do you trust me?"

She nods slowly, eyes wide.

"I think your dad is scared. Will you help him not to be so scared?"

Another slow nod.

"It means you have to be brave too. You have to do something really brave and trust me that it's for the best. Can you do that?"

"I think so," she whispers.

I riffle through my mom's bag. She packed everything we could possibly need for any hiccup. My fingers curl around the orange-handled scissors, and I turn back to the girl. "Are you sure you're brave?"

She stares at the scissors and nods.

"And you trust me?"

"Y-yes ..."

"Come here."

She shuffles her pink shoes toward me.

"Turn around."

She turns around.

I remove the ribbon from the partial ponytail on the crown of her head. Then I tie it low, right above the nape of her neck.

She jumps when I cut her hair just above the tied ribbon, and the rest of her hair falls into a short bob around her chin when she turns toward me.

I smile, ignoring her parted lips and bugged-out eyes. "Take this to your dad and tell him you are safe. Then tell him I am just a star. If he takes a step back, he'll see the whole galaxy."

She hesitantly wraps her hand around the tail of hair.

"One more favor?" I turn and squat in front of her. "Unzip my dress."

CHAPTER

One

Seven months earlier ...

I COULD USE a naked body with a pulse. This thought summarizes my love life as I approach Paul Turner, my first swipe right in over a month.

Full head of blond hair neatly parted to the side.

Clean shaven.

Jeans, white button-down, and a navy blazer.

He'll work. My standards are at an all-time low.

Paul sips his water and surveys the restaurant, blue-eyed gaze snagging on me as I weave my way through the chattering crowd, clinking dinnerware, and the tantalizing aroma of garlic. When he smiles, the tension vanishes, leaving nothing but relief. He not only looks like his profile picture; he looks better than his profile picture. This never happens.

"Josephine?" He stands.

"Paul?" I smile as he nods. "You can call me Josie."

Paul gives me a hug instead of a handshake. We've been chatting online for weeks. I don't get a lot of hugs, which makes it easy to sink into his warm body.

A warm body ... I could use one of those too.

Warm.

Naked.

With a pulse.

"It's nice to finally meet in person," I say, taking a seat across from him.

"You look better than your profile picture." Appreciation seeps through his words.

My grin doubles. "Funny. I was thinking the same thing about you as I approached the table." In less than thirty seconds, I have a good feeling about Paul Turner. He doesn't appear nervous or awkward. Confident, but not overly so.

"Can I get you something to drink?" he asks.

"Water is fine. Thank you."

"Are you sure? They have an amazing house wine here."

"I'm sure. Please, however, order yourself a glass of wine. I'm going to jump straight into an appetizer because I skipped lunch today."

He laughs. "Sounds good."

We order drinks and appetizers while I contemplate my main course. He smiles a lot. I smile a lot. All the good vibes buzz around us.

"Did your niece have a nice birthday party?" I ask, lifting my gaze from the menu.

He narrows his eyes for a second. "Oh, that's right. I forgot I told you about that. Yes. It was extravagant. I fear when she turns five, anything short of a trip to Paris will be an epic disappointment."

"Is she an only child?"

Paul gives me a few more details about his family, and his love for them bleeds through each word. He's originally from Vermont, and he's lived here in Chicago for five years as a cosmetic chemist. Paul swiped right because we both have degrees in the sciences.

"So how do you like Chicago? It has to be quite the change of pace from Des Moines."

My head bobs several times as my stomach growls waiting for the appetizers. "It is, but I feel at home with my job."

"And you like your job?"

I sip my water before nodding. "I do."

"That's good." Paul sets his menu aside and unwraps his silverware, depositing the cloth napkin on his lap. "It takes the right kind of personality to work in a lab. My friends think I have a cool job. I mean ... I formulate cosmetics, but when they find out I'm tucked away in a lab all day, it loses its luster. I bet you get the same thing."

"Yeah, it's not as uh..." I clear my throat "...glamorous as other jobs."

"I can imagine people perk up when they hear you're a doctor. You think doctor and immediately you think *saving lives*. But I suppose working in pathology you're catching things like early stages of cancer, and in some ways, you're saving lives as much if not more than other doctors. Right?"

Saving lives? Not exactly.

I find a subtle smile to accompany my slight nod. "I worked in surgery for just under a year. So I'd never take anything away from other doctors. I solve mysteries."

"What's the hardest part?" Paul asks, and I wish we could steer the conversation in a different direction. Talking about jobs this much on a first date is as disappointing as talking about the weather until the main meal arrives.

"The hardest part is dealing with the death of young children."

"Yeah, I can see that."

"So, Paul, do you travel much?" I make the conversation go in a more acceptable direction. Paul bites, gobbling up my questions like Pac-Man. There are no awkward moments of silence. We cruise through dinner and dessert with each topic of conversation smoothly shifting to a new topic. This is how a date is supposed to go, and I'm hopeful that it won't end when we leave the restaurant.

"I'm going to use the men's room quickly." Paul

stands after paying the check, even though I argue that the first date should be separate checks.

Feeling good about the start to my weekend, I watch his smooth gait drift toward the back of the restaurant.

"Josie Watts?"

No.

No. No. No.

That familiar voice at my back—familiar like a paper cut eliciting a grimace and a silent expletive— brings every hair on my neck to attention, ready for battle.

Turning, my lips find a neutral position short of an actual smile. That dark hair is as unkempt as it was the last time I saw it, nearly seventeen years ago. Same irritating smirk. Same glimmer of antagonism in his monster-like brown and gold eyes. He's a dimple shy of being that guy every girl swoons over in high school then despises the rest of her life. "Colten." His name still leaves a sour taste in my mouth.

"Wow! How long has it been?" he asks.

Not long enough is my answer, but I don't offer it to him.

"I heard you went to medical school."

"Did you?" I press my lips together for a beat. "I heard that too."

He laughs, angling his body a little more.

"Eating alone?" I eye his table set for one.

"I am. I'm comfortable in my own skin. Besides, I like listening to the interesting conversations around me. A pathologist. That's impressive, Josie. Well done. I can see you hunched over a microscope."

"Good to know you *heard* I went to medical school, and you can *see* me hunched over a microscope. Are your other senses working well too?"

Colten laughs again.

I've always been his favorite source of amusement. It started in fourth grade. The seventeen-year break from his torment has been nice.

"Still quick-witted. I'd forgotten how much I loved your feistiness."

"Ready?" Paul saves the day with his return.

"Absolutely." I stand, tossing my napkin on the table.

"Aren't you going to introduce me to your friend?" Colten has the nerve to ask me.

"No," I say, hooking my handbag onto my shoulder while glaring at him. More than a decade and a half should be long enough to bury all hatchets, yet I feel eighteen again and equally as livid. No scientist has been able to prove the existence of time, so in some ways, I am and always will be eighteen and despise Colten Mosley.

He knows what he did. And he knows where he can go for it.

As soon as I escape Colten and step out into the early June sunset, Paul invites me to his place. It's a no-brainer. I'm thirty-five. What I do with my body is no longer a measure of my virtue. However, when Paul makes me breakfast Saturday morning, it's a positive measure of his virtue. After a long kiss at his door, we make plans for dinner midweek. This might be something.

MONDAY MORNING, I sweat at Pilates, grab a breakfast sandwich and coffee, meet in the conference room with twelve other pathologists, and then gown up in the county medical examiner's locker room in time to meet my two bodies for the day.

A possible overdose and a suspected homicide.

I start with the suspected homicide because there's something about the missing legs that calls to me. An hour later, I nearly bobble the liver right onto the floor when I hear an unwelcome voice behind me.

"Never saw this coming. Dr. Josephine Watts, M.D. Assistant Medical Examiner? No fucking way." Colten Mosley chuckles.

I recover the liver before it slips past my clawing fingers and secure it at the end of the table where the decedent's legs should be. Then I glance over my shoulder while a masked Colten makes his way into my view—suit, tie, and that messy excuse for a hair-style. "What are you doing here?"

"Detective Mosley..." he flashes his badge "...homi-cide. I started last week after working in Indianapolis for five years. I wanted to move closer to home. The real question is what are *you* doing?"

"What does it look like I'm doing?"

"I'd say you're up to your elbows in vital organs, but you told your Friday night fling that you work in a lab. A nerd hunched over a microscope. This is ... not the same thing, Josie."

"I'm a pathologist. And I do have a lab with a microscope. What's your point?" I glance up and reach for my scalpel.

"*This* is not what your date pictured. I can guarantee that. Not gonna lie ... this isn't what I pictured either when my mom told me you got into medical school."

"I don't care what you pic—"

"I pictured..." he cuts me off, sliding his hands into his pockets "...a dress hugging your curves, stopping right above the knees, high heels, sexy lab coat, hair down, maybe nerdy glasses sitting low on your nose. Not this astronaut getup with a black apron, goggles, and a face shield. And I guarantee Mr. Friday Night didn't picture you in this. Unless ... did you tell him the rest? Did you tell him you're not *just* a pathologist, but a forensic pathologist who plays around in the cavities of dead bodies like a toddler in a sandbox?"

"What do you want, Mosley? I'm too busy with my real job to play cops and robbers with you today. So if that badge is real, then you'd better have a good reason for interrupting me." I glance around the autopsy suite for Alicia or one of the other assistants, someone to force *Detective Mosley* to get to his point and leave me alone.

"We canvassed the entire area, and we can't find a

weapon. I thought you might tell me what we're looking for."

"An eighteen-volt circular saw with a seven-and-a-quarter inch blade. Six-foot cord. Zero to fifty-one degree bevel angle range. Adjustable cutting depth. Red handle."

"How do you know the handle's red?" Colten asks.

I grin behind my mask and shield. I've waited for what seems like forever to be the one on top. "Because you don't saw off two legs without a little blood splatter. But really, your question should be how I know the cord is six feet long."

"How do you know that?"

Glancing up again, I wait for him to realize I just ate his lunch.

"Jesus ... you don't know shit about the weapon, do you?" he asks.

"Weapon or tool? If the cause of death didn't involve a weapon, then you're merely looking for the tool that was used to remove the legs. Now ... get out of here. When I know something that you need to know, I'll let you know. Breathing down my neck won't expedite anything."

"Oh, Watts, I'm not breathing down your neck." He heads toward the exit. "If I were, you'd feel weak in the knees."

"Or ... I'd vomit." My comeback bounces off the door that shuts before my words stumble out of my mouth.

I hate him. He's always one step ahead of me.

CHAPTER

Two

I MET Josephine Watts the summer before fourth grade. While I wasn't thrilled about moving to Des Moines, my dad landed the head boys' basketball coaching job at the high school, and the cost of living allowed us to have a bigger house—aka my own bedroom.

"Better stay out of trouble," Dad said, squeezing my shoulder as my older brother and I helped Mom unpack the dishes. "Our new neighbor is the Chief of Police. Just met him while he and his son were getting ready to go fishing. They hunt too."

"Great. Neighbors who are gun obsessed," Mom murmured.

"Not everyone hunts with a gun, Becca." Dad slapped her butt like he did to his players. Then, he winked at me like I needed to take notes so I could slap my wife's butt someday too.

"How old is their son? Do they have other kids?" Mom quizzed Dad. He opened the fridge as if some food fairy filled it before our arrival. No such luck.

"I don't know if they have other kids. I didn't ask. His son, Joe, is Colten's age."

"Really? My age?" I perked up. Hunting and fishing weren't my favorite pastimes; in fact, I knew nothing about either one. However, the idea of making a friend before school started easing my anxiety a bit.

As soon as Mom dismissed me from helping her in the kitchen, I ran up to my room. Mine. It was all mine. No more bunkbeds. No more of Chad's dirty underwear being tossed on my pillow, streak side down. No more "accidentally" breaking my Lego creations or wiping boogers on my baseball glove.

It took me the better part of the afternoon to get my room organized. Mom was a stickler on cleanliness, except with Chad. Apparently, his ADHD diagnosis gave him an exemption from hanging up his shirts and dumping his dirty underwear in the hamper.

I tacked up my final poster to the wall, Hank Aaron, while the neighbors pulled into their driveway. The police chief climbed out of the black pickup truck as his son jumped down from the other side. A fishing hat with dangling lures covered his head.

Tan, scrawny legs, baggy shorts, and a green tee— nothing like his intimidating father with shoulders twice

15

as broad as my dad's and calves the size of tree trunks. The kid had to be the runt of the litter. My enthusiasm lost momentum. My *one* friend for the first day of school wasn't going to be the most popular kid, that was for sure.

With no lack of confidence, I headed downstairs and straight to the door. "Mom, I'm going to meet the boy next door." Figured I might as well befriend him early. Without at least one friend, it was going to be a long summer. And I sure as heck wasn't going to rely on Chad to entertain me. All he did was play stupid video games. I wasn't sure his skin ever saw the sun.

"Don't play with any weapons," Mom replied.

I rolled my eyes. "Okay."

Their garage door was open, and my steps faltered for a second when two freaky eyes peered at me. It was a deer head mounted to the garage wall. Before I could make it to the front door, it opened.

"Hi. Are you the new kid?" A girl in jean shorts and a pink tee grinned at me. Her teeth looked extra white behind her deep red lips and tan skin. Hair as black as my brother's fingernail (the one Mom said might fall off) caught in the breeze and blew into her face as she peeled it away.

"Yeah. I wanted to meet your brother. I guess we're going to be in the same grade."

"I don't have a brother."

I stepped onto the stoop and shoved my hands into the pockets of my shorts. "Haha. My dad already talked to your dad, so I know you have a brother. And I watched him get out of the truck a few minutes ago…" I turned to point at my window facing the street "...from my bedroom window."

"That was me."

"Why are you being weird?" I tilted my head to the side. "I know what I saw. And my dad's not a liar. And I know your brother's name is Joe."

"You saw *me*. And my name is Josephine. My friends call me Josie. And my dad calls me Jo because I was supposed to be a boy."

I shake my head. "The kid who got out of the truck was wearing shorts and a green shirt."

"Yeah. And it smelled like fish, so I changed my clothes. Do you want to come inside?"

"Not if you don't have a brother."

"That's ..." She twisted her lips together as her fists perched onto her hips. "Rude."

"I'm not being rude."

"You don't want to be my friend because I'm a girl. That's rude."

"I don't play with dolls and dress up stuffed animals."

"Do you eat cookies and drink chocolate milk?"

After thinking about it for a few seconds, I nodded.

"Good. So do I. Come on." She turned and left the door open, disappearing to the right.

I glanced back at the street, giving a quick look right then left before taking slow steps into the house. More animal heads mounted to the wall peered at me along with a big fish and some kind of bird on a shelf that looked quite real.

"Where are your parents?" I asked, peeking around the corner into the kitchen as she poured two glasses of chocolate milk.

"My dad's rubbing my mom's feet in the bedroom. They're huge! She's pregnant, and I guess being pregnant makes your feet and ankles get really big, and that makes them hurt."

I nodded slowly while she climbed onto the kitchen stool and opened a Tupperware container of chocolate chip cookies.

"So what's your name?" Josie asked, setting a cookie on a napkin for me right next to hers.

"Colten."

"Where did you come from?"

"Across the street."

"Duh. Where did you live before you moved into the house across the street?"

I stammered a second. She had me flustered because she was a girl, a pretty girl, with as much if not more confidence than I had. "Houston, Texas."

"Are you a cowboy?"

"No. Why?"

She lifted a shoulder and dropped it just as quickly while dipping part of her cookie into her chocolate milk. "I thought there were a lot of cowboys in Texas ... which is weird because we have a lot of cows here in Iowa, but I don't see that many cowboys."

I couldn't start my first day of school with only one friend—a girl. But school wasn't starting for two months, so I didn't see anything wrong with being

Josie's "neighborhood friend" just until I found boys my age. After all, the cookies were the best thing I'd ever tasted, and I liked watching Josie.

Her smile.

The way she flipped her hair over her shoulder.

Even the way she whisper-counted to ten every time she dipped her cookie in milk.

"Have you ever seen the exoskeleton of a cockroach under a magnifying glass?" she asked before starting her silent count again with her next bite of cookie dipped into the milk.

"I don't know if I've ever seen a live cockroach."

"Oh, it's not alive, silly. It's dead. I have a lot of dead stuff in my room. Want to see?"

And just like that ... the hair-tossing and whisper-counting became the least fascinating thing about Josephine Watts.

CHAPTER

Three

"YOU'RE BREAKING MY HEART, Dr. Watts."

On the verge of grabbing my bag and heading home for the day, I glance up from my desk. The irony ...

I'm breaking his heart? I'm pretty sure he obliterated mine on more than one occasion, which proves one thing: he has no heart.

"Who keeps the citizens of Chicago safe while you're stalking me, Detective Mosley?"

"I bet it felt nice to put on makeup and wear a bra for your date the other night?"

I'm wearing a bra. *Asshole.*

Glancing down at my chest, I curl my shoulders inward when I notice my nipples. I'm wearing a *thin* bra.

But still ... he's an asshole.

"You were supposed to call me with the results of the autopsy."

"I talked to Detective Rains. Cardiac arrest due to major blood loss. The decedent was alive when his legs were amputated."

"Why?" Uninvited, Colten takes a seat in the chair across from me.

"It's extremely hard to profile a ghost. When you catch your killer, plenty of qualified people will dissect his life and motives."

"No." Colten shakes his head. "Why did you talk to Detective Rains instead of me?"

"Because I like him better than I like you."

"Oh ..." He nods and smirks. "So you do, in fact, like me?"

"I like your parents ..." My scowl softens as I keep my gaze on my computer screen. "I liked your parents. I haven't talked to your mom in years, but I was brokenhearted when I heard about your dad. I'm sorry, Colten."

"Good old dad hung himself." He blows out a long breath, staring at my framed certificates on the wall. "I didn't even come home for the funeral. Fuck it. If I mattered to him, he wouldn't have killed himself."

I deal with a lot of grief in my job. I talk to families daily, explaining *what* and sometimes *why* something happened to their loved ones. But suicide doesn't usually come with a clear "why" answer. "I know you weren't there."

Colten returns his attention to me. "My mom told

me you were at the funeral."

With a slow nod, I shut off my computer. "I wasn't there for you."

He grunts. "Of course you weren't. Nobody gave a shit about me, especially my dad."

"How rich of you to play that part."

"What part?" Those monster-like eyes narrow at me.

"You're fine with people being shit on as long as it's not you."

Colten's dark brows lift a fraction. "Oh, this is about that? You think I shit on you."

I *know* he shit ... shat ... crapped all over me.

"I'm referring to your mom and brother. When you don't show up to be with them—the living—that's pretty shitty. Even for you."

"I visited them the following week. I helped go through his stuff."

I open my mouth to say more, exchange another barb, but I close it just as quickly. "Detective Rains has everything you need to know. And for the record, I was right about the weapon. And if you find it, and it has a red handle and a six-foot cord, I expect something like a fruit and chocolate bouquet with a note that says I'm the goddamn queen of forensic pathology." Standing, I sling my bag over my shoulder, give him a tight-lipped grin, and fish my keys out of the side pocket.

"I knew you were smart to a fault, Watts. But this..." Colten stands and takes several steps toward the door before glancing over his shoulder "...is a godlike arrogance I never saw coming from you. I imagine you're a pain in the ass to work with. We should grab dinner sometime."

"Can't. I'm busy." I usher him out the door so I can close and lock it.

"I didn't say when."

"I know." I pass him on my way to the stairs. "I meant I'm busy *never* having dinner with you. Not having dinner or any interaction with you outside of work is officially my new pastime."

"Jesus, Watts. You're still boring as fuck if avoiding me is your pastime. But I'm flattered that you're spending so much time thinking about me. Feels like old times."

I race down the stairs. "I'm not thinking about you. I'm actively *not* thinking about YOUUUUUU!" My foot catches and I fall down the final four steps.

My head. Oh, my aching head. My fingers reach for the laceration at my temple.

"Josie, just ... don't move. You could have broken something." Colten flies down the stairs after me.

I broke something alright. My pride, her sister Dignity, and Dignity's cousin Self-Esteem. It's taken Colten less than a week to reduce me to the young, shattered-ego girl I was the day I left for college. He's a perpetual thorn in my side. He's necrotizing fasciitis—a flesh eating infection that can't be contained.

"I'm fine." I search for my feet to get them under me so I can make another mad dash.

"You really need to hold still and let me call for

help."

"When you..." standing, I grimace "...finish medical school, I'll let you give me advice on my health. In the meantime, just stay away. You're nothing but bad luck."

"Are you blaming your clumsiness on me?" Colten's jaw unhinges like I offended his fragile, Good Samaritan soul.

I blame everything bad in my life on Colten Mosley. Always have. Why stop now?

As I dig into my bag for a tissue, Colten grabs my arm and pulls me toward the restroom. The men's room.

"Let go of me. I don't appreciate being manhandled."

"Really?" He opens the door and forces me inside without checking for occupants. Luckily there are none. "Huh. You used to love my hands on you. Handling you."

Asshole.

"I have an open wound, and you think the best idea is to get me closer to urinals?"

He grabs a wad of paper towels and runs them under the water. "I'm pretty sure I can assess your wound and decide if you need stitches without an actual medical degree. Basic first aid training, Watts. Or did you become a forensic pathologist because you couldn't save lives? Did you get demoted to the morgue? Can't kill anyone if everyone's already dead."

"Asshole." I could only keep it in my head for so

long. He's the *worst!* And when I'm in his presence, I'm the worst version of myself too.

"You remember what I used to do when you called me that?" He presses the wet towels to my injured head.

He used to kiss me. I'd get mad. Call him an asshole. And he'd kiss me until I lost all my fight. He called me a stubborn overthinker. As if one can really think too much.

"You manhandled me. And I hated it." I frown, averting my gaze to the side.

"You loved it."

"That's what your inflated ego said to ease your conscience of the burden of truth."

"And what was the truth?"

I force myself to look at him. "You were a control freak. And clearly you never grew out of it."

He flinches.

Colten's mom called his dad a control freak. I know Colten doesn't want anyone comparing him to his dad, but it's the truth. It doesn't mean Colten will hang himself while his wife and oldest son pick up Friday night pizza. It's just an unavoidable mix of genetics and years of learned behavior.

"You'll need a couple stitches. Or glue. They glue shit now, right?"

I grab his wrist as he blots my temple. "Give this to me." Facing the mirror, I frown. "This is why you don't chase people downstairs."

"You're not seriously blaming this on me?" He lifts

his right eyebrow.

"I was trying to get away from you." I press the wet towels to my temple and open the door with my other hand.

"Why are you always trying to run away from me?"

I turn back toward him with such speed that he nearly bumps into me. "You're too old to be asking why the grass is green and the sky is blue."

Rubbing his stupid lips together, he hides his grin. They're stupid lips because I always stare at them. They were my first kiss. I still feel robbed.

"Look at you. You're a goddamn medical doctor, Josie. That's a shit-ton of school. So much hard work and determination. However, here you are ... assistant chief medical examiner in the third largest city in the US. Even if your job is creepy as fuck, it's a huge feat. Not very many people can do what you do. But a lot of people can get a bachelor's degree to be an accountant or some certificate to sell real estate. A lot of women get pregnant and forego their professional aspirations to stay home and a raise a family." He shakes his head slowly, face a little more somber. "You weren't that girl."

I never said I wanted to be that person. I hated him then and a part of me still hates him now for assuming he knows everything about me. Colten meant something to me, but he wasn't a drug that took away my ability to make sensible decisions. He's still so fucking full of himself.

"Oh my god." My head rears back. "Please tell me

you're not trying to take credit for who I am and what I've become."

"Well ..." he says slowly.

"You..." I jab my finger into his chest "...are still an asshole. I became a doctor, and you stayed an asshole."

He inhales my words like they give him some sort of high. It doesn't matter if it's a compliment or not. The bastard gets off on pushing my buttons. "I'll drive you to urgent care."

"You won't." I pivot and stomp my feet toward the parking lot.

"You're going to hold that to your head *and* drive?"

"Yes. And I might even chew a piece of gum at the same time."

He chuckles. "I wouldn't expect anything less, Watts."

Even when I'm showing strength and independence, he has a way of making it seem like I'm stubborn, which feels like a weakness. I can't explain it. And nobody else has ever noticed it. Everyone thinks Colten Mosley is a classic nice guy which means my reaction to his constant goading seems extreme.

I'm the bitch.

I'm overreacting.

I don't know how to take a joke.

Not true.

Not true.

Definitely not true.

I get along well with others.

I've always excelled at group activities.

And most people find my sense of humor endearing. I can laugh at myself.

Except ... when Colten pokes and prods at me. He toys with me like I'm a cat batting my paw at a dangling ball of yarn that only he and I can see.

"*Colten's going to miss you, Josie. He's making a sacrifice so you can pursue your dreams and he can find his way. It's noble. Friends do that for each other. You'll be better ... stronger for it someday.*"

My mom had *all* the great mom lines and philosophies.

Boys are mean to you when they like you.

Girls are catty because they are jealous of you.

You'll look back and be so grateful that you didn't try to fit in with the cliques.

You're smarter than them, and that's intimidating.

You might be the only girl in your class who hunts, but that just means you'd be the only one to survive if you're ever stranded on a desert island.

That one was always my favorite.

How many people actually get stranded on desert islands? I grew up in the Midwest. Was that really a danger?

I drive to urgent care, grab groceries after that, and get in a workout just to prove that I'm not anyone's damsel in distress.

Then I pull out my photo albums because I can't believe Colten Mosley actually got better looking with age.

I really, really hate him.

CHAPTER

Four

JOSIE WASN'T the worst friend ever—for a girl.

"You sure do like balls," she said as we rode our bikes to the batting cages.

I laughed. "That sounds bad."

"Why?"

I made a quick glance behind me as her dark hair blew in the wind. "Because it sounds like you're talking about parts of a body."

"You mean testicles? If I meant testicles, I would have said it. I know all the parts of the human body."

"Yeah." I faced forward again to hide my grin. "I know you do."

Josie didn't look like a nerd, but she acted like one. It's not that I didn't like to read, but that's *all* she did. Well, that and fish with her dad. I probably had no room to talk; I spent a lot of hours practicing piano.

Mom was determined to have one of her boys play the piano. Chad wouldn't even consider it.

"Am I your only friend?"

"No," she scoffed.

"Because I haven't seen you play with anyone else since I moved in next door to you."

"Do you stare out your window and watch me all the time?"

"No." Yes. Watching her house was my favorite pastime. Her dad seemed to like me. He ruffled my hair a lot the same way my dad ruffled my hair. Chief Watts looked intimidating in his uniform. He always appeared ready to crush something or someone. They had a two-stall garage attached to the house and another two-stall detached garage where he kept all kinds of free weights, a bench press, and a pull-up bar. Sometimes Josie would go ask him for permission to play with me while he was lifting barbells that I swore weighed more than Josie and I combined. Angry veins riddled his skin like the Hulk. And a really big one bulged along his forehead while his face turned as red as the cherry tomatoes Josie's mom grew in five-gallon buckets on their porch.

"Jenn and Adrianna, my two best friends, are gone for the summer to Jenn's grandparents' house. They have a cabin on a lake in Wisconsin."

"And they didn't invite you?" I made another quick glance back at her, not at all hiding my grin. I liked picking on Josie. Whenever my mom heard me doing it, she rolled her eyes and assured Josie I was just pretending that I didn't have a crush on her. Of course, I adamantly disagreed, but not because my mom was wrong.

She was right. However, I would rather have died than admitted it.

"They invited me. I just couldn't go."

"Why not?"

"Because Jenn's dad got arrested for drinking and driving, and now my stupid dad won't let me ride in the car with them, even though Jenn's mom was going to do the driving."

Why did it disappoint me that Josie had two best friends? Why did I secretly hope I was her only friend?

Oh, right ... I had a huge crush on her.

We locked up our bikes and headed toward the cages.

"My dad said to always be careful if you're here close to dark because a few years ago a boy our age was kidnapped. They never found him."

"Then how do they know he was kidnapped?" I asked.

"Because he's gone, stupid."

"Maybe he didn't like his family, and he ran away."

"He was nine. Where does a nine-year-old go?" She pulled my bat out of my backpack and turned quickly before I could grab it back from her.

"If I ran away, I'd hide in the woods during the night and get free samples at the grocery store during the day. Sometimes, the gas station will give you free pizza and donuts if it's the end of the day, and you pretend you forgot your wallet at home. They just throw them out anyway." I shrugged.

"He's dead. Someone took him and cut up his body. He's in the woods, buried in pieces."

I tried to hide my shock. Josie looked so innocent, but the things that came out of her mouth were not things most kids our age said. Her dad must have discussed his job around her. Of course, that didn't explain why she had a collection of dead insects in her room or why she liked to hang out around the funeral home in hopes of seeing Roland Tompkins, the undertaker, to ask him a slew of questions.

"Anyone die today?"

"Have you ever put two people in one casket?"

"Are you going to be cremated or buried when you die?"

"Can you put ashes in a casket if you want to be cremated but still want to be buried too?"

Roland tolerated her because she was the police chief's daughter. After the third or fourth question, he nodded toward our bikes and asked us if we had somewhere we needed to be. I would say "yes" at the same time Josie would say "no."

"Thanks, Josie. Now, every time I come here, I'll think about someone kidnaping me, cutting up my body, and burying me in the woods." I managed to snatch the bat away from her.

"Well, that's what I always think about when I'm here with you," she said matter-of-factly.

"You think about *me* being kidnapped or you?"

She didn't answer me, not until I was in the batting

cage hitting my third ball. Her fingers curled around the chain links as she leaned against the cage to watch me. "Both. I think we'll be kidnapped and killed together. Or ... what if our kidnapper makes us choose? What if only one of us can live? Would you choose me or yourself?"

"I don't know." I swung and missed. "Who would you choose?"

"I asked you first."

"I'm not answering unless you answer first," I said.

"Then let's answer at the same time. I'll count to three. Who would you save? One. Two. Three."

We both said "me" at the same time. Then we shared an offended look at the same time.

"You'd let me die?" Josie's jaw dropped.

I laughed and hit the next ball. "You'd let *me* die."

"Yeah, but ..." She had nothing.

"I don't think the kidnapper would let us choose. He'd make us run, and the fastest one would get away."

"Well ..." She took several steps back from the cage. "That means you would die."

"Uh ..." I missed the next ball because I was looking at her overly confident grin. "No. That means you would die. I can run faster than you."

"Why? Because you're a boy?"

"Yes."

"Let's race."

I shook my head.

"Scared you're gonna lose?"

"No. I just don't want you crying when I beat you."

"I won't cry."

"Fine." I dropped my bat and sighed as I exited the cage.

We found a strip of grass to the north of the fields and made a starting line with a few sticks pushed end to end. Then we did the same for the finish line.

"It's like capture the flag." Josie set a bigger stick right behind the finish line. "First to get the stick wins."

"Promise you won't cry?" I said as she hunched into a ready position at the starting line.

"Shut up, stupid. Mark. Set. Go!" Josie took off like a shot. Arms pumping furiously.

I can't lie. She nearly beat me. *Nearly.*

And maybe she would have had she not tripped three feet before the finish line and scraped her hands and knees along the ground until they were grass-stained and a little bloodied.

"Are you okay?" I tossed the winning stick aside and knelt beside her as she pulled her knees to her chest and inspected her hands. I couldn't see her face because her hair hung like a dark, silky veil around it.

"I'm fine," she said just above a whisper in a shaky voice.

"Are you crying?"

"No." She sniffled.

"If you are, it's okay. You're bleeding."

"I'm not crying!" Her head whipped up straight. She wasn't crying, but she had tears in her eyes, and she clenched her jaw so hard it made her whole upper body shake.

I didn't know what to say, so I grabbed the prize stick and handed it to her. "Here. If you wouldn't have tripped, you would have won."

She stared at the stick for a few seconds and sniffled again before taking it from me. "I'll be your girlfriend."

"What?"

She shrugged one shoulder. "I said I'll be your girlfriend. Your mom said you have a crush on me. And my dad said I should never like a boy who isn't nice to me. You did the right thing. I won, and you gave me the stick. So I'll be your girlfriend for the rest of the summer."

My young brain didn't know how to respond. She packed so much into her little speech. She wasn't faster than me. She simply got a head start because she said "mark, set, go" so quickly. And I never said I wanted her to be my girlfriend. Then there was the summer part. She'd be my girlfriend for the rest of the summer? Why? Why did I need a girlfriend for the rest of the summer?

"But you should get a skateboard. Jenn had a boyfriend last summer, and they rode to the skate park all the time. Sometimes they kissed. We're not kissing because you lick your lips a lot, and I'm not kissing your lips after you've licked them."

"No thank you." I stood and headed back to the batting cage to get my bat and bag.

"What do you mean *no thank you*?"

"If we're not going to kiss, then I don't need you to

be my girlfriend. And I already have a skateboard, but one of its wheels got busted off when my dad accidentally ran over it with his car. And you're not faster than me. And I shouldn't have given you the stick because now you're acting weird. Well ... weirder than you already are."

"Colten Mosley. What's that supposed to mean? You think I'm weird?" She chased after me.

"Yes. You collect dead stuff, and you talk a lot about death. That's weird."

"Maybe it's unique. My mom says I'm unique."

I shoved my bat into my bag and headed toward our bikes. "She says you're unique because your skin is not the same color as hers or your dads." I turned just before reaching our bikes. "My parents told me not to say anything to you in case you didn't know, but if it were me ... I'd want to know."

"Know what?" She crossed her arms over her chest and flipped out her hip.

"You're adopted. That's why your skin and hair are darker than theirs."

"I'm not adopted, stupid."

"Um ..." My nose wrinkled. "Yes. You are. My mom said it looks as though you have a little Native American in your bloodline. And don't tell anyone I told you. I don't want to get into trouble."

"My mom had sex with someone else. That's why my skin is darker."

"What do you know about sex?" I asked. I knew only

what my brother had told me. A man pushes his penis between a woman's legs and pumps his hips. I asked why. He said because it feels good like when I touch myself. But ... I hadn't touched myself in a feel-good way. Not yet. That came (pun intended) the following summer when Josie let me see her tits for three seconds in exchange for half of my Twix bar. I later learned it was frowned upon to trade things for glances at titties. They really needed a handbook for stuff like that. I couldn't keep track of all the unspoken rules.

"Sex is how two people make a baby, stupid. Why don't you know that?"

"I do know that." I ignored her "stupid" label. My mom, the relationship expert, said Josie calling me stupid was actually an endearing term—just a little immature and unrefined. Mom said "silly" might be a better word, but she assured me Josie didn't really think I was stupid.

"Then why did you ask me?"

I turned away from her and unlocked my bike. "Because my bro—" No. I stopped myself. I wasn't giving my brother credit for my knowledge of sex. If my mom was wrong and Josie did think I was stupid, I didn't want to give her anymore ammunition to tease me. "Because I'm pretty sure people have sex for other reasons too."

"Other reasons?" Josie eyed me as she unlocked her bike.

I didn't make direct eye contact because my cheeks

were catching fire from talking about something that felt taboo. "Yeah. Sex feels good."

"What do you mean?"

By that point, I couldn't remember how we got on the conversation of sex, but I would have given my right arm to talk about anything else. "You'll find out someday."

"Tell me."

"No."

We hopped onto our bikes.

"Tell me, Colten."

"Nope."

"If you don't tell me, I'm telling my dad you pushed me down."

I slammed on my brakes, skidding to a stop. My gaze flitted from her scraped knees to her grass-stained hands. Before I could say anything, I think she read my reaction and withdrew her threat. That was the first of what would be many withdrawn threats.

"Fine." She sighed. "I won't tell my dad that. Just ... tell me. If you don't tell me, I'm not going to be your friend."

Again, I gave her a look.

Again, she huffed a breath and withdrew her threat.

"We'll be friends, but I'm never coming back here with you. And that's no lie. So if someone tries to kidnap you, tough luck, Mr. Duck."

After a few more blinks, I laughed. "Tough luck, Mr. Duck?"

She hated it when I laughed at her, but I couldn't help it. Who said, "tough luck, Mr. Duck?"

Josie. That was who.

I was too young to recognize it, but I started falling in love with Josephine Watts before I had any idea what that really meant. By the time my adult self figured it out, she was gone, and it was my fault.

She frowned at me, a rain cloud ruining her baseball game, and wrinkled her nose while bolting ahead of me, down the street. I easily caught up to her.

"I'm kidding. Are you mad?"

"I'm kidding. Are you mad?" she parroted in a mocking voice.

"You're mad."

The second we turned onto our street, Josie kicked it into overdrive, dropped her bike in the front lawn, and ran inside her house.

"Did you and Josie have fun at the batting cages?" my mom asked as I kicked off my high-tops at the front door.

"I don't know."

She glanced up from the sofa, folding laundry and sorting it into piles around her. "Did something happen?"

I pulled off my baseball cap and hooked it on the banister before plodding my way to the faded leather recliner next to her.

"Don't sit on my folded bath towels."

"I won't," I said, managing to wedge myself into a small open gap next to them. "Josie's mad."

"Why?"

I shrugged. "She's a girl. Girls get mad about stupid stuff."

"Like?"

"Like I was joking about something she said, and that made her mad. And she said she'd be my girlfriend for the rest of the summer, and I said no. Maybe she's mad about that. I don't know."

Mom chuckled. "She offered to be your girlfriend for the rest of the summer?"

"Yes. Because I let her win a race."

"You're a little too young to have a girlfriend. And I really like Josie, so I think it's best that you stay friends."

I didn't mention that I would have said yes to her being my girlfriend had she not made the no kissing stipulation.

That night, my eyes were glued to the window, hoping to catch a glimpse of Josie. Just when I was about to give up and close my blinds, she ran out the front door and grabbed her bike. As she walked it toward the garage, she glanced back at my window. I jumped to the side so she wouldn't see me. My heart pounded, and I wasn't sure why.

What was the point of hoping to see her if I didn't want her to see me too?

Over the next nine years, I spent a lot of time at that window hoping to catch a glimpse of Josie Watts. Hiding from her. Hiding my feelings for her.

CHAPTER

Five

"Dr. Watts, do you believe in God?" Dr. Cornwell, the Chief Medical Examiner, asks me as he documents tattoos from the decedent on his table at the opposite end of the autopsy suite. A flock of interns surround his table, church mice with perked ears and curious eyes while four other forensic pathologists dissect their first cases of the day.

I focus on my table holding a male teenager who took a round of ammunition in his chest last night. "I like the idea of God."

"So that's a no?" Cornwell asks.

I glance up, eyeing him through my goggles and face shield—what tiny sliver I can see of him through the congested parameter of interns. "Depends. Do you define the word 'believe' as something you hold as a truth or opinion?"

"Does it matter?"

"Yes. I can be more liberal—in a nonpolitical sense —with my beliefs if others willingly interpret them as my opinions. But if they are interpreted as what I believe to be truths or facts, then I find it best to limit my beliefs to things that have little disputable evidence. So saying I like the idea of God is my way of saying I acknowledge that I can't prove God's existence, but I wish I could because it's comforting to think there's something greater than us ... than this life."

"Now, I know why you're still single," Dr. Cornwell says, eliciting some chuckles from the peanut gallery. "You don't always have to be right, Watts. Well, I need you to always be right here, when it counts. But outside of work, it wouldn't kill you to indulge a little."

I bite my tongue. I think he just implied I'm a prude or someone quite boring, not so adventurous. "I indulge."

"Now I'm curious. Tell me you follow your horo-scope or get your palm read. Do you avoid black cats and walking under ladders? Have you ever had bad luck after breaking a mirror? Do you believe in ghosts?"

"Vampires and werewolves. Not ghosts. Come on, Dr. Cornwell. Ghosts ... what are you? Eighty?"

He turns seventy next month, and he's really sensi-tive about his age, not as sensitive as he is about losing his hair, but still ... I think he'll always be young at heart.

"Have you ever autopsied a vampire, Dr. Watts?"

"No. That would be nearly impossible," I say.

"Because they don't exist?"

"No. Because they don't really die. I don't think they can be killed either. They have to be destroyed which means there would not be anything left to autopsy." It's my turn to elicit laughter from the peanut gallery.

God, I wish I could see Dr. Cornwell's face behind his mask. Is he smirking? He rarely smiles, so a smirk would feel like a total win for me today.

"Dr. Watts graduated top of her class. She thought she wanted to stare at diseased tissue all day through a microscope and diagnose diseases. Then she tried her hand at general surgery. Then ... she met me. I've trained a lot of young doctors in my life, but none have shown as much natural talent for ... dare I say, disassembling and reassembling the human body quite like Dr. Watts."

A few of the interns navigate from his table to mine. I'm now the interesting one in the room, and they're curious. What do I have that they might see in themselves?

"Spooky," I say.

One of the other pathologists uses a bone saw for a bit before the room returns to its normal white noise from the ventilation system.

"What's that, Watts?"

"Spooky. The first time you watched me perform my first solo autopsy, you said it was almost spooky."

He grunts. "It was. I think I also asked you if you'd lived on a farm and slaughtered animals. Nothing about the process seemed to phase you one bit. I'm not sure I've met anyone in this profession who hasn't taken a moment's pause when working with a dead body for the first time to let subtle realities sink in such as how cold the bodies are. You know it in your head, but it doesn't register until you actually feel it. Not with you. I didn't see you take a millisecond pause or so much as exhibit the tiniest of flinches. In fact, you whistled the whole time. You still do."

"Only when I'm alone." I follow the next bullet track.

"Not true. You were doing it just before I asked you if you believed in God."

"No. I wasn't."

"Can I get a witness testimony?" Dr. Cornwell asks the interns.

A few brave souls nod their heads and mumble, "You were."

"'Pumped Up Kicks,'" one of the interns adds. "Yesterday," he continues, "you were whistling 'If I Die Young' during your first autopsy of a young woman who died of a suspected drug overdose, and you whistled 'Pumped up Kicks' during your second autopsy—a gunshot victim as well. I assume you have certain songs for different causes of death."

I do?

How have I not realized this?

"Funny." I retrieve the bullet. "I never realized I did that."

"A song for different causes of death," Dr. Cornwell

says. "I like that. What do you whistle for heart attacks?"

I chuckle. "I don't know."

"Duh." The same observant intern pipes up again. "Demi Lovato's 'Heart Attack.'"

His fellow interns laugh, and I smile behind my mask. It's interesting how much we learn about ourselves from the observations of people around us. This shouldn't surprise me. I often learn more about the deceased from talking with their family than I do from performing an autopsy. There's so much in life that's not black and white—so many things that require explanation before one can make accurate inferences. What if we learned to reserve judgment until we knew the whole story? I think I'd like that world.

TWO HOURS LATER, I take my lunch outside, in need of some fresh air.

"Watts," Detective Mosley says my name and grins as I strut past him in the lobby. "Just the person I'm looking for."

"I'm on a lunch break."

He pivots and follows me outside. "Does your profession get a lunch break? I know mine does not. Is it hard to eat after seeing the things you see daily? I bet you're a vegetarian."

"I bet I'm not." I cross the gated entrance to find a spot on the grass behind the building's sign.

"Do you still hunt?"

"No." I take a seat and dig my sandwich out of my thermal lunch bag.

Colten slips his hands into the pockets of his suit. I never imagined him in a job that required a suit. I can see him in a uniform, but not an actual suit. It's weird. I don't let on that I'm the least bit interested in what he's wearing or anything else about him.

"Did you put 'field dressing a deer' on your resumé?"

"Did you put asshole on yours?"

"Ouch. That's harsh. You're not still holding a grudge, are you?"

Leave it to him to make my feelings seem ridiculous.

"What do you want, Detective Mosley?"

"What were your findings with Jacob Marsh?"

"Who's Jacob Marsh?" I know who he's referencing, but I'm not his personal medical examiner. Jacob Marsh was brought in this morning. I haven't autopsied him yet. And I wouldn't be surprised if Dr. Cornwell jumped in and stole him from me.

"Missing legs. Most likely a chainsaw. Seeing any connection? That's two in the past month."

"Good to know. I'll have to get back to you after I conduct the autopsy."

"Why didn't you do it this morning?"

I chew the bite of my sandwich and stare up at him,

squinting against the sun. "Because I was busy," I mumble with my mouth full.

"Don't you prioritize?"

"That's what your boss said when he wanted the results of this morning's gunshot victim. Now, he has to sit on his thumbs and wait for ballistics. I suggest you go see if your thumbs will fit up your ass too because I'll get to it when I get to it."

"Did you speak to my boss like you're speaking to me?"

Just his presence has stolen my appetite. I shove the other half of my sandwich in my bag. He's relentless. Always has been. I know he won't stop nipping at my ankles anytime soon.

"You can finish your lunch first. I'm not a monster."

"You are." I march back to the building.

He grabs my arm like he did before I fell down the stairs.

I yank it out of his grip as I turn back toward him.

"I'm sorry, Josie."

I don't want to be the person who holds a grudge. Not because he deserves my forgiveness, because I deserve to live without this awful feeling weighing on my conscience. Anger is an unrelenting weight on one's soul. It's suffocating. And it's been too long. I need to let this go.

"It's no big deal." It is. Or at least it was a huge fucking deal. He ended us—a near decade of friendship—and it crushed me. I told no one. I suffered in silence.

"Well …" He shrugs with an innocent and somber expression I haven't seen since our recent reunion. It's a glimpse of the Colten I once knew. And maybe that Colten is still inside of him, the way that young Josie girl still resides in my heart. "It was a big deal to me then. And you knowing that I'm truly sorry for how it ended … even if it was for the best…" his eyebrows pull together as he bites the inside of his cheek for a few seconds "…that means something to me now."

I don't walk away. It feels physically impossible. All these emotions that have been locked away for so long are on the verge of coming out. Things I should have said seventeen years ago. "Did you get married?"

His head eases side to side slowly.

Maybe that should make me feel better, but it doesn't. I hope he didn't get married because he *is* the asshole I thought he was, and no woman in her right mind would marry him. The thought of him searching for me in someone else, the way I've spent the last seventeen years looking for him in every failed relationship, makes me feel a little less broken.

"I have a daughter," he says.

Never mind. I'm shattered. Again.

"No wife. But you have a daughter. I hope you're just rejecting marriage and not a deadbeat dad who didn't stick around and do the right thing."

Colten winces.

I don't. Not externally.

If I nailed the truth on the head, that's his problem.

Not mine, although I find it disheartening to think that he fathered a child and abandoned her and her mom.

"It's complicated," Colten says.

"Yes. Children complicate things." I force myself to turn again and head back into the building. It's his life. *We* ended a long time ago. What he's chosen to do with his life is none of my business.

"Call me about Jacob Marsh. There's a killer on the loose."

"There's always a killer on the loose," I say as the door closes behind me.

CHAPTER
Six

I AGREED to let Josie be my girlfriend. Then she broke up with me right before school started. Two weeks later, Annie Nelson asked me to be her boyfriend. Being one of the new kids at school made me an enigma of sorts. All the girls wanted to be my girlfriend.

"You can't be Annie's boyfriend." Josie ran to catch up to me after the school bus dropped us off at the end of the street.

"Why not?" I didn't bother turning to look at her. The sting of her breaking up with me made it difficult to make eye contact with her. Unfortunately, our parents had become friends, and we lived across the street from each other, so totally avoiding her wasn't an option.

"Because she's so annoying."

"Maybe I think you're annoying."

"That's not very nice."

"But it's nice of you to call Annie annoying?"

Josie's shoes slapped against the sidewalk as I picked up my pace forcing her to jog behind me. "Because she *is* annoying. All she ever talks about is her stupid brother who plays football in college. *Ethan goes to school for free because he's so good at football. Ethan's going to be in the NFL and make millions of dollars. Ethan ... Ethan ... Ethan.* It's SO annoying!"

"What I do is none of your business, Josie."

"We're friends. So it's kind of my business."

"We *were* friends."

"Colten, we still are."

"You broke up with me."

"Yes. But I said we should just be friends."

I darted across the street to my driveway, hiking my backpack farther up my back. "I think we should just be neighbors."

"Colten ..."

"Josie ..." I mimicked her with the same tone she always used to mimic me.

"Derek asked me to be his girlfriend. I think I'm going to say yes," she goaded me. God ... she always goaded me.

I didn't give a shit about "Derek, brace-faced, thick glasses Hoffman." But his family was rich, and that made him one of the cool kids. It was too early to determine my status at school, but Annie was more popular than Josie, probably *because* her brother was a big deal, and that meant I'd be popular too if she was my girlfriend.

So I became Annie's boyfriend, and Josie became Derek's girlfriend. We didn't talk for the month she spent holding hands with Derek from the school to the bus stop, nor did we talk for the two weeks after they broke up while I was still Annie's boyfriend.

All that changed the Saturday Annie rode her bike to my house. My parents were gone, and Chad was supposed to be keeping an eye on me, but that was always a joke. I sneaked outside to meet Annie behind our garage.

"Hi." I grinned.

She looked pretty in her pink hoodie and jeans with flowers on the legs. She had straight blond hair and high bangs. The opposite of Josie's dark, unruly hair that always had waves in it and long bangs that she sometimes clipped to one side with a barrette.

"Hi." Annie smiled and wet her lips several times because the whole purpose of her riding her bike to my house the morning my parents were gone was to kiss me. And unlike Josie, I didn't mind kissing someone who licked their lips.

"Ready?" I asked because ten-year-olds asked to kiss each other. They excessively wet their lips. And they hid behind garages to do it.

"Are *you* ready?"

I nodded. I was ready. It had nothing to do with Annie and everything to do with kissing a girl before Josie kissed a boy. I wasn't one hundred percent sure she hadn't kissed Derek, but I felt pretty sure she hadn't kissed a kid with braces after her unwillingness to kiss me for licking my lips.

I leaned in a few inches. Annie leaned in a few inches. We stayed there, separated by another three inches for what felt like forever. Finally, I went the rest of the way and pressed my lips to hers. We both kept our eyes open, and that was really weird. She blinked, and I pulled away. There was no sound. No suction. I'm not sure it counted as a kiss, but she smiled like it did, so who was I to argue? I wasn't exactly an expert on kissing at that point.

"Oh my gosh!"

Annie glanced over my shoulder. Then, I turned around to Josie and her gaping mouth catching flies while her eyes swelled to big brown saucers.

"Did you really kiss her?" Josie tripped over her words.

"Get out of here," I said.

"I'm telling your parents." Josie pivoted and stomped toward the front door.

"I'd better go. I hope you don't get into trouble." Annie's face wrinkled.

Yes, we were hiding behind the garage to kiss, but not because I was worried about getting in trouble. It's not like my parents specifically ever told me I couldn't kiss a girl. I just didn't want my stupid brother to see us. Or Josie.

"I'll call you tonight," I said while chasing after tattletale Josie. She wasn't at my front door. She was, instead, running into the wooded area behind her house that backed up to a dirt trail where people walked their dogs or sometimes road dirt bikes.

"Josie ... stop!" I jogged after her.

She jumped up and grabbed the lowest branch of her favorite tree. Then she climbed up three more branches to her favorite perch where she often spied on people along the trail. It was also where she escaped to when her parents would fight. Josie climbed trees, fished, hunted, and rode a skateboard. She was the definition of a tomboy. She also wore girly clothes and painted her fingernails and toenails. She was a mix of ... perfection.

I never told her that.

"That's gross, Colten. Just stay away from me."

"Kissing a girl is gross?"

"Kissing Annie is gross. Why did you do that?"

I laughed as I climbed the tree and sat next to her, our legs dangling in sync. "Because she's my girlfriend. Why did you hold Derek's hand every day after school while walking to the bus?"

She kept her expression neutral and her tongue mute as she stared ahead at the empty dirt trail.

"Are you going to tell my parents?" I didn't care. Well, I kind of cared, but I didn't understand why she'd tell them. Did her parents know about the hand-holding?

"Why?" she whispered.

"Because if you're just going to tell on me, I'm going to tell them first."

"No." She shook her head. "Why did you kiss her?"

"I told you. She's my girlfriend."

"Ugh!" Josie maneuvered past me, nearly knocking me out of the tree to get to the trunk and shimmy down it. "I *hate* that she's your stupid girlfriend." She marched back toward her house while I hopped out of the tree.

"Why?" I ran behind her.

"Because."

"Because why?"

"Because now you can't be my boyfriend."

"You broke up with me."

"Ugh ... you're so stupid. Boys are so stupid." She ran up the deck stairs.

I was really confused. And I had no idea that moment was a tiny glimpse into a lifetime of not understanding women. I thought it was just Josie being Josie. Wrong. It was Josie being a female.

As usual, I needed my mom to interpret things for me. She spoke female.

"She likes you. That's why she's upset that you have another girlfriend," Mom explained as if it should have been crystal clear to me.

"But she broke up with me."

"Yes. But that doesn't mean she's ready to see you with another girlfriend."

"But she had a boyfriend for a month."

"Doesn't matter."

That made no sense to me. It *did* matter.

"You never said what made her mad to begin with.

Why did she run off to her tree? Did you say something? Did someone at school say something?"

I hadn't told my mom about the kiss behind the garage. Even if I didn't think she'd be mad, I also didn't think she'd exactly be happy either.

"I don't know," I mumbled as I escaped to my room before she asked anymore questions.

Taking my usual spot on my beanbag chair by the window, I pretended to read the book we were supposed to be reading for English while keeping surveillance of the Watts's house in hopes of catching a glimpse of the *stupid* girl I had a chronic crush on.

The next day, I broke up with Annie.

Josie still ignored me on the bus ride home, even though I sat right next to her. When the bus dropped us off at our stop, I waited for Josie to get her bag, and we exited the bus together. Instead of walking toward home, she just stood there, watching the bus close its door and pull away from the curb as the rest of the kids scattered in different directions toward their respective houses.

When it was just the two of us, I broke the silence. "Aren't you coming?"

Josie turned ninety degrees from the curb toward me. After a few slow blinks, she clenched the straps of her backpack, lifted onto her toes, and leaned forward, our lips pressing together. But this wasn't like the Annie kiss. This was different. It was a real kiss.

My lips moved, latching onto her top lip for a few seconds, and then her lips moved and did the same thing to my bottom lip. There was suction and movement.

It was definitely a real kiss.

When she dropped flat onto her feet again, she smiled. "Let's go home."

That wasn't the day she became my girlfriend, again. Not in any official capacity. That was just the day I started kissing Josie Watts.

We kissed a lot.

We held hands.

We hung out at the batting cages, in the woods behind her house, and in her dad's garage where he exercised or worked on his old Chevelle. That was the year I learned to change a tire and change the oil in a car. My dad thought I was a bit young when I told him, but I think he was just jealous that Josie's dad taught me instead of him.

Josie and I were friends, but of a different kind. At school, I had my friends, and she had her friends. I played sports and the piano. Josie stayed after school to help the librarian put the returned books back on the shelves. And sometimes, she lay in her front yard under the maple tree and read. Josie read so many books.

Then there was *our* time. It felt like everything else was just an obstacle to navigate to make it to our time. That place where our hands searched for each other. That place where she'd nudge my arm with hers, and I'd bend down to give her a quick kiss. We'd smile and I knew she thought the same thing I did: we weren't each other's world—the world was simply ours when it was just the two of us.

Josie Watts was unlike any other human I had ever met. She'd call me stupid one minute and bring me cookies she made with her mom the next minute with a handwritten apology.

Passionate.

I'd say she was passionate, even if at the time I didn't know what the word really meant. There were a lot of words that fit Josie that didn't come to mind until after I'd already lost her.

Inquisitive.

Generous.

Authentic.

"I heard something," Josie said one night as we were stargazing from her mom's hammock on their deck. Her parents were inside, tending to her baby brother.

"I didn't hear anything."

"No." She gently rolled toward me as I did the same, so we didn't fall out of the hammock. With her face a few inches from mine, her lips pulled into a sad smile. "I heard my dad telling my mom something about your dad."

I narrowed my eyes. "What?"

"I'm not sure I should tell you."

"You have to tell me. We tell each other everything."

"Yeah." Her gaze shifted to my chin. "But this is something that's sad."

"What? Just tell me."

She forced her eyes, the color of night, to look into mine again. "My dad said he saw your dad kissing a woman that wasn't your mom."

"That's a lie." I sat up, and Josie had to quickly put her feet on the ground, so she didn't fall off the other side.

"I'm just telling you what my dad said."

"Well ... he's lying," I murmured with my back to her, and my heart pounding against my ribs the way it did when I thought I was in trouble or when I jumped off the high diving board at the pool. It made it hard to breathe, and it felt painful and a little scary.

I was too young to understand, or maybe I didn't want to think about what that meant. "I have to go home."

"Don't tell your dad I told you. I don't want him to be mad at my dad or at me."

My unpredictable relationship with Josie should have prepared me for that moment—the one where things that seemed upright were actually upside down. Where the sky was green and the grass was blue. It was like Josie breaking up with me then kissing me. Maybe I wasn't supposed to understand everything; I just needed to nod and accept it. Whatever *it* was.

CHAPTER

Seven

"Wʜᴀᴛ's up with you and the detective?" Alicia, one of the morgue techs, asks me as we change into our PPE in the locker room.

"I don't know. What do you mean?"

She smirks. "I heard he calls and always wants to talk to you, not Dr. Cornwell. And I saw the two of you having lunch outside the other day."

"We weren't having lunch outside. *I* was trying to eat my lunch outside, and he insisted on ruining it by asking me questions about an autopsy I haven't performed."

"You sound angry." She laughs. "I take it you don't care for him?"

"Astute observation. We went to school together." I tie my black apron.

"I see. Childhood archenemies?"

"Not exactly. The enemy part came after we graduated and went our separate ways. For the most part, we were … friends growing up." Who am I kidding? We were more than friends. I would have been fine saying goodbye to my *friend* Colten Mosley after we graduated, but we were a lot more than friends. Or maybe that was a miscalculation on my part.

"What happened?" Alicia pulls her booties on over her tennis shoes and all the way up her legs, close to her knees.

"It's a long story." I lie. It's a rather short story. With the grace of a dirty bomb, he obliterated my heart and wished me good luck at college. There were a few pathetic moments that I blamed his dad. Had his dad been a better role model, maybe Colten would have known how to treat someone you supposedly love.

Maybe his dad didn't really love his mom, just like Colten didn't really love me.

"We should get a drink sometime, and you can tell me all about your long story."

"I don't drink alcohol." I shut my locker door.

"Why? You've seen too many ugly livers?"

I laugh. "Ironically, no. That's not it. I've just never had any desire to drink alcohol."

"Ever?"

I shake my head.

"Were either one of your parents an alcoholic?"

"Nope."

"You didn't drink in college? At all?"

"Nope. Cough syrup and kombucha is the extent of my alcohol consumption."

"That's ... crazy." Alicia follows me to the autopsy suite.

"I know. But it's true."

"Well, I've seen you eat, so we'll talk about your juicy past over greasy onion rings and two virgin margaritas."

"Deal."

I half expect to see Detective Mosley waiting for me in the autopsy suite because my first case today is another body missing its legs from what investigators believe was likely a saw. That makes three. By the end of the morning, we might officially have a serial killer on our hands.

Before I take lunch, I make a courtesy call to Detective Mosley.

"Circular saw. Red handle. Six-foot cord. Am I right, Dr. Watts?"

"Something like that." I roll my eyes and plop down into my desk chair, shaking my mouse to wake up my computer screen.

"Do I get brownie points for waiting for your call instead of visiting you?"

"I don't know, Detective. Are you a Girl Scout?"

"Just a do-gooder. Run-of-the-mill nice guy who happens to catch killers and put them in prison to keep citizens like yourself safe."

I should have left on my PPE; the shit's getting deep.

"You might catch the killer with the help of me and my team, but you don't put anyone in prison. I'm pretty sure that's the DA's job."

"I don't remember your ego being so sensitive, Watts."

"I don't remember your arrogance hogging all the credit, Mosley."

He chuckles. "Okay. I'd love to spend the day flirting with you like this, but I have a job to do. Give me the rundown."

I open my mouth to protest his ridiculous accusation that I'm flirting with him, but I, too, have things to do, so I get back to business and confirm everything he already suspects.

"Why cut off the legs if you're not planning on burying it or transporting it?" he asks.

"Well, I'm a forensic pathologist not a forensic psychologist, but it's possible that he or she had something happen to them in their past. If my husband beat me, *kicked* me repeatedly, and I decided to kill him, I might remove his legs."

After a few seconds, Colten hums. "Mmm … maybe. So you think the victims abused their killer at some point?"

"No." I chuckle. "It's unlikely the victims did anything to the killer. They just might have resembled someone who did do something to the killer."

"I've thought about that, but there's nothing that stands out other than all three victims are men. One black, two white. Ages twenty-three, twenty-nine, and forty-seven. One was married with kids. One was in grad school. And one just married his business partner in a civil service."

"Keep looking. There's something. There's always a *something*. But ... I have other mysteries to solve, so you're on your own now."

"Did you talk to the families?"

"I haven't talked to Matthew Roslow's family yet. Why?"

"Just wondering."

I frown. I don't have to see Colten to know from the sound of his voice that he's formulating a theory he's not ready to share yet. When we were younger, he used to torture me with his half-thoughts. He'd ask me something that seemed random and out of the blue, only to answer my "why" with "just wondering."

The bait's similar, but I'm no longer biting. Colten Mosley is no longer my keeper of secrets, my favorite confidant. And if my heart knows what's good for it, it will keep my relationship with him professional.

"I don't know if the family will give me anything they haven't already shared with the police, but I'll let you know. Otherwise, good luck." I cringe as I say those two words.

"Good luck, Josie. You're going to be a huge success." The past echoes in my mind.

"Thanks."

"Bye—"

"Josie?"

I bite my lips together and close my eyes. "Yeah?"

"How would you feel about getting dinner with me sometime? We could catch up."

Catching up with my past is a terrible idea. I'm still running from it. "Thanks, but I'm good. I feel all caught up."

"You still with that same guy I met at the restaurant?"

"You didn't meet him. I never introduced you to him. And yes, I still see him."

"And he knows your real job?"

"Bye, Detective." I end the call and give my phone the middle finger. Colten thinks he knows me. He thinks he knows my date whom he's never met. How is this possible? We've spent more time apart than we ever did together. Nine years together. Seventeen years apart.

Seventeen adult years.

Seventeen years of dating other people—having sex with other people.

And ... having a baby with someone else. I still can't believe he has a daughter.

"Wow! I didn't expect to hear from you again. I thought you were ghosting me." Paul's spot-on analysis of my behavior makes me cringe.

"Work has been crazy. That's all."

"Long days looking through a microscope?" he asks with a hint of sarcasm.

"I'm free tonight if you want to have dinner or just hang out."

Have sex. If he wants to have sex.

For some disturbing reason, the more interaction I have with Detective Mosley, the more I feel the need to have sex with … anyone. Well, not anyone. I'm not that desperate, *yet*. Someone. I want to have sex with someone.

Angry sex.

Revenge sex.

Screw-you-Colten-Mosley sex.

And I really want to have sex with someone and *not* think of Colten, but at this point, it's unlikely. That sucks too.

Still … *still* … after all these years, he has this invisible hold on me. I'm too educated, too mature, too confident to be this pathetic. It's because I don't like unsolved mysteries. I hate when I can't determine the cause or manner of death. I hate marking that stupid box. It makes me feel like a failure. And I hate that Colten broke my heart, and I don't know why. I *need* to know why, but I can't ask him. There's no way I'm giving him that level of satisfaction.

"We can order in pizza. Your place?" Paul invites himself to my place.

I think of a million excuses, then I think of Colten. "I'll order the pizza now. Can you be here in an hour?"

"I can. Should I …"

"Should you what?" I ask while picking up some dirty dishes around my kitchen.

"Should I pack an overnight bag?"

Why did he ask me? It knocked his confidence level down a good ten notches. *Don't ask if you're staying. Assume you're staying. Make me want you to stay—beg you to stay.*

"I don't know. Should you?" I try to flip it, acting flirty, giving him the opportunity to play along.

"That's why I asked you. It's your place. I don't want to assume I'm staying."

Sometimes ... just sometimes ... chivalry kills the moment.

"Actually, I have to meet someone early tomorrow morning."

"No overnight bag. Got it." Paul tries to sound cool. He's not. I'm not that cool either, so I don't judge him too harshly. We're both science geeks. "See you within the hour. Text me your address."

"I will. Bye."

Paul arrives in less than twenty minutes. I'm flattered that he's so excited to see me. Devoting more than a decade to achieve your professional goals leaves little time to cultivate meaningful relationships. I've started to feel broken in that area of my life. Can I find a man who finds my love for my job an attractive quality?

We'll see.

"The pizza is on its way. And I don't have a drop of alcohol to offer you. So make yourself at home on the sofa while I get you a bottle of water." I bite my lips together to hide my ridiculously embarrassing smile.

67

"You can choose sparkling or still." Not only have I neglected my love life for the past decade, but I've also failed to stock my apartment with anything that might make me look like a good hostess.

"I feel like living on the edge tonight, so I'll take sparkling. Thank you." Paul slips his shoes off just inside my door and saunters to the sofa.

His ass looks good in jeans. It looks good without any too.

"You okay?"

I glance up as he turns toward me just before taking a seat on my sofa. *Busted!* Yes, I was looking at his ass, and he knows it.

"I'm good." I tame my grin, but I'm sure he sees the truth in my flushed cheeks.

"Do you have some lime to go with the sparkling water?"

I open my fridge as if I'm checking, but I know the answer already. "Shoot. I think I used my last lime yesterday. I have a tangelo. Would you like a slice of that instead?"

He laughs. "No. I'm good."

I hand him the sparkling water and sit at the opposite end of the sofa as if I'm shy—as if we haven't had sex. My mistake. I should have kept things going, but I'm terrible at keeping shit alive. That's why I don't have house plants. It's also why I work with dead people.

"I've missed seeing you. I'm so glad you called."

I shake my head. "I'm terrible at dating. I'm

surprised you even took my call. I get so distracted with work. Really, I'm sorry. I should have made a better effort because I did enjoy..." I smirk and laugh a little "...hanging out with you."

Sex.

I enjoyed the sex. I enjoyed the company of a *warm, naked body.*

"Well..." he scoots a little closer to me, angling his body a few degrees to face me "...I enjoyed hanging with you too." Paul makes me feel good. Normal. Relaxed.

The pizza arrives, and we eat nearly the whole thing while sharing funny stories from our childhood. We were both a little "different." I've been searching for someone who is not like me—probably not a great strategy—so it's not surprising that I'm still single. Paul gets me. Or so I think ... until I slip up and overshare.

"Oh ... this feels good." I toss the crust of my pizza onto my plate and set it on the coffee table. "It was a long day. I needed this. I don't think I'll ever get used to having a child on my table." The second I say it, my sluggish mind catches up. Paul doesn't know. I can't keep it from him forever, but I'd planned on sharing the truth with a little more tact and a lot more explanation.

"Child? On your table? Do you still work directly with patients? I assumed you just worked in the lab."

My lips curl together, face wrinkled with a hint of a cringe. "I do work in a lab sometimes. I ... God, please don't take this the wrong way like I intentionally lied to you. I just feel like sharing the truth too soon ends things before they really begin."

"You're not a doctor."

I shake my head. "No. I'm a doctor. And I'm a pathologist."

"So ..." Paul raises a single eyebrow.

"I'm a forensic pathologist."

He blinks several times before nodding slowly. "That's ... you ..."

"I'm an assistant medical examiner."

Paul continues to inspect me between his slow blinks. He leans forward, setting his nearly empty bottle of sparkling water next to his plate on the coffee table. "You perform autopsies?"

"Correct." I smile softly.

"So the child on your table was ..."

"Deceased." I nod several times.

"That's ..." Paul clears his throat.

"Sad," I say. "But if you're referring to my job, it's necessary. There's actually a shortage of forensic pathologists in the United States." I shrug. "Somebody has to do it. It's not glamorous, but it's necessary."

"Of course. I just didn't see that coming. I had a vision of you in a lab."

"Well, sometimes I'm in the lab."

He scratches the back of his head. "How did you uh ... decide to become a medical examiner? Surely you didn't dream of it as a young child."

I really like Paul. And I think he likes me. This doesn't have to be a dealbreaker. And he deserves my honesty, but I think he needs it in small doses. I don't tell him that I'm incredibly good at my job. A natural at something so very unnatural. I have a gift for separating the body and soul. I don't see a person. I see a body that housed a soul. Even when I see a child on my table, it's only a little harder because I know there is a family (usually) who feels like the order of death didn't go as intended. Children shouldn't die before their parents. But sometimes they do. And that's life.

It's my job to determine the why and the how. And while it won't bring them back, sometimes it gives the family a sense of closure.

"The Chief ME, Dr. Cornwell, recruited me. He made me feel special and needed. He knew I could do what a lot of other doctors can't do. So no, I didn't dream of becoming a medical examiner. I don't think most people end up taking the path they dreamed of as a child. Did you?"

"Yes." Paul gives me a serious face for a few seconds before grinning. "It's true. I'm a purebred nerd. I've dreamed of being a chemist since I got my first chemistry set for Christmas when I was eight. But ..." He nods. "You're right. It's probably the exception not the norm that someone actually becomes what they dream about as a child. That probably makes me boring and tragically predictable."

It really does. I bite my bottom lip, and he leans into me, stopping just before our mouths meet. I grin, so elated that he knows the truth and it's no big deal. I'm so glad I called Paul. I should have done it sooner.

We kiss, letting the need build. He slides his hand from my leg to my waist, from my waist to my breast. I hum into the kiss. My hands reach for the button to his jeans, and I push him back onto the sofa, straddling his waist.

My shirt comes off. His shirt follows.

My hands work the zipper to his jeans. He grips my hips.

I smile. He ... cringes. Winces. Something *not* sexy.

His gaze goes right to my hands. "Is it weird for you..." he grabs my wrists to stop my hands from doing anything else "...to separate what you do at work from your personal life?"

My gaze narrows. "Uh ..." I shake my head. "What do you mean?"

"I mean ... you use these hands to cut open dead bodies. But now you're using them to touch me. I bet you've done things to a man's..." he nods toward his erection "...*part* that's not exactly sexy. Is it weird for you? Do you think about it when you're not at work?"

My hands, the same ones I use in my job, rub my face as I chuckle because it's better than what I really want to do—cry. "No. I don't think about work when I'm with you like this—the way male OBGYNs don't think about their patients' vaginas while making love to their wives." I drop my hands from my face and rest them on my legs to keep from touching him since it seems to make him uneasy. "At least, most male OBGYNs probably don't think about work when they're having sex."

"But you've seen a lot of naked men."

Oh my god. This isn't happening. "It's an occupational hazard. It's not a perk. And can I just say that a lot of doctors who work on living people see them naked. Surgeons cut into people. They hold their organs in their hands. They put them together and sew them back up. But for whatever reason, it's much easier for surgeons to get laid than forensic pathologists." As my words escalate in volume, I climb off his lap and pull on my shirt.

"I'm sorry." He sits up. "I know how ridiculous it is. And you're a great person ..."

Here we go. I refrain from rolling my eyes, but it's not easy.

"But I can't shut off my brain now. All I can think about is you opening dead bodies like it's no big deal."

"It is a big deal, Paul. It's someone's son or daughter. Someone's friend. Someone's significant other. Someone's parent. I don't ever take that for granted. And while I'm not saving their life, I'm finding answers to questions that might help give the family closure or comfort if they know their loved one didn't suffer. And you know ... sometimes I do save lives. Sometimes I discover a hereditary condition that the family can use as knowledge for early prevention. I help the police solve murder mysteries, and I help put dangerous people in prison. There's nothing about my job that I don't take seriously. There's never a day that I don't feel like I'm making a difference in someone's life. I never make a cut and think it's *no big deal*."

He tucks in his shirt as he stands, head bowed. "I'm so sorry. I'm a bastard. And this is one hundred percent me, not—"

"Me, not you. Yeah. Yeah. I've heard it a million times. Get the fuck out."

Paul's head snaps up, lips set into an O of shock. "Josie—"

"It's Dr. Watts to you. Get out. And pray you never show up on my table, or you will be the exception to my high level of professionalism as I gut you like a fish."

Paul keeps a sharp eye on me as he scurries to the door and shoves his feet into his shoes. "You're a crazy bitch."

Pressing my lips together, I nod a half dozen times while he flies out of my house. This is a first. I've never reacted like this before now. I've been rejected a lot, but never have I lost it. My usual MO is a few shy nods and a "thanks anyway" like someone's refusing to buy something I'm trying to sell.

If I'm honest, it's Colten Mosley's fault. He's had me on edge since the moment he said my name at the restaurant with Paul. I'm not mad at Paul. I'm mad at Colten.

And I'm sexually frustrated at the moment.

And I'm ... I don't know. Something. I'm definitely something at the moment.

CHAPTER
Eight

A WEEK after losing my shit with Paul, I have to testify in a murder trial. I *get* to testify. Dr. Cornwell hates this part of the job, but I don't mind it. I don't get nervous on the stand, and I find the whole legal process fascinating. If I didn't have to get back to work all the time, I'd enjoy watching murder trials all day.

"You're good."

I turn as the hair along my neck stands erect from the irritating sound of his deep voice. "Detective." I pull my shoulders back and challenge all my senses to act unaffected by Colten in his sharp navy suit and crisp white dress shirt. Perfectly knotted tie.

"On the stand, you're very put-together and confident."

I nod. "Of course. Why wouldn't I be? I'm an expert witness." My days of trying to impress Colten Mosley should be long over, yet they're not. I'm still singing my own praises with him. Only with him.

One side of his mouth lifts into a half smile that some women probably find sexy. I imagine.

Not me. Nope.

"I was actually a little nervous." He shrugs, looking innocent when I know he's far from it. "Rafferty can be a real dick on his cross examinations, regardless of your level of expertise. But you held your own."

"Thanks. I don't mind testifying, unlike Dr. Cornwell. I swear he's been passing any case on to me that he thinks might lead to giving testimony."

"I don't blame him. I hate being questioned."

"You hate someone questioning your authority, not necessarily questioning you," I say.

"Who does like having their authority questioned?" The elevator doors open, and we step into it.

"Me. I like when some hotshot attorney questions my authority and level of expertise. Because regardless of how much research they did in advance to sound intelligent while asking the right questions, they have a law degree and I have a medical degree with hundreds of autopsies under my belt. I like scrutinizing everything they say, looking for little discrepancies—an opportunity to show their lack of knowledge and therefore their vulnerability."

The doors open to the main floor. "You're sadistic."

"I'm not." I laugh.

"Which is weird..." Colten ignores my reply "...

because you were much nicer to people when we were younger."

There is a lot to unpack here. "You did not just say that to *me.*"

"It's true. You were honest but considerate of people's feelings."

I exit the courthouse and cringe when a blast of humidity fills my lungs and fucks up my hair. "Yes, *I* was considerate of other people's feelings."

"That's a jab at me. I get it. That's fair. I was an asshole sometimes." Colten follows me. "You should let me buy you lunch to make up for the past."

There's not much that leaves me speechless anymore. I've heard and seen just about everything, but Colten is certifiably insane if he thinks lunch makes up for what he did to me. Maybe ... just maybe something like his testicle catching a bullet or early onset male pattern baldness with a scalp covered in scaly eczema would make up for the past. I'm going to think on this one.

"Wow, that's kind of like a murderer buying the victim's family a puppy and calling it good."

"Now you're comparing me to a murderer?" His eyebrows shoot up his forehead.

"No. Murderers eventually put their victims out of their misery. I have to get back to work." I pivot, taking quick strides to my car.

"My mom's coming for a visit this weekend. She'd love to see you."

I slow my pace, closing my eyes for a brief moment.

He's not playing fairly. "Tell her to call me, and I'll meet *her* for lunch."

"That's just rude, Josie."

Glancing back at him, my lips pull into a tight smile. "Rude?" I nod slowly as if I'm giving his word choice some careful thought. I'm not. I'm giving myself a few breaths to remain calm because I could kill him about now. "Tell *her* to call me."

FRIDAY, I swipe right on the hottest guy I can find. I need to clear my mind after a week of sorting through the cluttered memories of Colten. Tonight, I'm a doctor, an ER doctor who's going to get some mindless, meaningless, sex.

Jared supposedly manages hedge funds. I'm not sure I buy it based on our brief conversation over dinner, but he's not lying about his obsession with working out.

A full head of hair, nice abs, and my favorite flavor of breath mints goes a long way when I'm feeling ... easy. Jared checks off all three of those boxes. The next morning, he passes up the coffee I offer him and opts to head straight to the gym.

"It was nice meeting you," he says on the way to my front door as I slide on my robe and practically crawl to the coffee maker.

Nice meeting me? We had sex. Granted, I'm not wanting anything beyond last night, but throw me a bone. Lie to me and say you'll call me, or message me, or something. Cordial is not the best morning attitude.

I much prefer the awkwardness of fake intentions. A simple "see ya around" is something I can work with even if I know he won't see me around.

"Yeah." That's my reply. I could have said "you too" and matched his level of enthusiasm, but with a caffeine deficiency in my blood, I just don't have the energy to go the extra mile and give him more than one syllable.

"Oh, excuse me," Jared mumbles and the expected *click* of my door shutting never happens.

I don't make it three steps before I hear the *click*. By the fourth step, I see an intruder in my entry ... and his mom.

"Becca ..." I say her name slowly.

"Josie!" She hugs me, and I hold out my mug of coffee so I don't spill it on her.

"What a surprise." I give her a tight grin and wide eyes.

"So good to see you, dear. I hate to ask, but do you mind if I use your bathroom? We had breakfast, and I should have used the ladies' room after my second cup of tea."

I nod. "Down the hall on the left."

As soon as the bathroom door shuts, I shoot Colten a scowl. "You'd better have a warrant, Detective. You're in my house uninvited. And what the hell? You brought your mom without a freakin' heads-up?"

"Watts..." his head gestures to my door, ignoring my rant "...that's not the dude from the restaurant."

"Brilliant observation. Chicago is so lucky to have you as one if its best and brightest on the force. Why are you here?"

"What does he know about you?"

"He knows I'm not married, and I supply the condoms. What more does he need to know?" I sip my steaming coffee when it's obvious that he's not going to answer my questions.

Colten's thick eyebrows inch up his tan forehead. "Giving it away, huh?"

I shrug a shoulder and pad my way back to the kitchen. "I can't sell it in Illinois. You should know that, Detective."

"I like when you call me detective."

"I like when you call before coming to my house *with your mom.* What part about 'have her call me' was most confusing?"

The bathroom door opens, forcing me to find a welcoming smile again.

"You have a lovely place, Josie."

"Thanks, Becca." I set my mug of coffee onto the island and readjust my robe's sash.

"Not a single hunting trophy." Colten shakes his head slowly. "Not even a bearskin rug."

I'm ready to mount his head on my wall and skin *him* for a rug. Instead, I ignore him. "Had I known you were coming, I would have made a point to be showered and dressed."

"Was that your boyfriend leaving? I haven't seen or talked to your mom in years to find out what you've been up to. Well, I saw your parents at..." Becca pauses for a second like she needs a big breath to continue "... the funeral. But I don't remember much from that day."

Colten's gaze affixes to the window with a hardened expression. I don't think he likes to think or talk about his father's funeral or anything about his father for that matter.

I contemplate reminding her that I was at the funeral as well, but I can read the room. It's not a subject that deserves anymore time. "Jared. That's the guy you saw leaving my apartment. And our relationship is fairly new, so I don't know if he's my boyfriend yet."

I will never see him again. When the most prominent photo of a guy on a dating app is of him with a towel hanging so low on his waist that half of his closely trimmed pubic hair is visible, it's a given that he's only looking for a quick hookup. He was a good way to get Colten out of my head for a night. I thought I'd enjoy a full cup of coffee while thinking of Jared's warm body and strong pulse.

No such luck.

Colten nods to the sofa for Becca to take a seat like it's his place. Then he collapses onto the cushion at the opposite end. Okay ... I guess they're staying for a bit. I need a shower to wash Jared from my body. Brush my teeth. Put on actual clothes.

Deciding to save those as an excuse to get them to leave after a bit, I sit in the armchair adjacent to the sofa, tucking my feet beneath me and holding my coffee mug with both hands while Colten eyes me like I'm his next case to solve.

"Has Colten told you about Reagan?"

Biting my lips together, my head inches side to side. Colten adjusts in his seat as Becca gazes at him for a few seconds with a soft smile on her face.

"Reagan is five. And she's the most beautiful little girl I have ever seen. I didn't think either one of my boys would make me a grandma. They've been too preoccupied with pursuing careers. So imagine my surprise when I found out I was going to be a grandma."

I study Colten's expression. The constant bobbing of his throat. His unfocused gaze flitting all around the room. His hands slowly rubbing his denim clad thighs.

"I'd love to meet her." The words fly off my tongue before I give them much thought.

Colten eyes me, his fidgety hands stilling for a few beats.

"Does she live around here?"

He says nothing. Not a single word. It's been seventeen years, but I can still read him. He's in pain. I'm not sure I'm ready to muster sympathy for him since I'm still dealing with my own pain that's been renewed with his reappearance in my life.

"Against my better judgment, he gave up custody.

But he sees her every month or so. Katy's very generous."

Colten clears his throat, but he only responds to Becca with a few tiny nods.

Her smile swells and excitement shines in her eyes, but I'm not sure why since he looks so miserable. "And she's coming tomorrow," his mom squeaks.

I can't contain my own smile. After seeing the lifeless expression on Becca's face at her husband's funeral, this is a nice contrast. Well-deserved happiness.

Colten forces a grin, giving her a quick glance.

"I'm staying for two weeks to watch her while Katy and her new husband honeymoon in Europe."

"That's awesome," I say, earning me a slight scowl from Colten. It only makes my enthusiasm grow. If he thinks he gets to show up at my house uninvited on a Saturday morning with his mother and earn an ounce of sympathy from me for his life's decisions ... he is delusional.

"The four of us should go to the zoo." Becca's palpable enthusiasm is hard to ignore.

Still, I need to ignore it. I'm happy for her. She's earned this joy a million times over. Colten? I'm not sure what he deserves. Clearly, he doesn't deserve his daughter if he gave up custody.

Colten's expression softens as he makes eye contact with me. "We should."

We? No. I'm not part of any "we."

"I'm busy, but I'm sure you'll have a great time." My

fake smile stretches my lips, exposing the teeth I need to brush.

"You and your blanket statements about being busy." Colten has the nerve to challenge me in front of Becca.

"Well, Detective, as someone who harasses me on a daily basis, rushing me to give you information, you should know I'm very busy. Then there's Jared and that budding relationship. I'm a woman in demand."

"Oh! Colten said you're a medical examiner. Years ago, your mom said you were going to medical school, but I never knew you were interested in working with dead bodies. That has to take a very special mindset."

"Josie's always had a special mindset. An affinity for dead things." Colten smirks.

Apparently, he's all smiles as long as we're not talking about his role as a father, or lack thereof.

"It's a very in-demand profession. It takes someone with a high level of intelligence, laser focus, and well-honed communication skills to do what I do. Often, studying death unravels many mysteries of the living. Colten's had the pleasure and good fortune to work with me and learn from my expertise."

Right there.

That look on his face is the most satisfying reward I've received in a very long time, and that's saying a lot because I do, in fact, find my job incredibly rewarding. I can't quite decipher his expression, but it's either a classic case of "cat got your tongue" or good old fashion defeat. Either way, it's beautiful.

"Josie ... I'm so proud of you. I bet your parents are too. You work with law enforcement. That has to make your father happy. And I'm sure Colten is smitten to reconnect with you after all these years and get to witness firsthand all of your accomplishments." Becca gives her son an expectant look.

Colten eyes her briefly before clearing his throat. It's reminiscent of the times she thought he hadn't been nice to me and made him apologize or say something kind.

Also like old times, I don't say a word. I wait patiently whether I deserve it or not. Only this time, we won't run out of the house to the back woods, climb the tree, and fight over who was really right or wrong.

One of us won't hold up a big sheet of paper to our bedroom window at bedtime with the words *I'M SORRY* scribbled in all caps. One of us won't offer a giant-sized Snickers bar as a truce.

"Smitten isn't the right word, Mom." Colten's gaze flits to mine, sliding down my face and over my entire body as he maintains a contemplative expression. There's a newness interwoven with the old familiar parts of Colten Mosley, a tiny glimpse of those missing seventeen years when he transformed from a boy to a man.

A lanky teen to a filled-out man with a thick scruff along his jaw and face.

A dreamer without purpose to a professional with stature.

A heartbreaker to ... what sometimes feels like a glimpse of the brokenhearted.

Did his daughter's mom break his heart?

"Happy," Colten says, returning his gaze to mine, the hint of a sincere smile touching his lips. "I'm happy that Josie has found her calling in life. It would have been a shame for her to settle for anything less than her dreams."

Fuck you, Mosley.

My dreams? Is he serious?

"How are your parents, Josie? I feel so out of touch since Trenton died. Is your dad still Chief of Police? Are they still in Des Moines? Does your mom still teach sign language at the community college?"

"My dad took early retirement two years ago, and my mom retired six months later. Dad sold the fifth wheel even though he still hunts, and they bought an RV. They still have their house in Des Moines, but they're on the road more than they're home."

Becca tries to smile, but it's a failed attempt. I always wondered why she stayed with Trenton after he cheated on her. More than once, I overheard my parents talking about it. I never caught the "why" part, but I remember my mom always saying Becca was a better woman than most. Years later, it occurred to me that my mom was giving my father a subtle warning that she would not be tolerant or forgiving if he was ever unfaithful.

"I always thought Trenton and I would move to Florida when he retired, maybe Sanibel Island."

The muscles in Colten's jaw work overtime at the mention of his father's name. This visit has reached its limit.

I stand. "I hate to be such a terrible hostess. Had I known you were coming, I would have planned accordingly, but I need a shower. My day is filled with plans."

"We really must have dinner when Reagan gets here," Becca says, taking Colten's proffered hand to help her up from the sofa. It's a kind gesture. He's always been a mama's boy.

I choose a smile as my response. It's friendly and noncommittal. There's no way I'm going down the Mosley rabbit hole again, but I'm not a complete asshole who says it to Becca's face.

"Do you remember when I used to make chicken enchiladas? Those were your favorite."

Tightening my smile, I nod once. My mom made the best baked goods, but Becca's meals were better. I basically invited myself to dinner on chicken enchilada night.

"I hope you enjoy your time with your grand-daughter."

"Oh, I can't wait." Becca beams like a bright star.

I remind myself that it's been seventeen years. Colten's level of discomfort with this conversation is not my concern. Whatever he did to fuck up his personal life is none of my business. But there's no denying that his daughter brings much-needed joy to Becca's life.

When we reach my front door, Becca pulls me in for another hug, leaving Colten in my line of sight over her shoulder. With his hands in the front pockets of his jeans, his gaze flits around the space, anywhere but meeting mine. Becca always loved me. By our senior year, I felt certain she thought I'd be her daughter-in-law.

And if I'm being honest and peeling back the scar tissue covering seventeen-year-old wounds, I'll admit I thought the same thing.

As Becca heads toward the street, Colten hangs back a minute, preventing me from closing my door. "Thanks. She really wanted to see you."

I nod.

"I'm glad you're well, Josie. Really." He lifts his hand and traces the healing cut on my forehead. A breath later, he drops his hand.

I manage one last nod. I much prefer dealing with Detective Mosley on my turf at work where I feel a good ten steps ahead of him unless he's chasing me down a flight of stairs. Bringing his mom to my house, uninvited, on a Saturday morning is out of bounds.

Just as I think he's going to say something else, his phone chimes, and he answers it. "Mosley." He winks at me and struts toward the street.

Closing the door, I march toward the bathroom to shower, feeling a mix of anger and that familiar attraction. That wink. That stupid wink. It's just like the first time he winked at me when we were younger.

CHAPTER

Nine

COLTEN MOSLEY, starting as pitcher for the varsity baseball team as a freshman, was a sight to behold. He exuded so much confidence, and nobody loved that confidence more than Heather Peterson, his girlfriend who was a year older than us.

I hated her. That was a given.

My relationship with Colten flickered on and off more than the dying florescent light in the laundry room. It was easy to blame Colten. He was guilty of so many things.

Too cute.

Too nice.

A stellar athlete.

Coach Mosley's son.

And he played the piano like Hélène Grimaud.

Of course, nobody our age knew who Hélène

Grimaud was, except Colten. Our neighbor said he played with a similar "expressive freedom." Whatever that meant.

After the team's first win of the season with their freshman pitcher, Heather Peterson squealed while throwing herself into Colten's arms the second he emerged from the dugout with his lucky glove and shit-eating grin.

"Baby!" She just had to call him baby.

I rolled my eyes, taking slow steps descending the top of the bleachers with a cherry Tootsie Pop in my mouth, squinting at *him* as he stared at me over Heather's shoulder.

That was the first time he winked at me.

That asshole had the nerve to wink at me while hugging *her* to his sweaty body. I knew they'd already kissed. Heather had told Ronnie as much, and telling Ronnie was the equivalent of announcing something over the PA system.

The only thing I hated as much as Heather Peterson was that wink. The first of many. And he always did it over the shoulder of some girl hugged to him like a bear in a tree.

After games.

The homecoming dance.

In the school parking lot.

Just outside of the locker room.

The problem with Colten Mosley's stupid wink was I never saw him do it to anyone but me. Not once.

"Thanks for coming to my game," Colten yelled as I

scuffed my sneakers along the dirt toward the parking lot.

Halting, I turned slowly, bringing my sucker out of my mouth with a *POP!*

"Baby, I'm going to talk to Jenna and Ronnie. Meet you at my car." Heather blew him a kiss before blowing me off without so much as a smile or a "hi."

Colten stopped his dusty cleats mere inches from my sneakers as he eyed me with a smug satisfaction. He had an older girlfriend who called him "baby," and she had her driver's license. So what?

"Watts."

"Mosley."

"Need a ride home?" he asked.

"My mom's picking me up."

"Heather and I could give you a ride."

I scoffed. "I'd walk home before I'd get in the car with that psycho."

"Psycho?"

"She backed into the dumpster behind the school last month. Ronnie told everyone she barely passed Driver's Ed. And she rear-ended Mr. Leach at the four-way stop after last Tuesday's softball game."

"You think you're going to be a better driver?" Colten stole my Tootsie Pop and sucked it into his mouth—the same mouth he used to kiss Heather Peterson.

"I start Driver's Ed next week. But I already am a better driver. My parents let me drive everywhere. My dad lets me drive his truck. I've backed his fishing boat onto the trailer in and out of the loading ramp a million times. It's a stupid question and you know it."

Colten rolled my Tootsie Pop in his mouth while canting his head to the side. "Are you wearing lip gloss?" he mumbled over the sucker.

I rubbed my lips together. "No. It's from the red sucker, stupid."

"Looks like lip gloss."

So what if I was wearing lip gloss? Heather wore a whole paint palette on her face.

"Never seen you wear makeup before."

It irked me that he had to point out all the ways I was different than the other girls ... the girls who hugged and kissed him. The girls who cheered from the fence by the dugout and squealed while throwing themselves into his arms. The girls who called him "baby" and dissed me because I was younger.

"We're the same age in case you've forgotten. If you can play varsity baseball and suck face with the worst driver in the whole school, then I can wear lip gloss or an entire mask of makeup for that matter, without you making such a big deal of it."

Colten pulled the Tootsie Pop from his mouth. "I know." He shrugged a shoulder before bringing the sucker to my lips, a mischievous glint in his eyes daring me to put it back into my mouth.

"Colten!" Heather called.

My lips parted, accepting the sucker. His grin spread wider than I'd ever seen it.

Two seconds after brushing past me, he turned.

"My mom's making chicken enchiladas tonight. She felt bad for missing my game, so she promised to make my favorite dinner to make up for it. You should come."

"Three's a crowd, Colten. I don't think Heather wants to have dinner with me."

"Who said I was inviting Heather?" His tongue slid out to wet his lips before he rubbed them together as if he needed to hide his grin.

As Heather the angry badger charged in our direction, doing a terrible job of hiding her distaste for me, I smirked around the sucker and mumbled, "See you at dinner."

"Josie, come in, hon." Becca opened the door, a yellow kitchen towel draped over her shoulder as she smiled before heading back to the kitchen. "You don't have to knock. You know that."

"Smells amazing." I ignored her comment. Colten had a girlfriend who was not me. I no longer felt like I should enter their house unannounced.

"Colten's upstairs. Dinner will be another twenty minutes or so."

"Okay. Thanks." I crept up the stairs as I had done many times before.

"Mosley," I leaned against the doorframe of his bedroom as he scribbled on a page of music at his keyboard.

Becca bought him a keyboard after his dad took a sledgehammer to the piano when Colten called him a "fucking bastard" for cheating on his mom. Trenton Mosley wasn't a patient man by nature. After spending years trying to destroy his marriage, his career, and all credibility with his two sons, the last thing he expected was his youngest son having a moment of brutal honesty after reconciling with Becca.

"Watts." He glanced over his shoulder, flashing me a big grin.

"Where's your dad and brother?"

That beautiful grin? It fell right off his face, a big chunk of an iceberg breaking off and falling into frigid waters. "Don't know. Don't care." Returning his attention to his sheet music, he continued to scribble notes.

Padding my way to him, I glanced around his room, looking for signs of Heather. A photo. A gift she might have given him. A friendship bracelet since she wore approximately a dozen on each wrist. "Play me something," I said, sitting next to him in the opposite direction on the edge of the narrow bench.

"What do you want me to play?"

I shrugged. "Anything."

His long fingers rested on the keys, caressing them lightly before pressing a single key. Then he started to play the very familiar beginning to "Fallin" by Alicia Keys.

How ironic.

Did I keep falling in and out of love with Colten Mosley? It was too early to say. Still, I'd known him for what felt like forever. Living across the street for five years, same school, sharing a seat on the bus, spending every free moment with him ... it made it hard to remember what my life was like before he and his family moved to Des Moines from Houston, Texas.

"Do you play that for Heather?"

He stopped playing as if my words made him forget the notes. Glancing over at me, he narrowed his eyes a fraction. "Heather hasn't been in my bedroom."

"Well, she's been to your house."

"Are you spying on me, Watts?" One corner of his mouth turned up into a slight grin.

I rolled my eyes. "You wish. I'm not spying on you. I'm simply not blind. I've seen her car in your driveway. That's all."

He maintained his smirk of skepticism. Did I once (maybe twice) use binoculars to spy on him to see if he did, in fact, take Heather to his room? Maybe. If I had, I never would have admitted it to anyone.

"You did good today. Freshman starting varsity. Can you believe it? You know you'll get lots of offers to play in college. Right?" Once again, I managed to say something that dissolved all joy from his handsome face.

"Yeah, I mean ... it's possible. My dad sure thinks so."

"I'd imagine he's pretty proud of you."

Colten grunted, flipping off the power switch to his keyboard. "His pride is the least motivating thing in my life. In fact, when I think about something making him happy or proud, all I want to do is the exact opposite."

"Sounds like a great plan for completely blowing your future."

He sighed, scooting off the bench before moseying to the window, stuffing his hands into the pockets of his sweatpants. "Baseball isn't everything. There are a lot of happy and successful people who didn't choose to play baseball in college."

"True ..." I stood and followed him, stopping a foot or two from his backside. "But a very small percentage of the population has your talent at playing baseball."

He turned, eyeing me for a few seconds. "You've said I'm good at playing the piano."

I nodded several times.

Colten's head slanted to the side. "You said I'm good at climbing trees and skateboarding—almost as good as you."

It became increasingly difficult to not offer a submissive smile as he listed off his talents.

"Maybe I'm one of those people who will be good at whatever I set out to do."

Lifting a shoulder like I didn't want to give him a total pass on ignoring the obvious fact that he would be pursued hard by colleges wanting to recruit him, I offered a murmured, "Maybe."

"Not everyone's future is mapped out from birth like yours."

"What are you talking about?" I took a step backward to give us some space. It was hard to be in his *space* and not feel transparent with my feelings.

The jealousy.

The envy.

The true feelings hidden beneath mounds of stubborn pride.

The fear of telling him the truth only to be rejected.

"A hunter. A goddess like Artemis."

I scoffed at Colten's comparison. "Are you seriously still reading Greek mythology? I can recommend much better books."

"Ancient literature, thank you very much. And yes, I'm still reading it. So don't roll your googly eyes at me. I'm complimenting you. I realize there's a little controversy when it comes to Artemis, but true scholars believe she was fiercely protective of those who were considered weak. Reclusive but passionately defensive. A champion of purity ... the virgin kind." He smirked. "However, she was quite temperamental and rather unsympathetic to men. Sound familiar?"

"No. Not really. I'm very sympathetic to men. I mean ... we're still friends, right? Something tells me Heather wouldn't be near as tolerant of your nerdy side. She's a fan of your jock side. You know, the side you actively try to repress and secretly despise just to spite your father?"

"Look at you effortlessly proving my point, Watts. Again, just like Artemis, you possess a lack of mercy and an overabundance of pride. Sadly, those were her greatest weaknesses, and I think they're yours as well."

"I don't possess a lack of mercy." I scoffed.

"You kill Bambi." Colten's nose wrinkled.

"Bambi's dad, dumbass. Nobody kills Bambi, not even my dad. Hunters have compassion, Mr. High and Mighty, who gives not a single thought to the true brutality your double cheeseburger lunch suffered to make it into your fast-food sack next to a pile of cold fries and ten billion packets of ketchup."

"Dinner, kiddos!" Becca called upstairs.

We stared at each other through a series of silent blinks. It wasn't the first time the dinner bell interrupted our meaningless conversation. Neither Colten nor I ever participated in debate club, but we both would have excelled. We spent hours, sometimes days, debating the most ridiculous topics.

"Do store-bought chickens suffer more than hunted chickens? I think the enchiladas are made with store-bought chickens. I've never seen my mom snap a chicken's neck, so I assume it died by some other means. Lethal injection? Personally, I think I'd prefer the injection to someone snapping my neck."

My head eased side to side. "You don't see the neck snap coming. No fear. Just ... *snap*. Done. Dead. No suffering. But you know something bad is about to happen when you're restrained, and a needle's shoved into your vein. Ticktock ... the end is slowly approaching, and you can't stop it. The fear is terrifying and crippling. And no ... chickens don't die from lethal injection."

Colten had a way of looking at me for several silent seconds after I'd speak. And just as his face threatened to morph into amusement, he rubbed the pads of his fingers over his lips to erase all signs of a grin because he knew I'd lose my shit if I thought he was making fun of me.

"Do you think you'll ever let me give you a compliment without it turning into the most ridiculous argument?"

"We're not arguing," I ... *argued*. "Do you think you'll ever give me a compliment without presenting it in the form of a saga?"

"You're a skilled huntress." He gave me a sharp nod, a nonverbal period to his simple compliment.

It was my turn to hide my amusement. Huntress. Everything about that word implied something mythical in my head. "Thank you." I almost choked on those two words. I wanted to tell him the word huntress was a little extreme for me. I occasionally went hunting or fishing with my dad. I'd never been hunting on my own for anything besides insects, okay ... I might have happened upon some roadkill here and there.

"You're welcome. Let's eat."

As he reached the door, I spewed the words I told myself I wouldn't say. "Why did you wink at me? After the game, Heather hugged you, and you winked at me. If you were my boyfriend, and you hugged me while winking at another girl, you'd be my *ex*-boyfriend."

Colten turned a few degrees, his head twisted but not fully looking at me. "I've been your boyfriend ... a lot. And I've been your ex-boyfriend ... a lot. And when

I was your boyfriend, I never winked at another girl." He shrugged a shoulder.

I bit my tongue because I didn't have the courage to tell him that I never felt like the girl he deserved. He could spin things all day long, trying to explain away my personality and passions under the guise of mythical goddess likenesses. Guys like Colten Mosley were genetically bred to be with Annies and Heathers, even cheer squad captains like Kaitlyn.

The Josephine Wattses of the world (of which I knew there were very few) didn't fit in with anyone.

CHAPTER

Ten

"JUST A PRELIMINARY GUESS, but I don't think this is a homicide case, Detective Mosley," I say without glancing up from the body on my table, ignoring the few students crowded around me.

"The victim's mom swears on her life that it wasn't suicide," he says.

"Bereaved mothers don't want to believe their children are capable of suicide, of hanging themselves. It takes premeditation. Preparation. Even a little practice to get the right type of knot, secure the ... extension cord in this case ... to something that won't break or collapse under their weight, and execute it without fail. But ... his face was paler than his torso which means the blood supply was cut off to his head, and therefore it's likely that within seconds he lost consciousness which means he didn't suffer that long. It doesn't always go that way."

When Colten doesn't respond with a single word, I meet his fixed gaze.

Shit.

His dad hanged himself.

"I'll talk to the family," I say.

Still, he doesn't move.

"Detective Mosley?"

Nothing.

"Colten?"

His head jerks, eyes on me.

"I'll talk to the family. Is that all you needed?"

In another delayed response, he nods slowly.

When we finish up with the sixteen-year-old boy who made an impulsive, irrevocable decision to take his life, I strip out of my PPE, complete some paperwork, and take my lunch break outside in my usual spot. Two bites into my sandwich, I slip in my earbuds and call Colten.

"Detective Mosley," he answers in a clipped tone. Either he didn't look at his screen closely or I'm not saved under his contacts.

"It's Josie. I uh ... just wanted to make sure you're okay. Earlier, I said more than needed to be said because I was in work mode, talking through things aloud for the students, and I completely spaced on your dad. I'm sorry."

"Don't worry about it."

I shouldn't worry about it because it was an honest

mistake, and I don't owe Colten special treatment seventeen years after he made me feel anything but special. We've exchanged so many barbs over the years, they should no longer break the skin. We should be calloused to them. But I didn't mean to cut him, not with the tragedy of his father's suicide. Even I know there are lines that shouldn't be crossed. Sometimes I just ... don't see them.

"Is Reagan with your mom?"

"Yeah."

"That's good. I'll ... let you go. Just wanted to make sure—"

"I'm fine, Josie. He was a fucking selfish asshole for as long as I can remember. I shouldn't have expected his death to be any different than his life. Did you talk to the family?"

I pick at the crust to my sandwich. "I will this afternoon."

"You should come to dinner tonight. I'm picking up pizza on the way home. Then we're watching a princess movie."

"I'm not a big princess movie person."

"But you love pizza."

"I used to love pizza."

He chuckles and I let the sound of it *not* irritate me this time because I need to know I didn't unearth too many memories of his dad's suicide. "Josie, there are a few things in life that you love forever no matter what. Pizza is one of them."

And the boy next door ...

103

"Popcorn too. I'll even see if I can scrounge some deer jerky to go with it."

"Shut up." I chuckle.

"She's perfect, Josie." His voice softens. The chattering in the background disappears. He's moved away from the people around him. "I look at her and I can't believe she's part of me. She's just too perfect."

Leaning my head back and closing my eyes against the sun, I try to imagine what a little female version of Colten would look like ... or act like. "No onions."

He laughs. "Cheese. She's five. It's just cheese. I'll text you my address. Six work?"

I nod to myself and smile. "Yeah."

COLTEN'S unfairly using his daughter and his mom to get me to spend time with him outside of work. And for whatever reason, I'm letting him. It's nothing more than curiosity. His having a daughter who lives primarily with her mom has my curiosity piqued.

"Josie! Come in, honey. Colten isn't home yet, but he's on his way."

"Daddy!" A little girl comes barreling down the stairs, long, flowing dark hair pulled partially away from her face and secured with a red bow.

"No, sweetie. It's not your daddy."

Reagan hugs Becca's legs and peeks up at me with rich brownish-gold eyes and long lashes. Those are

Colten's eyes and his full lips that seem to smile a little crooked on one side.

"Reagan, this is your daddy's friend, Josie. She met your daddy when they were just a few years older than you."

"Hi, Reagan." This is awkward. I'm a little intimidated by a five-year-old because I work with adults and dead people, and I have no children of my own. I used to be better with kids when I had to babysit my little brother. That was a long time ago.

"Are you going to marry my daddy?"

My eyes bug out. Every word I was going to say dies on the end of my tongue and evaporates into thin air through my parted lips.

"Mommy married Sean. She said Daddy didn't want to marry her."

Well shit. This girl's a little too smart for her own good.

Becca doesn't seem to offer words either. Her cheeks flush as she clears her throat. "Oh, sweetie, it's not that your daddy didn't want to marry your mommy. They just had different plans for the future. And sometimes grown-ups have to raise their kids apart while they follow their dreams and work hard to buy little girls cute stuffed animals and big swing sets for the backyard."

That's a terrible explanation, but I applaud Becca for thinking on her toes and finding literally anything to say. I still have nothing.

"Um ..." I fumble my words. "Reagan, I'm your

dad's friend. He might get married someday like your mom got married, but he won't marry me. We're just friends."

Friends is a stretch at this point, but she doesn't need to know the finer details of how her daddy broke my heart. She'll probably have her own version of a Colten Mosley to teach her those hard lessons in life. For now, she can leave her daddy on a pedestal. I'm not a dream crusher.

Becca gives me a sad smile. I think she always imagined me with her son—forever. I imagined it too.

"Hello. Hello ..." Colten's voice carries from another door.

Reagan sprints toward him. "Daddy!"

Becca gestures for me to follow her.

For someone who doesn't have custody of his daughter, he sure has her love. We turn the corner into the kitchen where Colten has Reagan hugged to him with one hand and a pizza box in his other hand.

Becca takes the pizza box from him, and he winks at me.

"I just want you to know that no matter what girl lays claim to me, I'm still yours, Josie."

I can't help it, not that I want to. A big smile spreads across my face. Reagan is his girl. *The* girl. I'm not sure why he's winking at me.

Relinquishing a grin, I give him a slight headshake and eye roll.

"Daddy, your friend is here, but she's not going to marry you."

Jesus, little girl ... you're killing me.

He sets her on her feet, eyeing me the whole time. "Is that so?"

I laugh it off and file it under "kids say the darnedest things" as I nod. "She's correct."

Colten loosens his tie, eyeing me head to toe. "A shame," he mumbles.

I clear my throat, turning my attention to Becca as she tries to slow down Reagan's grabby hands reaching for the pizza box. "What can I do?"

"Plates are in the cabinet to the right of the oven," she says.

"Got it." I head to the cabinet.

"I'm going to run upstairs and change my clothes. Save me some pizza," Colten murmurs as he saunters toward the stairs looking unfairly handsome in his suit. I have a flashback of seeing him in a suit for the first time at a piano recital. He hated it, but Becca insisted he wear it.

By the time Becca and I get the plates, pizza, and drinks set on the dining room table, Colten emerges in a pair of jeans and a white tee.

"Sit by me, Daddy."

"Of course, Button." He bops her nose, and she scrunches it.

I sit across from him, next to Becca, as he gets Reagan a slice of pizza on her plate and starts to cut it into pieces with a fork.

"No, Daddy. Don't cut it."

His eyebrows lift a fraction. "Sorry. I didn't realize you were such a big girl now."

Reagan's little lips pucker to blow on the pizza before taking a tiny nibble. Colten drapes a paper napkin onto his leg while eyeing me and wearing a cocky grin.

I avert my gaze to the pizza on my plate.

"How's your boyfriend?" Becca asks.

I press my napkin to my mouth to keep from spitting it out at her unexpected question. Boyfriend ... she means hookup, only she doesn't know that's what she means.

Colten smirks, and I give him a quick narrowing of my eyes—one or two daggers shot at him.

"Uh ... that didn't work out. Most all dating these days is online dating, and to be honest, it's pretty brutal out there. Sometimes, I'm just looking for a night out with good conversation."

"Well..." Becca lowers her voice, talking like a ventriloquist as if Reagan won't pick up on anything if she talks that way "...he was at your place the next day. I assumed that meant it was serious."

Colten coughs, fisting a hand at his mouth.

"Yeah, well, I might have read that wrong." I shrug. "So what did you and Reagan do all day while Colten was at work?"

"We had tea and cake!" Reagan spits a little pizza out of her mouth with her excitement.

Becca and Colten chuckle.

"Colten made us reservations at a tearoom. So we

got dressed up and had three o'clock tea. Scones. Little sandwiches. And cakes. It was really ..." She eyes Colten and I swear I see tears in her eyes. "It was a wonderful gift. I raised such a thoughtful young man."

We're just going to agree to disagree on that one for a while, even if I find it really sweet that he did that for his mom and daughter.

"What about you, Josie? Did you have a good day?" Colten asks as if he didn't see me this morning and talk to me on the phone at lunch.

I nod several times, eyeing him suspiciously. "You?" I feel compelled to ask in return.

He takes a bite of pizza and chews it while nodding. "It was okay. Better now that I have my three favorite girls all at the dinner table with me."

No. Nope. Uh-uh. He's not allowed to say that. Seventeen years. Seventy years. Five hundred lifetimes. It doesn't matter. He crushed me, and I'll *always* feel it.

Becca gives her son the expected adoring gaze. Reagan's too busy eating her pizza in micro bites to pay any attention to his comment. I ... well, I ignore him, gulping down my water like I haven't drank a drop all day.

After dinner, Becca takes Reagan upstairs for her bath while I help Colten clean up the small mess from dinner.

"I talked to the family this afternoon." I hand him the last plate to load into the dishwasher. "It was incredibly hard, but I think reassuring them he probably didn't suffer was a little comforting. I don't know how long it will take for them to really process that it happened in the first place."

"Never," Colten mutters, closing the dishwasher. "You never fully process it."

I wipe my hands on a towel before setting it aside and sliding my fingers into the pockets of my gray linen capris. "I wanted to call you. After it happened, and you weren't at the funeral, I wanted to call you. But ..." I press my lips together, not really sure how far I can or should go with this. Where will it end?

"But you hated me."

Staring at my feet, I inch my head side to side. "I didn't have your number."

"And you hated me. You did. You *do*. I won't make you say it. And I take full responsibility. I can't change it. And I haven't decided if I would change it if I had the chance."

The only thing worse than feeling rejected is hearing his confession that it wasn't an accident. It was intentional. No remorse.

He hurt me, and he feels no remorse.

"Tell your mom and Reagan goodbye for me. I'm going to head home."

"Josie ..."

I make my way to the front door without actually running, but I want to. Boy, do I ever want to run away from Colten Mosley and never see him again. With him, I'm not a doctor. I'm not a well-respected medical examiner. I'm barely a woman. With Colten Mosley, I will always be the girl in love with the boy. The girl who he thought was a boy. The default friend.

"No. Just ... no." I bolt out the front door, slinging my purse over my shoulder.

"Josephine Watts, *look* at yourself." He takes long strides, following me to my car. "You are more ... so much more than I imagined. Without me, you became everything you never were *with* me."

I stop at the driver's door, keeping my back to him, taking one deep breath after another.

He's right, but not in the way he thinks. I will *never* tell him that.

"If we choose to live with regret, then I have to regret Reagan. I have to regret my job. I have to regret too many things that are good in my life *because* my life went in directions no one could have ever imagined. And I'm tired of regret. It's the heaviest anchor, the most unbearable feeling of drowning ... of suffocating. My dad tied a rope around his neck because of regret. If I regret, then I'm chasing a ghost. If I regret, it might be *my* neck inside that noose."

Pressing my fingers to the corners of my eyes, I wipe away every outwardly physical sign of pain. My other hand grips the door handle. "If I can't look back, you are nothing more than a detective like Detective Rains. I don't eat dinner with him. I don't visit his mom and meet his children. So..." I open the door "...good night, Detective Mosley."

CHAPTER
Eleven

W<small>HEN</small> J<small>OSIE SAID</small> my dad had kissed another woman, I was mortified.

Angry.

Embarrassed.

But mostly ... confused.

I ran home without another word to her and tore through the house looking for my parents.

"Where's Mom and Dad?" I quizzed Chad.

He was too deep in his video game to acknowledge me.

"Where's Mom and Dad?" I plucked the controller from his hands.

"Hey! I don't know." He lunged for me.

I tossed the controller onto the floor, and Chad dove for it like a lifeline. Feeling frantic and confused, I checked the basement, the backyard, and finally the garage. Upon hearing raised voices, I cracked open the side access door less than an inch.

"I'm sorry, Becca ..." I barely recognized my dad's voice, the desperation and the way each word sounded like a stutter because he was crying. It was the first time I witnessed my father crying.

Mom stood in front of him with a blank expression, gaze fixed on his chest like it was too unbearable to look up at him.

"Honey ..." He grabbed her shoulders, and she jerked away from him, stumbling back a few steps until the Volkswagen door stopped her from going any farther. "It just happened. It wasn't planned."

"Did you fuck her?"

Mom didn't swear ... ever. And even if my young mind could have imagined a cuss word falling from her lips, it never would have been the F-word. The king of all swear words. I felt pretty sure I was not only forbidden to say it, but forbidden to even think it.

What confused me the most was what she meant when she said it. I had heard the word a few times. I knew it was bad and forbidden. But I'd never asked anyone for a definition. The few times I had heard someone use it was "fuck you." And not in a nice way. It was an angry "fuck you." So if my mom was asking my dad if he fucked "her," the woman I assumed he kissed, then he must not have liked said woman that much. So why did he kiss her?

I had so much to learn, and hindsight ended up being one very haunting bitch.

"Becca ..." my dad said, just above a whisper. I didn't recognize him. The strict father. The militant coach. The man of the house.

"How c-could y-you?" She sobbed.

Things were bad. How bad? I didn't know until I started to close the door and the hinges squeaked, drawing their attention to me.

"Jesus Christ ..." Dad mumbled, wiping his face while turning his back to me. "Go to your room!"

"Colten ..." Mom chased me as I did what my father told me to do.

In the house.

Up the stairs.

Door slammed shut.

Face planted into my pillow.

And then ... I cried.

"Wait up!" Josie called as I marched toward the bus stop the next morning.

Mom tried to console me for nearly an hour the night before, but I didn't want to talk, so I pretended to fall asleep.

The next morning, there was no sign of Dad. Mom's eyes were swollen, but she put on a fake smile and tried to serve Chad and me French toast like every-thing was okay. I wasn't hungry. And it wasn't okay.

I envied Chad's ability to tune out the world so easily, or so I thought. Come to find out, Chad absorbed everything; he just processed it differently. Not better, but differently.

"Colten?" Josie's shoes slapped the sidewalk, and she ran to catch up to me. "Hey, why are you ignoring me?"

"I'm not ignoring you. I'm getting on the school bus."

"You're ignoring me. Is this about last night?"

"Just ... shut up, Josie. I don't want to talk about it." As soon as the school bus pulled up to the curb, I raced onto it, taking the first available seat.

Two seconds later, Josie plopped down next to me, hugging her pink, black, and green camo bag to her chest. Slumped next to the window, I closed my eyes, hoping she would not say another word.

A few blocks later, she slid her hand under my bag and grabbed my hand, giving it a squeeze while keeping her eyes trained to the front of the bus and her mouth shut.

I lost track of how many times Josie squeezed my hand over the next few years after my dad moved out.

After my mom had a breakdown.

After my brother tried to set a stranger's house on fire.

Every little silent squeeze seemed to say *I've got you. You're not alone. This will pass.*

CHAPTER

Twelve

"You're welcome," Dr. Cornwell says to me the second I arrive in the conference room to go over reports for the day. The other pathologists greet me with hairy eyeballs. Yes, I'm a little late. Neugen Cronk gives me the hardest glare. We were hired at the same time, but he has more experience. Cornwell thinks I have more of ... everything else, and that pisses off Cronk.

Cornwell is quicker than the rest of us at deciding which ones will require autopsies and which ones won't. Sometimes the cause and manner of death can be determined just by reviewing the medical record.

"What should I be thanking you for?" I ignore my colleague's silent animosity and pour a cup of coffee.

"Christ ... have you not seen the news?" Dr. Cornwell asks.

The news. Yes, I watch the local news. Most of the time. This morning, I spent too much time convincing my get-Colten-out-of-my-head hookup from last night that he needed to leave my apartment. No time for the news.

"Our serial killer strikes again."

I perk up before a single sip of coffee.

He smirks. "She's all yours."

"She?" I narrow my eyes while taking a drink of coffee.

"She. You need to find something, Josie. I'm sure you'll have several detectives breathing down your neck before you even get on your PPE."

Colten.

He means Detective Mosley will be breathing down my neck.

It's been five days since I walked out of his house, fumbling with my emotions and tripping over the parts of my ego that are still a little jagged.

Thirty minutes later, I'm in the autopsy suite with a nice gathering of students.

"Dr. Watts is the best I've seen," Dr. Cornwell announces as he passes my table on his way to an eight-year-old girl found dead in her room just after dinner last night. "Want to know why?" he asks the peanut gallery.

Cronk mumbles something just before speaking into the microphone hanging above the table to dictate. I know it was a jab at me.

"Because she thinks like a detective," the young

male student just to my right says, his eyes alight with confidence.

Cornwell and I have played this game. He's prouder of the "correct" answer than I am.

"Partial credit, Hoffler. All forensic pathologists have to think like detectives. It's the part that should come naturally in this field. Dr. Watts thinks like a killer—*that's* what makes her so special."

"My parents prefer 'hunter,' but thanks, Dr. Cornwell. I'm honored you think so highly of me."

The students laugh.

Alicia winks at me when I glance up from my camera lens. I roll my eyes, swapping her the camera for my sketch pad and blue pen.

Over the next hour, we lose three of the students. Newcomers. There's something about a mutilated body mixed with the stench of feces and stomach acid that gives even the most devoted students a moment's pause. Or ... a few moments to vomit or come to after passing out.

I finish my two assigned autopsies, shower in the locker room, and eat my lunch in my office while typing up case notes.

"Bet you expected to see me sooner." Detective Mosley pokes his head into my office before taking a seat opposite me.

I lean to the side, eyeing him behind my computer monitor. "Or not at all." I frown before returning my attention to my screen. "Did Detective Rains break up with me?"

"He has one of those..." Colten snaps his fingers several times "...camera up the ass appointments."

"Colonoscopy. Good for him. Early detection is good."

"You couldn't pay me to do that shit."

Again, I lean to the side, peaking a single eyebrow.

He shrugs, drumming his fingers on his legs clad in black pants. "Listen, about the other night ..."

I clear my throat and take a bite of my sandwich, finding refuge behind the monitor again while mumbling, "You mean ... about this morning. Did I find anything? Yes. I found a fetus. Fifteen weeks."

"Jesus ..."

Chewing another bite of my sandwich, I nod a few times. "They're alive. All of the victims have been alive when their legs have been amputated. You have an angry killer on your hands."

"Angry? Are you implying some killers are not angry?"

I shrug. "You know the answer to that. Kevin Gleason. Necrophile. Lust killer."

Twisting his lips, he nods slowly.

"Sorry," I say. "I haven't found anything to connect the victims. I'm afraid this will be on you. Friends. Family. Co-workers. What do you know about them? Did the victims belong to the same gym? Shop at the same grocery store? See the same massage therapist?"

"You're assuming we're dealing with an organized killer? Seems pretty random at the moment. Wrong place. Wrong time. Voices in their head."

"You have no DNA that does not belong to the victim or the victim's family. Four bodies. Always in a dumpster. No camera footage. Nothing. I think you have a highly intelligent person who is methodical, cautious, and patient."

"What are you doing tonight?"

My nose wrinkles. "What?"

"I'm taking Reagan to the park for a little T-ball practice."

"Okay. Have fun." I wad up my sandwich wrapper and shove it into the sack.

"I thought you could come with us. Unless ... you're hooking up with someone tonight."

"Detective Mosley, I'm pretty sure my personal life is none of your business."

"Listen, I couldn't care less if you go with us or not. It was Reagan's idea."

"Bullshit." I flip up the straw to my water bottle and take several long swigs while eyeing him.

"Ask her yourself."

"Sorry, I don't have her phone number."

"Call her dad around six, and he'll let you speak to her. Say 'Hi, Reagan. It's me, Josie. Do you want me to play T-ball at the park with you and your dad?' And I promise you she'll say yes."

"Why did Katy marry Sean instead of you?"

The gleam in Colten's eyes dies along with his smile. "Wow." He stands, buttoning his suit jacket. "You really know how to ruin a good day, don't you?"

"I'm the person who tells families how their loved

ones died. Ruining people's days is kinda my thing. And I don't really care why you didn't marry Reagan's mom. I'm just reminding you that we are not friends, so your incessant attempts will always be met with my incessant need for answers."

He shakes his head while finding the door to my office, stopping at the threshold with his back to me. "She asked me if I loved her."

I glance up at the door.

"I hesitated," he says. "Two seconds ... maybe three. Then I started to answer, but it was too late. She said she would never marry a man who hesitated ... but more than that ... she wouldn't marry me *because* she had to ask."

Leaning back in my chair, I hug my arms to my chest. "Text me the park and the time."

I HIDE behind a tree like a creeper watching Colten and Reagan play T-ball. This was a bad idea. Everything that involves being with Colten Mosley outside of work is a bad idea.

Some things never change. I spent most of my childhood entertaining bad ideas when it came to Colten.

On a deep breath, I step into view and smile at Reagan as she runs the bases of the small field.

"You came." Colten's smile gobbles up his whole face.

I shrug. "It's a nice night. Not as humid. And I could use a little fresh air."

"Daddy, it's her." Reagan runs right into Colten's leg, hugging it while pointing at me.

"Yes, it's Josie."

"Hi, Josie!" She gives me a quick wave before grabbing the bat.

"Hi, Reagan."

Colten sets the ball back on the tee. Reagan smacks it and starts running the bases again, stopping at third base to chase a butterfly.

"No attention span." Colten shakes his head.

I chuckle.

He slides his hands in his pockets and watches her. "Do you remember when we said we'd never have kids?"

Yes. I remember. Colten said he'd never bring children into the world because he was afraid he'd inherited the loser dad gene. I just ... never wanted to be a mom even though I've had a great family. I wanted a career.

And Colten ... I wanted Colten Mosley. Had he wanted to marry me and have ten kids, I would have said yes.

"Well ..." I clear my throat. "I didn't have kids. She's all yours."

His head inches side to side several times before looking at me. "What about now? Are you dating a new guy every night because you're looking for love? A husband? A family?"

Rubbing my lips together, I shake my head and watch Reagan and the butterfly. "Just sex, Mosley. I don't want or need a husband. And we know I'm not exactly maternal, so I'll leave the childrearing up to women who are more nurturing."

"Occupational hazard?"

I smirk. "Something like that."

"Well..." he blows out a long breath "...I hope the sex is good."

I snort. "Yeah. I'm sure you do."

Reagan runs toward us, and Colten hunches down, letting her tackle him. "Oof!" He falls backward, and she straddles his chest, pressing her hands to his cheeks.

"Love you, Daddy."

"Oh, Button." He jackknives to sitting and grabs her tiny head, giving her a loud smooch on her forehead. "I love you too."

"I'm hungry."

"Okay. Let's hit a few more balls then we'll grab dinner."

Reagan softens all his rough edges. I need those rough edges to remind me to keep a safe distance from him. The dad version of Colten Mosley is too much.

We find some great Tex-Mex a few blocks from the park. My treat. Then he fastens Reagan into his Tahoe and starts the engine before stepping outside with me again, back resting against the closed door. "Thank you for meeting us tonight."

I cross my arms over my chest and nod several

times. "It was fun. Reagan is great. I'm amazed at how close you two are given the fact that you don't have shared custody."

"We FaceTime almost every day." His brows knit together as he stares at his feet for a second. "I gave Katy full custody because it was better for Reagan. No need to shuffle a baby back and forth between two homes. And I trusted that she'd do the right thing when Reagan got older."

"The right thing?"

He glances up at me. "Katy is a better person than I am. Even if I couldn't love her like..." his gaze averts to the side "...like she deserved to be loved; it wasn't a reflection of her. I trusted her to either let me into Reagan's life if it was best for our daughter or to raise her with someone else. She chose me." He shrugs a shoulder.

"You're not your father. That's why she trusted you. That's why she chose you."

When his gaze meets mine again, he smirks. "You giving me a compliment?"

"I'm ..." I hold up my hands and take a step backward. "I'm ... leaving. That's what I'm doing."

"Got a date tonight?"

I shake my head. "Why? Are you jealous?"

Colten scratches his jaw. "Watts ... I'm not sure there will come a day that the idea of you with some other guy doesn't make me a little jealous. It's in my DNA."

I study him, looking for an ounce of sincerity. Then

124

I turn and make my way to the driver's side of my car. "You hesitate." I glance up at him as I open my door.

His eyes narrow.

"You're a single dad because you hesitate. You pause. You always leave the door cracked open. Certainty is sexy. Nobody wants to be anyone's second thought."

Me. I was his second thought.

CHAPTER
Thirteen

I TURNED thirteen two weeks before the start of eighth grade. My dad was out of town for a camp. Mom was recovering from an appendectomy. And Chad managed to pull his head out of his ass long enough to help Mom while Mrs. Watts (Savannah) made me a birthday dinner and cake.

"How's your mom?" Chief Isaac Watts asked as I strode up their driveway. He was working on his 1970 Chevelle SS 454. Blue. White striped hood. His true baby.

"She's okay. Chad's with her."

"Your dad still gone?"

I nodded.

Chief Watts frowned for a second before ducking back under the hood. He didn't approve of my dad's extramarital affair or the way he failed to teach me and

Chad basic skills like changing a tire, fishing, or how to use a gun.

"Sports aren't going to help you in the real world," Chief Watts would casually say when our families got together to grill or play yard darts.

My dad always had the same comeback. *"Colten's going to go pro someday. He'll pay someone to fix his car. Hire a bodyguard. And eat at fancy restaurants where someone else caught the fish."*

Go pro? In what? I wasn't sure. Literally any sport. All coaches had big dreams of their kids achieving what they never could. I had no interest in letting my dad live vicariously through me or making him happy at all for that matter.

"Need some help?" I asked Chief Watts.

He glanced back at me and grinned. "Dinner won't be ready for a bit. Might as well get your hands dirty first."

I didn't care to fish or hunt. But I liked his Chevelle and how willing and patient he was to show me everything about it.

Only minutes later, Josie opened the back door. "Oh ... you are here." I bumped my head on the hood because her voice startled me. It did things to me every time I heard it.

"Yeah, I'm helping your dad."

"You could help too, Jo," Chief Watts said.

She sighed, taking a seat on the garage step. "I could, but that's why you have Colten until Benji gets older. Oh ... and happy birthday."

Savannah offering to make me birthday dinner didn't come at the best time. Josie hadn't talked to me in three weeks. I called her bluff on an ultimatum. She wanted me to lie to her parents if they asked about her whereabouts the night she said she was supposed to be with a friend but was actually with Roland Tompkins at the funeral home. Of course, she told Roland her parents said she could help him prepare things for a visitation that night.

They did not.

So ... when I said I wouldn't lie for her, she broke up with me. It was something like breakup number ten billion and one. Our relationship changed like a blinking red light.

On.

Off.

On.

Off.

I don't remember falling in love with Josephine Watts. I just remember the day we met and the day I let her go for good. For me, she wasn't really my girlfriend. She was my everything. Every other girlfriend was just a game to get her back. Every fight was a prelude to treehouse kisses, "I'M SORRY" signs in the window, and shared cookies and milk.

I lived with my family, but I lived *for* Josephine Watts.

"Thanks, Josie." I played it cool like my birthday wasn't a big deal. Like her mom making me dinner or her dad letting me work with him wasn't a big deal.

Like *she* wasn't a big deal. Who was I kidding? If my birthday was the excuse she needed to break her silence, then that was the only birthday present I needed.

"Isaac? I need you to start the grill," Savannah said before shutting the door.

As he passed Josie perched on the stair, he gave her ponytail a little tug. "Be good."

With a dramatic eye roll, she mumbled, "Duh."

I grabbed a rag and wiped my hands while Josie rested her elbows on her knees and her face in her hands.

"My mom said your dad is gone for your birthday. That's pretty lame."

I shrugged. "I don't care."

"What did you get for your birthday? A new bat? New glove?"

"Nothing. I'm not sure my dad even remembers that it's my birthday, and since my mom was in the hospital, she hasn't had time to get me anything."

Josie's nose wrinkled. "That sucks. What do you want for your birthday?"

"Nothing."

"Liar."

"I'm not lying."

"Can you believe you could be driving by this time next year? My dad said I can drive his car when I turn fourteen. Jealous?"

Jealous? Yes. I was always jealous of Josie and her family.

"No."

"I'll go to the batting cages with you after dinner."

Again, I shrugged. It didn't come naturally to me, but I sure as hell tried to act unaffected by her.

"Jo, go inside and help watch your brother while your mom tends to the burgers on the grill. I need to finish up so I can take Colten for a ride after dinner." Chief Watts ruffled my hair before taking the rag from me.

"Really?" I couldn't help my excitement.

"We're going to the batting cages. Right, Colten?" Josie said, cocking her head to the side. A test. The head-cock was always a test.

My gaze flitted between Josie and her dad. "Uh ... we can go to the batting cages anytime. But your dad's not working tonight, so ..."

"So what?" Josie played hardball.

"We might find an empty parking lot where you can get in a little driving practice," Chief Watts said, showing me exactly where Josie got her persistence and competitive nature.

What was she going to do? We were already broken up.

"Batting cages tomorrow," I said.

Chief Watts gave me a wink.

Josie stormed into the house.

"Give her time. She's spicy just like her mom. But she'll come around. She always does. Right?"

I nodded slowly.

Josie didn't even look at me during dinner. She

didn't sing "Happy Birthday" when I blew out the candles on the cake. And she took her cake and ice cream to her bedroom, ignoring her dad's offer to go for a ride with us.

As promised, Chief Watts let me drive his car in the empty parking lot of the community college. There was something really cool about the chief of police breaking the law with me.

"I took leftover cake to your mom and brother," Savannah said to me when we entered the house.

"Thanks. Um ... where's Josie?"

"Out back."

"I'm going to go check on her. Thanks for a great birthday dinner."

Savannah picked up Benjamin and kissed his head. "Anytime, Colten. Happy birthday."

"And thank you, Chief Watts. It was awesome."

"You can call me Isaac."

I shook my head, eyes wide.

He chuckled. "Whatever. Go tell Josie she needs to come in by nine."

"Okay." I shot out the door, but Josie wasn't in the backyard. She was past the trail in her tree.

"Go away. You chose my dad over me."

I jumped up to grab the branch and pull myself up into the tree with her. "I chose driving over the batting cages."

"Same thing." She pouted.

"It's not. Besides, what are you going to do? Break up with me?" I laughed.

She did not laugh.

"I break up with you, so you don't break up with me first."

"That makes no sense."

"It does. Amy said Josh said you feel sorry for me, and you're afraid of my dad. That's why you let me be your girlfriend. I don't want you feeling sorry for me."

"I never said that. Josh is an idiot."

"Well, you must have said something like that. I'm sure he didn't make up a lie for no reason. Just be honest … do you think I'm weird? Do you think it's weird that I hunt with my dad? Do you think it's weird that I hang out at the funeral home? Do you think I'm ugly because I don't wear makeup like the other girls?"

"No."

"Then why do you want me to be your girlfriend?"

Thirteen wasn't the best age for me. The whole girls-mature-faster-than-boys was never more magnified than in that moment. I had no clue. Well, I had a little clue, but it was nonsensical. So I blurted out the first thing that popped into my head, which wasn't a lie, but it wasn't totally true either. "Because you keep telling me I'm your boyfriend. And I like you, so I say 'okay.' Then you get mad at me and tell me we're breaking up. So I say 'okay' because I just don't like it when you're mad at me. And I don't like it when you let other guys hold your hand and kiss you."

Josie took a moment to stare at her dangling black Nikes, and I waited for her to tell me what to do. Life was easier when Josie was happy, and when she told me how to make her happy instead of making me guess what I did to upset her.

"Why don't you like it when other guys kiss me and hold my hand?" she mumbled, keeping her chin tucked.

"Because it's what I like to do."

Ever so slowly, she glanced over at me and grinned. "Do you want to kiss me now?"

Wetting my lips, I nodded.

"Okay," she whispered.

Leaning to the side, my lips brushed hers. I closed my eyes. And ...

"Collltennn!"

Thunk!

Josie fell out of the tree.

"Oh, fuck!"

It took me a few seconds to move my body and climb out of the tree. I wasn't expecting her to fall. And I definitely wasn't expecting her to say the F-word.

"My arm ..." She cradled her left arm to her chest and cried.

"Josie! Oh my god. Are you okay?"

"M-my a-arm ..." She cried more.

"Is it broken?"

"I don't k-know."

"Can you stand? Do you want me to get your parents?"

She sobbed and nodded. I assumed it was a yes to getting her parents, so I ran to the house.

"Josie fell out of the tree and hurt her arm," I

blurted the second I charged into the house, but nobody was in the room. Panicked, I ran up the stairs. Her brother was already asleep in his room with the door cracked, and his white noise machine playing.

I didn't think. I really *really* should have thought before opening her parents' bedroom door without so much as a knock.

Up until Josie asked me if I wanted to kiss her, the highlight of my thirteenth birthday was Chief Watts letting me drive his car. Then Josie said those words, and I forgot about the Chevelle.

Until she fell ...

That was the new unforgettable memory from my thirteenth birthday.

Until ...

I barged into Josie's parents' bedroom and witnessed Chief Watts standing in front of the television with the remote in one hand and Savannah's ponytail in his other hand. Her on her knees. His penis in her mouth.

The infamous blow job.

I had only heard about it from friends. Never experienced it. Never witnessed it.

"Colten!" Chief Watts boomed.

"Oh my god!" Savannah scurried to her feet and ran into the bathroom.

Me? Oh, I couldn't tear my eyes from the chief's larger-than-life penis. He reeled that long thing back into his pants with the swiftness of a fire engine after the last ember was extinguished.

He was angry.

Josie was sobbing in the woods.

Yet, all I could think was will mine be that big?

God, I hoped so.

Benji cried. For some reason that was what brought me back to reality, that and Chief Watts's big hands on my shoulders guiding me out of his bedroom.

"What the hell are you doing, Colten?" There was a tightness in his voice that I hadn't heard before. A constraint.

"Oh ..."

Savannah, with her flushed face breezed past us to Benji's room. "Shh ... it's okay, baby."

"I ..." My gaze gathered enough courage to look Chief Watts in the eyes. My new idol. "Josie fell out of the tree. I think she broke her arm."

He winced. "Shit ..." he murmured, brushing past me to the stairs.

"Josie?" Savannah called behind us as I followed Chief Watts to the woods.

With the strength, only a large-penised man would have, he carried Josie straight to his truck.

"Josie ..." Savannah held a grumpy Benji while kissing Josie's head before Chief Watts put her in the back seat.

"We'll get an X-ray, and I'll call you," Chief Watts said to Savannah. "Get in, Colten."

He wanted me to go. Why? I wasn't sure, but I had a sneaking suspicion it had something to do with the infamous blow job.

135

I sat next to Josie, and she leaned her head on me as she occasionally sniffled and whimpered. My hand slid to hers and squeezed it.

"So what exactly happened?" Chief Watts asked as we headed toward the emergency room.

When Josie remained quiet, I cleared my throat. "Well ... we were in the tree, and she fell out."

"Why did she fall out?" He eyed me in his rearview mirror.

"Because I said he could kiss me for his birthday," Josie murmured.

I felt less intimidated watching Chief Watts shove all three feet of his penis back into his pants than I did as he scowled at me in the mirror. I'd kissed her so many times before that day; it wasn't a big deal. She showed me her tits. That was kind of a big deal, but not anything Chief Watts needed to know.

Why did Josie rat me out? Was it payback for me not lying to her parents about the funeral home?

"B-but ... I didn't. We uh ... we didn't ... Sir."

Chief.

Master.

King.

Please don't put me in jail!

He grumbled something indecipherable.

While the nurse took Josie for an X-ray, Chief Watts pulled me aside in the waiting room. "Listen, Colten ..."

I had run a lot of bases, sprinted many fifty-yard dashes, but never had my heart pounded so quickly and violently in my chest as it did beneath the formidable man towering over me.

"I don't know if your parents have had 'the talk' with you, but ..."

I nodded then shook my head. "No. I mean ... yeah, I know about *that*. I should have knocked, and ..."

"You saw something you weren't supposed to see."

"I-I'm ... sorry." I closed my eyes and shook my head.

"Hey, look at me."

Again, I dragged my gaze to his. "I need you to make me a promise."

I nodded at least a half dozen times. Anything. I would do anything if it didn't involve going to jail.

"You forget about what you saw."

More nodding.

"And you never kiss my daughter again."

I kept nodding. His words barely registered.

"So we're clear? We're good?"

A hundred more nods. "Y-yeah ..."

He rested his hand on my shoulder and squeezed it. "I'm going to talk to your dad. I think it's about time you learn how to use a rifle."

Forget about the large penis.

Never kiss Josie again.

Use a rifle.

Got it.

CHAPTER
Fourteen

"I'VE NEVER FELT NORMAL. But what is normal? How does one end up in this profession?" I ask.

Alicia sips her drink while I stir my lemonade with my straw. I've needed this girls' night out, especially since I don't have a lot of girlfriends. Never have.

"I have a seven-year-old son who tells his friends I sew up dead people." She rolls her eyes.

I laugh.

Alicia shrugs. "Someone has to do it, right? It's not for everyone, that's for sure. I wasn't exactly a 'normal' child either. I didn't hunt with my dad like you did, but I was never grossed out by things. Not gory movies. Not grotesque odors. Nothing."

"Did you have a fascination with death?"

She shakes her head. "No. Did you?"

I think about it, eyes narrowed at my drink.

"Kind of. Yeah. I hung around the funeral home. I asked my dad a slew of questions every time I overheard him talking about a death. I wanted to know all the details. When I'd ride my bike near ponds or creeks, I'd scour the area for dead bodies."

Alicia snorts. "You grew up in Iowa, right?"

"Yes. I didn't say I found any dead bodies, but ..."

"A girl can dream, right?"

My eyes widen as she returns a wry grin and shrugs. "If you know, you know."

On a chuckle, I nod. "I brought home a dead badger from the woods behind our house when I was seven. My mom was beside herself. Later, I overheard them talking about the incident, saying it was something one might expect from a dog, not a young girl."

Alicia gives me a wide-eyed, unblinking stare. "A badger?"

I nod and shrug a shoulder. "I wanted to see if I could find its heart."

"Why? Had you watched something on television that made you curious? Did one of your parents have a zoology book lying around the house?"

"No. One night, our neighbor's Bichon got attacked by something. They had to put it down. My dad suspected it was a badger. He said badgers can be 'heartless bastards.' Well, I didn't believe any animal could live without a heart, so I wanted to see for myself."

Choking on her drink, Alicia coughs and pats her

chest as laughter assaults her ability to speak or breathe. "You're ... k-kidding."

"No. That was when I learned everything about rabies and all other diseases carried by animals. My dad told me I could no longer bring home anything that wasn't a bird, snake, or fish since they can't carry or transmit rabies."

"Oh my gosh ... your dad is too much. I can't imagine what it must have been like to grow up as the police chief's daughter. Were you allowed to date before you went to college?"

On a slight chuckle, I shake my head. "It wasn't easy. The only boy he cared for was the neighbor boy, but he didn't want me with him. He simply wanted a son my age. My dad adored him. Took him under his wing. They worked on my dad's Chevelle together. When we were in high school, my dad worked out with him. Morning runs. Weight lifting. They became quite competitive. Never got him to hunt, but he taught him how to shoot a gun."

"You must have been envious of the neighbor boy."

"Mmm ... I had strong feelings for him, but I'm not sure envy is the right word."

"You liked him?"

I nod. "Too much." Do I tell her it was Detective Mosley?

"But your dad wouldn't let you date him?"

"No. Well, I don't know the answer to that. We had a unique relationship where his loyalties were split between my dad and me since my dad made him promise to never kiss me again after an incident. So whenever our relationship breached the more-than-friends zone, we had to keep it from my dad. And I'm not going to lie ... I was all over the place. Protecting my heart wasn't easy. I kept him at arm's length, which kept me miserable for years."

Alicia frowns. "What happened when you graduated? Were you friends or more than friends?"

"We were ..." I stare at the bar over her shoulder, wondering if abstaining from alcohol all these years was a good idea with Colten Mosley living rent free in my brain. "We were over. He ended us. Blew up my heart. Ran over it with his car. Poured gasoline onto it. Then flicked a lit match at the wreckage."

Nose wrinkled, Alicia mouths the word "ouch."

"Yeah."

"Have you seen him since then? High school reunions? Facebook friends?"

Really, I should tell Alicia it's Colten, but I don't want her to think I'm still pining for him ... because I'm not.

"Yes, we've run into each other."

"Was it awkward? Is he married with a family? Really successful? A total loser?"

I chuckle while the waiter brings us our food. "A mix of all of the above."

After the waiter leaves, Alicia pops a cherry tomato into her mouth. "You're so successful and brilliant at your job; I'm sure he's envious of you. I'm sure he regrets everything he did."

"Sadly ... no." I dig into my meal.

After dinner, I offer to give Alicia a ride, so she doesn't have to take the train.

"It's out of your way."

"Nonsense." I reach into my purse as we round the corner of the building to the parking lot.

Alicia makes a weird noise behind me, and I turn.

Her eyes bulge from her head as a man in a hoodie holds his hand over her mouth and a knife to her throat.

"Wallets," he says. "Nice and slow, sweetheart. Or your friend won't see the sunrise."

Alicia drops her purse on the ground.

He kicks it a few feet to the right and nods to me to toss mine there as well.

With my hand still in my purse, fingers wrapped around my key fob, I shift my hand to my gun and quickly toss the purse. His gaze follows my purse instead of focusing on my hand ... on the gun.

The bullet hits his knee the second he releases Alicia to grab our purses.

"AHH!" Alicia screams when he releases her.

He grunts and falls to the ground like a wounded animal. "You shot me, you fucking bitch!"

Keeping the gun aimed at him, I sidestep and retrieve our purses.

"Oh my god!" Alicia shakes, hands cupping her neck where the knife had been.

With my free hand, I call 9-1-1.

An hour later, we're at the police station, giving our

statements. Alicia's husband picks her up, and I stay a little longer since it was my gun. To make my night better, my old neighbor shows up.

"Watts … did you shoot a man tonight?"

Resisting an eye roll, I angle in my chair to see Detective Mosley at the door to the office, looking smug as usual.

"She's all yours." The officer questioning me grins at Colten.

I stand and exit the office, brushing past Colten. "I'm not his," I murmur.

"How's Alicia?" He tails me.

"Shook," I say, reaching the elevator.

"How are you?"

I shrug as the doors open. "Fine. Why?"

He follows me as I step into the elevator. "Because you shot a man tonight. Doesn't that give you a moment's pause?"

"I didn't kill him."

Colten lifts a single brow. "No … but still. You discharged your weapon. I didn't know you carried."

"Sorry. Had I mentioned that earlier in our reunion, would you have given me more space?"

Colten stands next to me, giving me very little space while staring at the doors. "He's going to be fine. The guy you shot. If you were concerned."

"Pfft … of course he's going to be fine. I didn't shoot to kill."

"Have you shot anyone before?"

143

The elevator doors open, and I make a mad dash for the exit. "Not to my knowledge."

He chuckles. "That's not exactly reassuring."

When I get to my car, I turn because I sense him less than two steps behind me. Colten engulfs nearly all the space between us. It's hard to breathe in his close proximity—another thing that hasn't changed in seventeen years.

His smile fades a fraction. "You were brave. And a little stupid. You didn't know he was alone. There could have been someone else. They could have had a gun. If he wanted your wallets, you should have given him your wallets and not risked things escalating."

"Thanks, Dad." I turn to open my car door.

"Josie ..." He rests his hand on my hip.

I freeze. The perpetrator didn't frighten me, but Colten Mosley's touch scares me to death.

"Are you okay?"

"He didn't touch me. I'm fine."

"Your voice is shaking. That doesn't tell me you're fine."

I clear my throat and force confidence into my voice. "How exactly did you find out? I don't think homicide is called for an attempted robbery and a shot fired that doesn't result in ... homicide." Turning to force his hand away from my hip, I hug my handbag to my chest. A shield from him.

"When the assistant ME shoots a man in the leg, news travels fast."

"Gossip."

"Official Chicago PD notifications," he says, but his words are nothing more than mumbled syllables with no meaning behind them because he's too busy staring at my mouth, and that's mind-numbingly distracting.

"I'm gonna kiss you, Josie."

"Don't tell me. Just do it."

"I'm not going to kiss you." He grins.

I scoff. "Why would I think that?"

"Because you drag your teeth along your lower lip when you think I'm going to kiss you ... when you want me to kiss you."

"Seventeen years ..." I turn and open my door, forcing him to take a step backward. "It's been seventeen years. You know nothing about me. A lot has changed." I slide into the driver's seat.

Colten wedges himself between me and the door, resting his forearms on my car. "Sure ... you've turned into a successful doctor. Maybe you've even mastered dating apps and finding random guys to hook up with, but that look..." he bites his lower lip, dragging his teeth along it to mimic me "...time will never change that look."

"People often see what they want to see, not what's really there." I start my car.

"Take the day off tomorrow. You need to process what happened tonight."

I laugh. "If you shot someone in the knee, would you take a day off to process it?"

"That's different."

"I'll be at work tomorrow. If you need to take the

145

day off, then do it. You're clearly more bothered by the incident than I am."

"I bet Alicia takes the day off," he says.

I glance up at him. "She had a knife at her throat. I did not."

"Had it been you with a knife at your throat, would you take the day off?"

"Bad people don't scare me." I reach for the door handle.

"Well they should."

"Well they don't."

"That's fucked-up, Josie."

"It's just me. See ... you don't remember me as well as you think you do."

Colten steps back and lets me shut the door. I make the mistake of giving him one last glance. Of course, he knows me. And I know him. That's what makes this seventeen-year reunion a recipe for disaster.

When I get home, I jump on my stationary bike for forty-five minutes before showering. As the hot water washes over me, I attempt to make a mental and emotional assessment of myself.

The conclusion? I feel fine.

Maybe I'll have nightmares about the situation, but I doubt it.

CHAPTER
Fifteen

CHIEF WATTS ASKED me to take his daughter to the homecoming dance. Neither Josie nor I were dating anyone else. It was our sophomore year, and, honestly, I was fine not going to the dance. However, at the last minute, Ryan Wilkenson asked Josie to the dance.

A senior.

Josie said yes.

Chief Watts said, "Over my dead body."

I agreed with her dad, but I didn't tell her that. Ryan was a player in every sense. Not that I wasn't a player in my own right, but I wasn't in the business of collecting V-cards like Ryan.

"Dad! I hate this. You don't trust me. He's two years older, not ten. We're just friends."

I helped my mom bag yard waste while listening to Josie and her dad in their garage.

"Colten?" Josie yelled my name.

Shit.

"Tell my dad that Ryan Wilkenson and I are just friends."

Since Josie broke her arm, I refused to be her official boyfriend. Yeah, I made a promise to her dad, and I valued my life, so I kept it as best as I could. She still unofficially decided when we were together and when we were not.

Did she kiss me just to torture me? Absolutely.

Did I want her to kiss me? Did I love the torture? Absolutely.

Did I date other girls just to piss her off? You betcha.

As a result, she used me to manipulate her dad. Fair? Probably.

"They're just friends," I mumbled.

"He can't hear you!" She was ... fiery. "Come here, please."

Mom smirked at me.

Drawing in a long breath, I blew it out while crossing the street.

Josie sat perched on the step to the back door, her usual spot, while Chief Watts finished wiping down his Chevelle with a rag.

"Tell him," she repeated.

I rolled my eyes. "They're just friends."

"Don't care," Chief Watts said in a tone that sounded as uninterested as my own. "My little girl isn't going out with a senior."

"I'm not your little girl."

"Then whose are you?" He shot her a stern look over his shoulder.

Josie grumbled.

"You take her to the dance, Colten," Chief Watts said. "Problem solved."

"I ..." I shook my head while Josie's smile took over her face. "I'm not going to the dance."

"Yeah, Dad ... he's not going," Josie said behind her dad's back while running her teeth along her lower lip, that thing she did when she wanted me to kiss her.

"Either Colten takes you, or you're not going."

"I already bought a dress." She made an amusing attempt at batting her eyelashes at me.

I shook my head. "I'd have to see if one of my parents could drive us."

"I'll drive you in the Chevelle." He turned around and winked. "Your very own police escort."

Josie immediately played the disgruntled daughter. "Fine. Guess I'll have to tell Ryan that my dad doesn't trust him." She stormed into the house, slamming the door behind her.

An act ... it was all an act.

"Thanks, son." Chief Watts rested his hand on my shoulder and squeezed it. I wasn't his son, but most days I wished he were my dad. Except then Josie would have been my sister, and all of our kissing would have been really inappropriate.

Two weeks later, Chief Watts drove us to dinner. He and Savannah sat two tables away. It sucked not having our driver's licenses yet.

An hour and a half later, he dropped us off at the dance. We had until midnight. We spent most of the time chatting with friends and fast dancing. When the DJ played a slow song, Darren Hayes's "Insatiable," I asked Josie to dance.

She smelled like cool mint gum and a really strong perfume. Josie wore a white strapless dress; and her hair was straighter than usual and silky. Her eyes had a bronze shadow and her lashes were heavy with mascara.

"After this song, let's leave," she said while draping her arms over my shoulders as I kept my hands a safe distance above her butt.

"Your dad's not picking us up until midnight. It's only ten."

"When my dad picks us up, he'll take us home. You'll go to your house, and I'll go to mine. How are you supposed to kiss me goodnight?"

"It's not going to take me two hours to kiss you goodnight."

She smirked. The pink lip gloss she wore earlier that night had worn off. "Then you're not doing it right, Mosley." That was the sexiest thing Josie had ever said to me.

I grinned. "I think our ride is here now."

Josie's grin matched mine. I took her hand and led her to the exit.

"It's cold, Josie. Where are we going?" I slipped off my jacket and draped it over her shoulders.

"You don't trust me. That sucks for you." She pulled me toward the football field and under the bleachers where there was a folded blanket hidden at one end.

"Did you leave this after the game last night?"

She nodded, handing me the blanket. I shook it out and wrapped it around my back before taking a seat against one of the rails. Josie hiked up her dress and straddled my lap. I hugged her with the blanket, wrapping us in a cocoon.

"I'm gonna kiss you, Josie."

She grinned, leaning in and rubbing her cold nose against mine. "Don't tell me. Just do it."

That was an awkward time in our lives. We were either fighting, pretending to ignore each other, or making out like our existence revolved around each other's tongue probing the other one's mouth.

The problem?

Josie gave me a perpetual hard-on. The way she hummed when we kissed.

Her fingers in my hair.

Her warm crotch and thin panties just on the other side of said hard-on and strained fly.

We didn't move against each other at that point, but surely, she felt the difference between first sitting on me, and thirty seconds later when her tongue slid against mine and every ounce of blood in my body shot straight to my dick.

I only knew of a handful of boys in my class who had already lost their virginity. All of them to girls a year or two older. I wasn't going to have sex with Josie, probably ever, if Chief Watts got his way. Had he known where we were that night and what we were doing, I would have been a lifeless body in the cemetery just down the street from our houses.

As if she could read my mind, Josie pulled away a fraction, breathless, eyes wide, lips slightly parted. "I want you to be my first," she whispered.

I shook my head half a dozen times.

Josie grinned. "Not now. Just ... when it happens, I want you to be my first, and I want to be your first."

"Your dad will kill me."

On a laugh, she threw her head back, fingers laced behind my neck. "Duh, Colten. We're not going to tell him when it happens."

Never. *If* it happened, we would never tell him.

But fuck ... did I trust her not to let it slip? After all, everything changed when she felt the need to tell him she fell out of the tree because I leaned over to kiss her.

"What if I'm dating someone else when that time comes? Or what if you have a boyfriend?" I asked.

She shrugged a shoulder. "Doesn't matter. We agree to be each other's firsts, and that's that."

"So ..." I narrowed my eyes. "If I have a girlfriend and she wants to have sex with me, I have to find you and have sex with you first?"

Josie gave me a firm nod. "Yes."

It was my turn to bark a laugh. "And if you have a

boyfriend, you think he's going to be okay with you telling him you have to have sex with me before you can have it with him?"

"I'll just say tough luck, Mr. Duck."

I tried to conceal my amusement. She hadn't said that in years. "You can't say that to him."

"Why?" She slanted her head to the side.

"Because you say that to me."

She nipped at my lower lip and whispered, "You don't own me."

I rested my hands on her ass. "Not all of you." My lips found her neck, and I kissed my way to her bare shoulder. "Just the best of you."

CHAPTER
Sixteen

"YOU GOOD?" Dr. Cornwell asks when he saunters into the conference room.

"Of course. Not Alicia, though."

"One shot, right to his knee. You never cease to amaze me, Watts." Dr. Cornwell slides on his reading glasses and taps his tablet as the others file into the room.

"I've been called to testify. It's kind of last minute. I'll be back after lunch. If you're not done—"

"Go." He shoos me with one hand while keeping his focus on his tablet.

I grab my handbag and a case file from the table for court. "Is it weird that shooting a man in the knee didn't faze me?"

Several of my asshole colleagues mumble a "yes."

"Weird?" Cornwell eyes me over the top of his reading glasses sitting low on his prominent nose.

"Should I feel remorse? Fear of retaliation? Shock that I did it so easily? Something? I mean ... I don't really feel anything about it. I didn't panic. I just did it like someone does something on autopilot or instinct. Gave my account to the police. Drove home. Cycled. Showered. And slept like a corpse."

After a few silent seconds, he removes his glasses. "Frankly, I don't know. I've never shot anyone. I don't own a gun. I've removed too many bullets to feel like I'd ever want to put one into another human being. But consider all the people who think we are emotionless because of the job we do. Nothing could be further from the truth. We are methodical and controlled with our emotions. I'm sure that carries over to other parts of your life. My wife says I ground her because she's a ball of unchecked emotions, and I'm silently contemplative to the point she often feels the need to see if I still have a pulse."

I chuckle. "I don't feel so bad now." I head toward the door.

"Because I'm your idol?"

"Sure, sure, sure ..."

AFTER A MORNING OF TESTIMONY, I grab lunch at a food truck and head toward my car. I half expect Detective Mosley to call me, but he doesn't.

Not today.

Not the following day.

Or the following day.

I'm good. Or so I tell myself. How does his new existence in my life transport me back to the young girl spying out my window, waiting for Colten to come home from baseball practice?

On my way home (*so* far out of my way), I drive by his house, slowing down to see if I see anyone through the front window. When I don't, I continue to the end of the street.

My phone rings. I hit the handsfree button on my steering wheel when I see it's Detective Moseley. Does he have a sixth sense that I'm spying on him?

"Hello?"

"You're a little out of your neighborhood, Watts. What's up?"

I cringe, glancing in my rearview mirror just as he pulls into his driveway. "Uh ... I know your mom is leaving soon, so I was going to say goodbye, but it didn't look like anyone was home, so ..."

"I'm home."

On a nervous laugh, I nod to myself. "Yeah. I see that."

"Reagan and my mom go home tomorrow. You should come for dinner."

"It's your last night together. I'm not intruding on that."

"The way I intruded on dinner at your house

nearly every night for months after my parents separated?"

"That was different. My mom invited you."

"True. Hold on a sec ..." I hear a few indistinguishable sounds then the click of a door shutting. "Hey, Mom ... can Josie come to dinner?"

Oh my god ...

I'm embarrassed, and I'm not even in the house. He's acting like a child inviting a friend to dinner.

"She said yes. Come over. After the old and the young go to bed, you can hang out in the garage with me."

I turn the corner to circle around the block. "I'll come to dinner, but then I have to go home."

"Curfew?" he asks.

I grin. "Something like that."

When I pull into the driveway, he's standing on his porch, tie loose, jacket open, and his hands planted in his front pockets.

He's ... a sight.

"I'm intruding," I say for a lack of other words as I approach him.

"My mom would be disappointed if she didn't get to say goodbye. It's like you knew."

I offer a genuine smile as he opens the door.

"You have the best smile, Watts. You really should show it off more often."

I slip off my shoes. "I smile a lot ... in the right company."

"I used to be the right company." He slides off his suit jacket and heads toward the stairs.

"You used to be a lot of things," I say, feeling a million more emotions than I did the night I shot a man in the leg because my friend had a knife held to her throat.

Colten pauses, but he doesn't look back at me. "Have I mentioned how proud I am of your accomplishments?"

It rubs me wrong ... in the worst way. He keeps parroting that sentiment. "Have I mentioned that you had nothing to do with my accomplishments?" I head toward the kitchen and the sound of a five-year-old giggling.

"Josie!" Becca smiles, setting a steaming casserole dish onto the stove. "I'm so glad you could join us." She takes off her oven mitts.

"I feel like I'm intruding, but I wanted to get a chance to say goodbye before you left. Hey, Reagan. I heard you're going home with your mom tomorrow."

She glances up from her coloring book and nods. "Uh-huh."

"Well, it's been fun getting to know you. I hope we get to see each other again."

"Uh-huh."

"Reagan, go see if your dad wants a salad with his dinner," Becca says.

"I'm coloring."

Becca shakes her head. "You're killing my knees with these stairs."

"I'll go." I wink at Becca.

"Thanks, dear."

When I reach the top of the stairs, I glance in each bedroom. The primary bedroom is the last on the right. And the second I realize that, I'm staring at a half-dressed man. Jeans on but unbuttoned with the zipper down. A gray tee with his arms through it but not pulled over his head yet.

Damn ...

Everything about Colten Mosley is all grown up. I much prefer a living, breathing, *perfect* human specimen.

After my gaze goes right to his unbuttoned jeans, it slides up a few inches to the long scar on his abdomen.

"Watts?"

My gaze snaps up to his, and I swallow before clearing my throat. "Do you want a salad? Your uh ... mom wants to know."

"A salad sounds good." He threads the shirt over his head and pulls it down his torso before buttoning his jeans. He wasn't this muscular the last time I saw so much of his body. I've seen a lot of bodies, so it's strange that I'm visually enamored with his, but ... I am.

Since my brain has decided to completely go off the rails, I go ahead and take a quick scan of his bedroom.

King bed.

Striped bedding.

Tall dresser.

Nothing special.

No photos on the wall, just a coat of gray paint.

How many women has he had in his bed? More than the number of men who have been in mine? Am I really thinking it's a competition?

"I'll tell her I want a salad if you need a few more minutes to check out my bedroom."

"No." I refocus on him and shake my head. "I'm going. Take your time."

"Did I ever tell you what I saw the day you fell out of the tree and broke your arm?"

I turn back toward him. He rubs his fingers over his lips like he's trying to hide his grin.

"What you saw?"

He nods, taking a seat on the end of his bed. "I ran into the house, but nobody was downstairs. So I ran upstairs. Benji was in his bed, and I was panicked over you, so I opened the door to your parents' bedroom. I didn't knock because it was an emergency, and really ... what would they be doing anyway?"

My nose wrinkles. I'm afraid of where this is going.

On a nervous laugh, he runs a hand through his dark hair. "I witnessed your mom giving your dad head."

Blink.

Blink.

Blink.

I didn't hear him correctly. I was crying in the woods with a broken arm, and my mom was giving my dad a quick blow job before my curfew ended? I have seen and smelled the most grotesque and vile things, but this image that's now in my head is far worse.

"It was kinda crazy," Colten continues.

I don't know if I want him to continue. I think I want him to stop. Better yet, I would have preferred he never *ever* tell me this. He hates me. This proves it.

"You were injured, waiting for help, and I was supposed to be the one getting help, but then I walked in on them, and your mom ran into their bathroom, while I just ... stared at your dad's cock. I had never seen one so damn big."

A little bile works its way up my throat as I shake my head repeatedly, silently pleading for him to stop. My dad peed a lot on our hunting and fishing trips, but his back was always to me. I never saw his penis, until now.

Now, I'm imagining the largest penises I have ever seen and mentally placing them onto my dad like part of a Mr. Potato Head. I'm ruined. Scarred for life.

Colten Fucking Mosley.

"At the hospital, while you were getting an X-ray, he made me promise to never mention what I witnessed. And that's when I had to promise to never kiss you again, and he suggested I learn to shoot a rifle. As of this very moment, the rifle promise is the only one I kept."

In med school, I had to help separate two people who were stuck together. His penis piercing got caught on her tongue piercing, and very sensitive skin was ripping apart. That image is more pleasant than the one Colten just planted in my brain.

"I need to tell your mom that you want a salad, and you need to never speak to me again." My head continues its back-and-forth swivel. "Like ... ever. Got it?"

Colten takes several steps toward me, fingers tucked into his front pockets. "Did you ever think of me? In the past seventeen years, have you thought about me much?" He glances at the floor for a second before returning his gaze to mine. It's the innocent, boyish thing he used to do. He's no longer a boy nor is he innocent.

I purse my lips for a moment.

"I did," he says before I find my answer. "I thought about you so many times. I wondered how you were doing. I hoped you were okay."

"Okay?" I ask, grunting a tiny laugh. "Did you think I wouldn't be okay without you? Did you honestly think you were my everything? If that's what you thought, then it only makes the way you treated me that much crueler. Doesn't it?"

Pursing his lips to the side, he takes a quick glance over my shoulder and nods slowly before meeting my gaze again. "I knew you'd be fine without me. I never doubted that. I knew that no man, including me, would be the be-all and end-all of your life and success. That didn't make me think about you any less. Other things can happen in life that might make one *not okay*. A car accident. Someone pulling a knife on you. Cancer ... so many things. When we graduated, my mom said if I was going to let you go, I had to *really* let you go. She didn't tell me much about your life, and I knew she kept in touch with your parents for a long time."

He shrugs. "I assumed she'd let me know if you died, but beyond that ... I had only my thoughts, my curiosity, and my hopes that you were, in fact, okay. I'm not sure I've gone a full day without thinking of you."

Why is he telling me this?

"I'm going to tell your mom you're having salad." I turn and head toward the stairs.

"Josie?"

I ignore him. For someone who can't look back with any sort of regret, he sure does have a lot of things to say about the past.

"He wants salad," I announce just as Becca sets the casserole on the table along with a serving spoon.

"That took a while." She eyes me with a knowing look on her face. I'm not sure what she thinks she knows, but probably as much as I do.

"He's chatty."

She chuckles. "He has his best friend back in his life. The last time I saw him, he wasn't this happy."

I transfer the plates from the counter to the table. "Miss Reagan is here. Happiness personified."

"I know his Reagan high. This is different." Becca transfers salad from a bag into bowls. "You owe him nothing. I love my son, but I've always thought of you like a daughter. So as someone who shares a motherly love for you, believe me when I say you owe him nothing. Unless …"

I set the last plate in its spot and glance up at Becca while Reagan shoves her crayons back into the box. "Unless what?"

She shakes a bottle of ranch dressing. "Unless you feel good about him being back in your life too."

"I'm here for you, Becca. I don't have dinner with him alone. He's in my life as someone in my work world. That's it."

"Daddy play piano!" Reagan runs to Colten as soon as he comes down the stairs.

"After dinner." He picks her up and tosses her over his shoulder, and she giggles. When he sets her down at the table, he nuzzles his face into her neck and kisses her over and over.

Reagan squeals and giggles more.

Becca leans in and whispers, "I don't think that's how one looks at someone in their work world," while brushing past me to the table with three salad bowls in her hands.

I quickly glance away when she looks over her shoulder and gives me another knowing look. It's as familiar as the looks Colten gives me. Becca used to settle fights between us and gave me a look when I said I hated Colten. The look that said she knew I was crazy about him, and that's why I let him under my skin so often.

"Coming to Texas for Labor Day?" Becca asks Colten as we take our seats for dinner.

"Can't. Working."

"Halloween?" She follows up with him.

"Working."

"Thanksgiving?" She frowns.

He lifts a shoulder while dishing up casserole for Reagan. "I can put in for time off for Thanksgiving or Christmas, but not both."

"Well, choose whichever one you can bring Reagan with you."

"That might be neither." He eyes his mom.

She gives him a slow nod and sad smile. He has no official custody of her. Whatever time he gets with his daughter is granted by her mom.

I can't purge this one little thought from my head. It's on a continuous loop.

Colten Mosley is a dad.

CHAPTER
Seventeen

"WANT TO GO FOR A DRIVE?" Colten asks as he makes his way down the stairs after reading Reagan a bedtime story.

"I should go. When your mom comes back downstairs, I'm going to tell her goodbye and head home."

"She decided to take a shower because I told her we were going for a drive, and you'd say goodbye when we got back."

I frown. "Pretty presumptuous of you."

"Hopeful." He grins.

"Colten ..."

"Quick drive. We'll be back in twenty minutes. It will take my mom that long to shower and get ready for bed."

This is a terrible idea, but I find myself nodding.

With that winning smile that I've never been able to resist, he nods toward the door, opening it for me.

"This way." He heads toward the garage while I head toward his car.

"I'm not riding on the back of your bicycle, Mosley."

Colten chuckles. "You used to be more fun, Watts." He digs his keys out of his pocket and opens the side access door.

As I step behind him, he flips on the light, causing my next step to falter. There's a sunken floor and a car lift with a Corvette suspended in the air.

"Doesn't look drivable."

"Not yet." He eyes me over his shoulder and smirks.

I follow him around the car, stopping in my tracks for a second time when I see a blue Chevelle. Not *a* blue Chevelle, my dad's blue Chevelle. I don't know this for certain, but my gut tells me it's the same car, or maybe it's the beaming expression on Colten's face that leaks the truth.

"You bought my dad's car? When? Why? How did I not know this?"

"He sold it to me when I went into the police academy after serving in the Marines."

"You kept in touch with my dad after you enlisted?"

"Sure."

Sure ... he says it like it's no big deal.

"Do you remember when your dad took us to homecoming our sophomore year in this car?"

167

I nod several times, ambling around the car, giving it a slow inspection.

"Remember when we left early?"

My gaze finds his over the top of the car. Colten grins. I do all I can to keep my face neutral.

"Under the bleachers?" He continues to ask questions that don't need to be asked.

That's it. No more eye contact for him. There's nothing wrong with my memory, and he knows it.

"I'm trying hard to figure out," he continues, "how we spent nine years together and seventeen apart, but I feel like my whole life has been defined more by those nine years than the following seventeen." He shakes his head, running his hands through his hair. "You taught me so many things about life ... about love. And I didn't fully see those revelations until you were gone."

"Well..." I release a nervous laugh "...no regrets. Right? Your words. I don't recall saying those exact ones, so I didn't have *that* big of an impact on your life." I make my way around the car in the direction that will keep me the farthest from him. There's no way I'm getting in that car with him. "I bet your mom is out of the shower. And it's late ..."

"And I could have taken a job anywhere, so could have you. Still here we are in the same city, working in professions that overlap on a regular basis. Really, Josie, what are the odds of that?" He catches up to me just as I reach the door.

His fingers slide around my wrist.

And just like that ... I'm eighteen.

I can't breathe.

The deafening thud of my heart makes it hard to focus on anything but how his touch didn't age one bit. I've not acquired an ounce of immunity to it.

"Seventeen years, Josie ..." he whispers. "You can't stay mad at me for *seventeen years*."

Wrong.

My grudge is the eternal kind.

On my headstone, they'll write:

Josephine Watts
Mother of zero.
Loved by a few.
Friend to several.
Good with dead bodies.
Emotionally humiliated by Colten Mosley.

"You don't know anything about me," I say.

"I know the best parts of you."

God ... why does his warm touch feel so good? Oh, that's right ... dead bodies for a living.

I'm not going to forgive him. I'm sure as hell not going to forget what he did to me. But I might let his touch linger a few more seconds.

Colten tugs my arm a little until I face him. He takes a tiny step closer leaving no more steps to take. His hand slides up my bare arm, and I feel my resolve slipping. I don't like that feeling.

I need the anger.

The resentment.

The grudge.

Without it, I am too vulnerable.

"You killed the best part of me," I whisper.

His other hand cups my cheek. "I set it free."

My head eases side to side. "I hate you."

"If only it were that easy." He tips my head up and ducks his, pausing a breath from my lips.

Certain feelings, deep emotions—the haunting kind—can't be outrun. Colten has been the unshakable shadow of my existence since the day I met him.

"If only ..." I echo him.

We kiss.

And it's ... purgatory. It's poison. So why has my soul never felt more at home? *What is wrong with me?*

He's only feeding the hate and the resentment, even while my hands thread through his hair.

While I lean into his body.

While I let him back me into a slat wall of coats, coveralls, and hats.

"Josephine Watts," he mumbles, kissing down my neck, his hands palming my ass. "Jo ... se ... phine ... Watts ..."

I don't care how much agony his words hold; the grudge is eternal.

Hate sex was invented for this exact situation. Yes, my mind skips ahead a few steps to sex. It's not that I've been waiting seventeen years to have sex with Colten Mosley. Well, that's eighty percent true.

Kicking my heart to the curb to wait for me at a safe distance from Colten, I reach for his belt, giving it a hard tug to unbuckle it. He lifts his head from the crook of my neck.

He's going to stop me. That's his MO. I can see it in his eyes.

I blow out a long breath, unable to hide my frustration. "Some things never change," I murmur attempting to escape the confines of his much larger body pinning me to the wall.

His head cocks to the side as he smirks. "You don't know anything about me." He tosses my words right back at me while his gaze slides down my face to my chest. In the next breath, his fingers flick the button of my shorts, and he eases down the zipper.

Curling my fingers around the hem of his shirt, I work it up his torso. He grabs it with one hand and shrugs it off, letting it fall to the floor beside us while smashing his mouth to mine again.

Yeah ... I definitely waited seventeen years to have sex with Colten Mosley.

My hands return to his pants, unbuttoning them and giving the waist a slight nudge, sending them a few inches over his ass to his thick thighs.

His tongue makes a slow stroke against mine while his right hand sneaks inside my panties, palming my ass again.

Gone are the days of the cautious teenager, scared to death of my father. Where was this Colten when I needed him?

This changes nothing. This doesn't erase the jilted lover I've been for seventeen years. Still, it makes me deliriously happy to get the one thing he never gave me before we ended.

He spins me around, pressing my chest to a thick winter jacket. Hunching behind me, his fingers curl into my shorts and panties, slowly sliding them down my legs; his lips press to the curve of my ass while he hums.

"You are fucking perfection," he murmurs.

He's ...

So intoxicating.

So sexy.

So everything.

My eyes close, teeth digging into my bottom lip when I draw in a sharp breath and arch my back. He nudges my legs apart until my shorts and panties stop them, and he grips my ass with his hands, his lips skipping over my flesh, teasing me.

"Colten?" Becca says, opening the garage door two feet to our left.

History has a way of repeating itself. It's not a cliche. It's true.

Colten abandons me.

Abandons. Me!

He yanks up his jeans in less than a second and snags his shirt from the floor.

"What is it, Mom?" he asks her from beneath his shirt as he tugs it over his head.

My hands dive for my shorts and panties and wiggle them over my hips with my back to Becca. I cannot turn around.

Ever.

A few seconds of silence blankets the room. Why is

it silent? Are they talking in sign language? Is it a stare-off? Are they waiting for me to swallow the last drop of my pride and turn to face them?

"I'm going to bed. I wanted to say goodbye to Josie. Do you two need a few more minutes?"

Pinching the bridge of my nose, my face wrinkles into a grimace. A few more minutes? Is she serious?

"Maybe another ten?"

I whip around when Colten makes his stupid request. The floor becomes the most fascinating part of the garage. Giving it all my attention, I shuffle my feet to Becca and glance up only when I have her in a hug. "I should get going. It was great seeing you. Have a safe trip home."

That's it.

I release her and escape out the garage in one quick move.

CHAPTER
Eighteen

MOM and I spend a good minute or two staring at each other. I'm fairly certain thirty-five-year-old men can't be grounded, but she might prove that theory wrong.

I hear Josie's car door shut and her car pull out of the driveway. Mom tilts her head a fraction like she's listening to the same thing.

"Thought you two were going for a drive."

I return an easy nod. "That was the plan."

"And ... what happened? Your pants fell down on the way to the car? And ... you were helping Josie pull up her pants because you're a gentleman like that?"

Clicking my tongue twice, I wink at her. "Exactly."

She frowns. My humor's not everyone's taste.

Crossing her arms over her chest, she flicks out her hip. "Do you know what it means to court a woman? Because I feel like I failed you as a mother. You've never had any control around Josie. And I have a granddaughter (whom I love beyond words) because you think sex is the equivalent of holding hands. It's not."

"It was Josie's idea."

"Colten Wilson Mosley, you are a grown man. Stop blaming Josie for everything like you're still a child."

I've taken a life. Twice. Once as a Marine and once on the police force. I know martial arts. I have elite combat skills. I track down killers, risking my life to keep the public safe. How am I having this conversation with my mother?

I rub my mouth to keep her from seeing my grin.

"You have to grow up and take responsibility for your actions. You are a father now. And Josie deserves a man who's got it all together."

"I take offense to that. I have it together. I have a job. I pay my child support on time every month. I take my own bags to the grocery store. And I always have a condom in my pocket. Katy wasn't a one-night stand. We were dating."

Mom's expression wrinkles into a map of confusion. "So you were dating Katy, but you didn't love each other enough to get married for Reagan's sake?"

"I asked her to marry me."

Her jaw unhinges.

I nod several times before blowing a quick breath out my nose. "She didn't sense my love for her was what she deserved, and she was right."

"Why didn't you ever tell me that?"

I shrug. "Katy and I felt a little irresponsible, and we felt like it wasn't anyone's business. She knew her parents would try to talk her into marrying me, and I ... well, I wasn't sure what you would say."

Pursing her lips, she offers a slow nod. "Compare Katy to Josie."

My head inches side to side. Then I lace my fingers behind my head and gaze at the ceiling. "Apples and oranges. Really, I can't compare them. Katy is the mother of my daughter. Josie's the ..."

"The what?"

"I don't know," I whisper. "I never saw this coming. Her path and mine running side-by-side again. And when I see her ..." I return my attention to my mom. The gravity of my feelings seems to wipe the amusement from my face. "When I see her, I feel like our story is still untold. Seventeen years feel like seventeen seconds."

I can't remember the last time my mom looked at me with anything but concern on her face. She's always been worried that I'd be my dad. I'm not him.

"Go to bed, Colten."

Again ... I'm thirty-five, but I nod and shut off the garage lights behind us.

CHAPTER
Nineteen

THREE DEAD TEENAGERS waiting in the morgue.

Not my idea of a perfect Monday morning.

"Everybody gets a gun. You get a gun. She gets a gun. Every human gets a gun."

If I didn't already know where Dr. Cornwell stood on gun rights, I do now.

Alicia eyes me as she assists him. It's the you-saved-my-life-with-your-gun look. I don't think I saved her life. I think I saved us from being robbed, but I know from her incessant thank-you's that she feels like I saved her.

"If drugs were decriminalized, we wouldn't have to do this so much," I respond while removing drugs in the tied fingers of latex gloves.

"Guns *and* drugs, Watts? How did I not know about your dark side?" Dr. Cornwell laughs.

JEWEL E. ANN

I smirk behind my mask. "We all have a dark side. I carry a gun. You hide a large bag of beef jerky in your desk next to a bag of peanut M&Ms. I'm likely to take someone else's life. You're likely to take your own."

I love Cornwell's chuckle. It's genuine, like a father finding his daughter's antics amusing. "Touché."

When my exhausting morning bleeds into the afternoon, all the way until two o'clock, I retire to my office for lunch and reporting.

"Oh god ..." I murmur to myself when I spy Detective Mosley waiting outside my office. Head bowed to his phone. One leg crossed over the other.

When he glances up, I bite my lips together, lifting my eyebrows in a silent question: *What are you doing here?*

"Hi." He grins. "I was about ready to give up on you."

"Three teenagers riddled with bullets were waiting for us this morning. I've been busy." I unlock my door and squeeze past him. "Last I heard, you worked homicide. Shouldn't you be busy too?"

"That's why I was about to give up on you. You've been ignoring my phone calls and texts. Don't you think we're too old for that?"

"Just the opposite, Detective." I take a seat at my desk and fish my lunch out of my bag. "I had more time on my hands when we were younger. Now, I'm busy. I'll give you five minutes. What do you need?"

"Have dinner with me tonight."

"Terrible idea."

"I could shut your door, and we could finish what we started in my garage."

Opening the lid to my nori rolls, I shake my head without giving him the tiniest of glances. "I've blocked that near mistake out of my head. Are we done here? Three dead teenagers ... do you have a suspect in custody yet?"

"We don't. State took over, anyway. I feel like the mistake we made was not accepting the extra time alone my mom offered us."

I chew my bite of food and blot my mouth with my folded paper towel. "I had a temporary lapse in judgment. I let my feelings for your mom and your adorable daughter blur my true feelings for you."

"True feelings?" One side of his mouth curls into a smile.

"I hate you. But your mom and Reagan humanize you."

"Ouch." Colten grips his shirt, pulling the invisible knife from his chest. "Hate is a strong word. Just say you have strong feelings for me after all these years and let me interpret those strong feelings on my own." He stands, moving in the wrong direction around my desk to me. When he leans his backside on the edge and crosses his arms over his chest, I scoot a bit to my left.

"We're here for a reason. You're back in my life for a reason," he says.

My attention remains affixed to the computer screen with the occasional glance at my nori roll. "I'm in Chicago. We're in the same city. I fear you're reading into that."

"If my mom would have had better timing, we would have—"

"Thank god for your mom. She had perfect timing." I frown, picking a carrot sticking out of my nori roll. "Well, perfect timing would have been five minutes earlier before we ..."

"Kissed? Lost our clothes?"

I grunt, shaking my head. "Lost our minds."

"What are you afraid of, Josie? Are you afraid if we go too far, you won't be able to hate me?"

"No. I can go as far as I want *and* hate you. I'm good at multitasking."

"Great." He knocks on the top of my desk twice. "My place at eight. I won't even buy you dinner first since there's no point."

My head whips in his direction as he saunters to the door. "You can't tell me what to do."

He glances over his shoulder. "I can. It's my turn."

"Your turn?"

"After you broke your arm, you said I could be the bossy one in approximately twenty years. It's been twenty-one years since you promised me control. It's past due. Eight o'clock. If you're late, I'm going to handcuff you to the bed."

My lips part, fresh out of words, and he exits my office with a frightening level of confidence.

AFTER WORK, I do what any good self-preserving woman would do—I line up a last-minute date for the night. Garrett is a nice guy. We've chatted off and on for months. It's time I do the irresponsible thing and invite him to my place after dinner.

He says something funny as I unlock the front door and toe off my shoes.

"The fuck ..." Garrett stiffens, glancing over my shoulder when I turn on the light.

My hand dives into my purse, fingers curling around my gun as I whip around.

Shoulder casually propped up against the wall, arms crossed over his T-shirt-clad chest, Colten returns a frigid look to Garrett before glancing at his watch. "It's nine o'clock."

Tipping my chin up and easing my grip on my gun, I narrow my eyes at him. "Go home."

"So you can fuck this dude?"

"Yes."

"Um ... I thought you were single," Garrett says. "And you have a gun?"

"I am. And I do."

"Then who's this guy?"

"Nobody," I murmur.

My response draws a tiny grin from Colten. "Do you have a gun on you?" He eyes Garrett.

"N-no ..."

"Well, I do and so does Josie. So I'm thinking you should go home, have some warm milk, jerk off to your favorite porn site, and forget about her."

Garrett takes a step back, closer to the door. Without looking behind me, I grab his shirt and make a tight fist. "Stay, Garrett. Detective Mosley is out of his jurisdiction and out of his mind."

"*Garrett* ..." Colten clicks his tongue a few times. "You are a placeholder. A stand-in. A knockoff of the real thing. Go before you embarrass yourself anymore."

Garrett breaks free from my grip. "I'm out of here. I'm not down with this stupid shit."

When Garrett's no longer at my back, and I can't seem to find a word to say, Colten shifts his attention from Garrett's vacant spot to my unblinking eyes. He shrugs. "You were right. We can't end."

CHAPTER
Twenty

BY THE END of our junior year, Tessa was the flavor of the month—Josie's label, not mine.

A senior, Tessa Hart declared her intention to give me her virginity after just three weeks of dating.

"I'm going to college in the fall. I don't want to be a virgin. And I don't want a boyfriend. You still have a year left. And you're experienced, so what do you say?" Tessa pinned me to the side of the concession stand with her big boobs after my first baseball game of the season. Her fake fingernails teased my groin area, and she frowned when she realized my cock was safely tucked into my jock strap and covered with a cup.

Just the thought of her trying to touch me there had my dick at attention. As for her assumption that I was experienced ... I didn't know where she heard that.

And what was I supposed to say? That I needed to go have sex with Josie first?

Did I mention Josie had a boyfriend?

"Say yes, Colten," she whispered, lifting onto her toes and licking my lower lip until I took the bait and kissed her.

"Get a room," Tami said as she and a group of girls turned the corner of the concession stand, sports drinks and candy in their hands.

Bringing up the end of the cluster of giggles? Josephine Watts. But she wasn't giggling. Or smiling. The look on her face could only be described as murder.

"Maybe we will get a room. My bedroom. Maybe this weekend when my parents are at the lake," Tessa said, looking at me, but the volume of her voice was unmistakably announcing her intentions to the rest of the world—or at least to the group of girls.

My relationship with Josie was complicated … flat-out fucked-up by that point. I felt loyal to baseball. My mom and her desire for me to get a musical scholarship. Chief Watts and keeping my balance on the tall pedestal where he put me. And … there was Josie.

The reason my unconventional relationship with Josie seemed to work was because there was nothing conventional about Josephine Watts.

One minute I thought she understood my need to keep my promise to her dad (or at least the illusion of it), and the next minute I feared that she would take my life long before her dad ever got the chance to do it.

To say I had a love-hate-fear relationship with the Watts family might have been a gigantic understatement.

Tessa kissed me, closing her eyes.

I kept mine open, watching Josie toss her drink and bag of licorice into the trash before sprinting toward the parking lot.

"I gotta go," I said, turning my head to break Tessa's suction on my mouth before grabbing my duffle bag and running after Josie.

"Colten!"

Ignoring Tessa, I sped up. "Josie!" I smacked the side of her red Honda Civic as she sped out of the parking lot. "Fuck ..." I mumbled, dropping my bag to the ground in the cloud of dust she kicked up speeding past me.

By the time I made it home, Josie was in her house, and Chief Watts was home, sorting through his tackle boxes in the garage. As soon as I grabbed my bag from the back seat of my blue, rusty Chevy Silverado, he called my name.

Every time he called me into his garage, which was quite often, I dragged my feet, wondering if that was the moment he was going to break the news to me that Josie told him everything about us.

Break the news to me that he no longer thought of me as his son, and I would have to make amends with my own dad.

Break the news to me that I would soon die because I knew what Josie's nipples looked like.

There would be no lenience for staying out of her pants. I would die. And Roland Tompkins would cremate me and keep Chief Watts's secret because Roland had three daughters and would kill anyone who violated his daughters.

For the record, I didn't violate Josie.

"Congrats on your win," Chief Watts said.

I breathed a sigh of relief, knowing I'd live another day. "Thanks."

"Josie ran into the house mad as hell. Savannah is gone for the evening with Benji. Would you mind talking to her? She won't talk to me."

Jabbing my thumb over my shoulder, I fumbled my words. "Uh ... I ... it's ... my mom's waiting on me. Dinner. And homework."

"Five minutes, son. Just find out what happened so I know if I need to deal with someone or if it's just stupid friend stuff."

Deal with someone ...

Calling me "son" only tightened his grip on me, on my loyalty to him.

"Five minutes. But if she's really upset, she might not talk to me either." My shoulders curled inward while making my way to the door.

"I appreciate you trying."

"Mmm-hmm ..."

As soon as I shut the door behind me, I froze. Josie stood in the kitchen, a glass of milk in one hand, a cookie in her other hand, and that same evil glare boring a hole into my head.

I opened my mouth to speak, but before I could get a word out, her head shook several times in a sharp motion while making her way to me. "I hope Tessa has herpes or crabs or something that kills you. Then I'm going to dissect you and bury you in the woods next to my favorite tree so I can spit on you every day for the rest of my life." She tossed her whole glass of milk in my face.

And I stood there and said nothing while she took a slow bite of her cookie, giving me a blank expression for a few seconds before pivoting and heading upstairs.

"She's not in the mood to talk to anyone," I said to Chief Watts, not skipping a beat as I trod my way past him.

"Colten, what's all over you?"

"Milk." *And rage.* I kept walking.

"She threw her milk on you?"

"Mmm-hmm."

I managed to sneak past my mom without her focusing on my milk face.

"Sorry I missed your game, sweetie. How'd you do?" she called from the laundry room next to the kitchen.

My feet stomped their way upstairs. "Fine."

"Hungry?"

"I don't know."

It was a stupid question but so was my answer. I was always hungry. There was only one force stronger than my hunger— Josephine Watts's wrath.

The second I emerged from the bathroom, freshly

showered, Mom shouted upstairs. "Colten? Tessa called and Josie's here."

That sentence rubbed along my nerves to the point of making me shudder. Tessa and Josie in the same sentence just didn't belong. Oil and water. Heaven and Hell.

"Go on up, Josie. Tell him I put a frozen pizza in the oven for him, and it will take about ten minutes," Mom said as I stood at the top of the stairs contemplating going down them or climbing out my window, risking my fate from a second story jump and hoping I could wobble my way as far from home as possible.

Instead, I crossed the hall into my bedroom and took a seat at my keyboard, playing Beethoven's *Moonlight Sonata*.

Josie stood silent in my doorway.

Then she sat on my bed.

Finally, she made her way to the piano bench beside me, sitting in the opposite direction as usual.

I didn't skip a beat. Not a single note.

"My dad said I had to come apologize to you for the milk incident."

I ignored her, my fingers caressing the keys as my body swayed ever so slightly like the easy bob of my head.

"But I'm not going to apologize, and we both know why."

Did I though? I wasn't so sure.

After I played a few more measures, she sighed.

"I'm not ready to have sex, so you can't have sex with Tessa. Sorry."

For the first time since she came into my bedroom, I lost track of my location in the song, and my fingers stopped, idly hovering over the keys for a few breaths until they dropped to my thighs.

"Tessa's here!" Mom called, an official declaration of God's contempt for me.

"Oh ..." Tessa's voice chimed at my back. "What are you doing here?" she asked Josie in a catty tone.

"Whatever I want."

I grimaced at Josie's response even if it made me want to puff out my chest in pride that she stood up for herself with another girl from school, an older classman at that.

"What's that supposed to mean?" Tessa moved in on us.

I glanced over my shoulder and started to speak, but Josie cut me off.

"You are a placeholder. A stand-in. A knockoff of the real thing. Go before you embarrass yourself anymore," Josie said while standing, hands planted on her hips, chin up.

Tessa's jaw unhinged as she looked to me for confirmation that Josie was my official spokesperson. "Colten, are you and *her* a thing?"

We were *something.*

"Can I call you later, Tessa?"

"No," Tessa *and* Josie replied in unison.

Gritting her teeth, Tessa pointed a stiff finger at

Josie. "I am not a placeholder. A knockoff. I am the real thing. So why don't you go home and find a better way to stuff your little training bra so it doesn't make your chest look so lumpy. Then go ask your boyfriend to take a little pity on you and tell you about the birds and the bees. Colten, tell her to go home and leave us alone."

Focusing on my fingers, I continued my sonata. "Tessa, go home."

She gasped. I wasn't sure what Josie did, but if she had a reaction, it was silent.

"We. Are. Over!" Tessa stomped down the hallway and right down the stairs. A few seconds later, the front door slammed shut.

I moved to the middle of the song, leaning into the increasing tempo of the homophonic texture. Josie leaned her head on my shoulder.

"Are you the real thing? Does every other girl hold your place?" I asked her.

She drew in a slow breath and released it even slower. I couldn't see her eyes, but I imagined them drifting shut. "I hope so."

With that reply, I leaned my head on hers and finished the song. After the final note, her hand slid to my lap, taking my hand and guiding it to her stomach.

Beneath her shirt.

To her chest.

Into the cup of her bra.

Another girl was giving me an erection that day, only it wasn't just any girl. Josephine Watts was *the* girl.

My hand remained idle for several breaths, her chest pulsing in and out ... faster, deeper. When the pad of my thumb brushed her nipple, she released an audible breath.

"Close your bedroom door," she whispered.

She didn't have to ask me twice. I slid off the bench and closed the door. When I turned back toward her, she was sliding down her shorts *and* her panties, leaving her shirt on as she sat on the piano bench again. Her hands rested on her bare legs, her gaze struggling to meet mine as she chewed her lower lip.

"Have you had oral sex?" she asked, forcing her gaze to meet mine while her voice wobbled with uncertainty.

I shook my head slowly, unsure where I needed to keep my gaze. It wanted to track south.

"Do you want to?" I had never heard Josie sound so afraid, so nervous.

I nodded since my voice seemed to be on vacation. If this was her idea of an apology for the milk incident, I welcomed our next fight. My heart thrashed around in my chest so violently I thought it might explode while I took a few steps toward her.

"Here?" I whispered. The bed seemed like a more logical option, but for whatever reason, she sat back down on my piano bench after exposing herself.

Josie returned several tiny nods, lips pressed together while she took a hard swallow. I lowered to my knees in front of her. Her eyes flared, unblinking.

JEWEL E. ANN

Leaning forward, my hands rested on the bench beside her.

We kissed.

Josie was familiar, but not "the same." Nothing about her got old. In fact, she grounded me. Even on the days she left me dizzy with her rules and sudden mood changes, I was unequivocally the best version of myself.

Our kiss was slow. So was her hand guiding mine between her legs, inching it along her inner thigh.

Up ... up ... up ...

With every micro-movement, whooshes of air pushed out of her nose. I wasn't as well versed in oral sex as some of my friends, so I had a little apprehension, hence the long kiss. When the tip of my finger reached the apex of her slightly spread legs, she gripped my hand, a vise stopping me from going any farther.

Our kiss broke, and we breathed into each other's mouths. Had she let go of my hand, she would have felt it shaking as much as her legs. If she wasn't sure about me touching her with my fingers, how was she going to let me put my mouth in that very spot?

I nearly came in my pants just thinking about it.

"Maybe I should do it to you first," she whispered over my lips.

"That's ... um ... f-fine. If you ... uh ... want to." How did I think I was going to have sex with Tessa (who thought I was experienced) when I could barely express a coherent thought with Josie? I couldn't imagine Josie giving me a blow job, if I were being honest. I never asked Chief Watts what Savannah usually did with his load. Did it go into her mouth? Was swallowing involved? My friend, Bart, deposited his jizz onto his girlfriend's chest. But Josie had her shirt on. Was I supposed to ask her to take it off? It couldn't go onto her shirt. Savannah would see it in the laundry. I had a hand towel tucked under my mattress, but if I grabbed it, Josie would've seen how well-used that hand towel was, and I wasn't ready to be *that* honest with her.

"Or I could just touch you with my fingers," I whispered back to her. We seemed to be stuck mere millimeters apart, my hand still *so* close to the goal line. I considered saying, "I could finger you," but I wasn't sure that was an expression girls liked to hear. It was commonly referenced in the boys' locker room, but so were a lot of other crude comments.

"Can you make me come?"

I gulped and thought about that for a second. My instinct was to say yes. Sex was one of the most basic acts of humanity; I couldn't imagine making a girl orgasm required any sort of special sorcery. Then I considered how many times I fell off my bike before learning to ride without training wheels. Biking seemed pretty basic too.

"I guess there's only one way to find out." I faked sixty percent of my confidence and managed a smile that matched at least forty percent of that confidence.

That made Josie relinquish a tiny grin and loosen

her grip on my hand just enough to enter uncharted territory.

By a fucking millimeter at the very most.

Because ...

My mom decided to come into my room. Nope. I did not lock the door. I never locked my door because it was an unspoken rule to knock. I wasn't five anymore. It was a given that behind a closed door someone could be half naked. If the bathroom door was closed, we knocked. We never just opened the door.

Etiquette.

Rules.

Protocol.

Come on!

"Oh!" Mom gasped.

Really, everything happened at once.

The gasp.

Josie closing her legs so damn tight, I could barely withdraw my hand from between them. Then she lurched forward, grabbing her shorts and panties while I stood with my back to my mom so I could adjust my dying erection.

My dad used to say my mom spewed the most nonsensical things at the worst moments. I wasn't sure what he meant until that moment.

"Condom. Do you have ... do you want me to get a condom? No! I mean ... this is wrong. Colten, this is wrong!"

When I turned around, her hands were covering

her face.

"Mom! Get out." I grabbed her shoulders, turned her around, and guided her out of my room.

"Dinner's ready," she squeaked.

I closed the door behind me and leaned against it. My head eased back while I closed my eyes to Josie zipping her shorts with frantic hands.

"Your mom has impeccable timing."

When I opened my eyes, Josie rolled her lips inward into a closed-mouth grin.

"Are you going to be in trouble? Do you think she's going to tell my parents? Should I tell them first before she gets a chance to tell them?"

"No!" I shook my head a dozen times. "Do not tell them anything. I'll talk to my mom. She won't say anything. Just promise me you won't tell them."

"Colten touched me between my legs. I was half naked on his piano bench, and we decided to do the finger thing instead of having oral sex. What's that, Dad? Oh ... you're getting your gun. What are you going to do with your gun?"

"Colten, I want to tell them before she does. I can make them understand."

"She's not going to tell them. And what's to understand? How are you going to sugarcoat what just happened?"

Josie shrugged a shoulder. "I'll tell them we were heavy petting. That's what their generation called it. And no one can get pregnant from heavy petting, so it's not the worst sin in the world."

Seriously?

I'd felt my life slipping through my hands years earlier when Josie ratted me out for kissing her when she fell out of the tree. Heavy petting? Every cell in my body physically ached and shook with fear at the thought of what Chief Watts would do to me for that.

"Josephine Watts ..." I took two big strides forward and cupped her face, tipping her head back so she had no choice but to give me her full attention. "Do. Not. Tell. Them. We will be over. We won't even be friends. We'll be nothing. Less than nothing. Is that what you want?"

She blinked several times before easing her head side to side the tiny fraction my hands allowed.

"Go home. I'll talk to my mom. And we won't ever discuss it again."

"K," she whispered.

I released her and blew out a big sigh of relief.

"Colten?" She stopped at my door.

"Yeah?" I looked up at her as I followed her lead.

"We can't end."

I didn't know what that really meant for sure, but I nodded anyway.

"I never felt normal and accepted until I met you. So ... we can't end."

CHAPTER
Twenty-One

"You ended us. We are over," I reply to Colten's regurgitation of the words I fed him so many years ago. "There is no *we*. There is you, and there is me. Even if you've managed to run off my date tonight, it doesn't change anything."

He studies me in silence for several seconds. "Do you remember Tessa? The day she came to my house, and you were there?"

I remember everything. Every word. Every breath. Even the tiny spaces between breaths. He doesn't need to know that, so I give him nothing but several bored blinks and a straight face.

Easing his head side to side, he grins. "I was fucking drowning. Trying to figure out who I was, where my life was meant to go, why my dad was such an asshole, and how to be what my mom needed me to

JEWEL E. ANN

be. Then there was you, Josephine Watts. When I was with you, nothing else mattered. Until Reagan came into my life, I couldn't imagine ever meeting someone who made me feel so ..." His face contorts into a slightly painful expression while he averts his gaze to the floor for a second. "I ... I can't even find the right word. It's not 'important' or 'purposeful.' It's like I just knew I was meant to be your friend, the way I just knew when I held Reagan that I was meant to be her father. Not that you needed me or that she needed me. Just that I knew I was part of something ..."

His gaze meets mine, and I hate him for not being awful. I'll forever hate him for so many reasons. "Something life-changing," he whispers. "And I felt so damn lucky. Always have. Always will."

Colten has never played by the rules, not that I ever have either, but I have a healthy respect for them. I'm more judicious when it comes to breaking them. He dives in before checking to see if the pool is two feet or ten feet deep.

"You ran away. *That* was life changing. Being with me?" I shake my head. "That was nothing special to you."

"Yes—"

"No!" I cut him off. "You took a nine-year friendship ..." I steady my words, needing them to be as clear as they've been in my head for so many years. "It was more than friendship. You ended it with ten fucking words. And then you went to the one place you knew I wouldn't follow you. And you never made an effort to speak to me again." As my words rip from my chest, they lose all confidence. Seventeen years has done very little to mend the broken pieces of my heart.

"I don't watch baseball. I don't own a bike. I can't stand listening to the piano, let alone Beethoven. I haven't had milk and chocolate chip cookies in seventeen years. You took everything that was wonderful in my life and made it ugly and painful."

He winces. "I'm so sorry."

"Nope. You don't get to be sorry. Not now. Sorry expired approximately a year after you left. I thought ... surely you'd get homesick for me. You'd realize your fake altruism was nothing but fear. You'd be back. You'd call. Write. Something ..." I shake my head slowly. "Undergrad. Med school. Residency. Your dad dying. Your mom moving. Your brother stuck in treatment. Earthquakes. Hurricanes. Fires. Terrorist attacks. Mass shootings. The world going to shit. Nothing triggered your need for me. So now that we've stumbled into each other, you think the universe is telling you that I'm in your life again and ready to spread my legs for you?"

The smile has vanished from his face.

"Colten, you are a drug. I won't deny that. I've seen the catastrophic side of addiction too many times. I'm no longer your addict. You knew I was destined for greatness, right? Your words? Well, here I am. Being great all by myself. I didn't ..." The lump in my throat swells, exposing my weakness. Him. "I didn't need you ..." I blink back my tears. "I just really wanted you."

I have *never* felt this vulnerable.

The pain in my chest breaking free with those five words that have been looping in my head for years.

"I'm going to fix this." With two steps, he gazes down at me.

My eyes focus on his chest for a few seconds before risking a glance up at his sad face. "Some things can't be fixed. That's my area of expertise. I study all the things that went wrong. I answer questions. I solve mysteries. I might even give a little peace of mind and closure, but none of it fixes anything. We died."

"What if we didn't?" Colten whispers, eyeing my lips, the ones I won't give him again. "Or what if death isn't the end?"

"What's after death?"

He studies me for a few breaths before slowly shrugging one shoulder. "A second chance. A fresh start where the past doesn't matter because ... time stole the anger, the resentment, the grief, the heartache."

Rubbing my lips together, I return a single nod. "We'll talk in another life, but eternal is eternal, and my feelings toward you are eternal." I sidestep him and toss my purse onto the floor along with my shoes.

Colten opens the door. "So you'll love me forever."

"I'll hate you forever."

"Not without loving me more. We were young. Young people are malleable, impressionable. What happens to us when we're young leaves a bigger mark than anything that happens to us as adults. Those nine years were an infinity to the following seventeen years." The door clicks shut behind him.

After running my fingers through my hair ...

After wincing at my heart constricting in my chest ...

After grumbling like I did as a child ...

I turn and run after him, but I don't get a step farther than opening the door. He's less than a foot from me, smirking like he knew I'd cave. I'm not caving. I just need to ask him—

He grabs my face and kisses me like he did in his garage only harder, obliterating my thoughts. My conscience feels the sting of submission while my body refuses to listen to reason. It wants Colten Mosley naked. Right. Now.

We back into the house, his hands keeping a death grip on my face as mine grab his shirt and wad it into my fists.

His shirt ... off.

My shirt ... off.

I'm not thirty-five. I'm not a doctor. Or a well-respected professional.

I'm a teenager driven out of control by hormones and all the impulsive emotions that go with them.

Our legs tangle, and his hand shoots out to grip the wall, holding me to him with his other hand while keeping us from falling to the floor.

Doesn't matter. We hit the wall and melt to the floor anyway.

Colten hovers over me, hitting the pause button for

a few labored breaths. He's not a homicide detective. He's not the young man who left me. He's not a father. He's … the teenaged boy who I chased, pushed away, hated, loved.

Dipping his head, he kisses my neck while cupping my breast over my bra. My hips lift off the floor as if my body's entire purpose in life has been to feel Colten Mosley between my legs.

While his lips brush the swell of my breast, he releases a soft chuckle.

"Shut up, Mosley," I murmur as heat fills my cheeks. I'm a lot of things, but immune to his physical touch is not one of them. "Just shut …" I lose my words and my breath when he yanks my bra cup to the side, and his hot mouth devours my flesh.

My other breast.

My abdomen.

He unbuttons my pants and removes them along with my panties.

If his mom magically appears, I might take her life.

His right hand slides up my stomach, squeezing my breast again while his left hand grips my leg, guiding it to the side while his mouth plants between my legs.

"Dear godddd …" I arch my back, and he pinches my nipple.

Lick. Suck.

One finger. Two fingers.

I'm dizzy. So … damn … dizzy.

Colten's not the hesitant sixteen-year-old who played Beethoven like a boss only to nervously inch his fingers up my inner thighs as I sat on his piano bench with shaky legs and racing breaths.

I close my eyes, and I swear I can still hear *Moonlight Sonata*.

I gasp ... then I moan, lips parted, hips rocking into his touch. One hand grabs his hair while my other hand covers his hand on my breast, squeezing it.

He pinches my nipple until my body jerks from the pain.

A good pain.

That pain crashes into an explosion of pleasure when his tongue and his fingers move faster, harder ... and just ... so ... perfectly ...

"Col-Colten ... Colten ..." I chant with the arrival of my orgasm.

He slows his tongue while lifting his hips and working the button and zipper to his jeans.

I chided him for hesitating with Katy when she asked him if he loved her. I said women like confident men.

With all the confidence in this world, and maybe a few other worlds too, Colten fits between my legs. Kisses me with breathtaking vigor. And drives his cock into me with a hard thrust.

"Fuckkk ..." I cry.

He groans into my mouth, but he doesn't slow down. Not one. Single. Bit.

Has he thought about this for seventeen years like I've thought about it? Has my name and image popped into his mind with every other woman he's been with? Did he think of me the night he conceived his daughter? And if so, how would I feel about that?

I'm going to have bruises on my back consistent with fucking on a hardwood floor. If I die in the next twenty-four hours, that's not what the medical examiner will write in his notes, but that's what he'll think.

"Jesus ... Josie ..." He breathes in my ear before biting my earlobe. "This can't end ... I want to fuck you all night ..." His teeth dig into my shoulder next.

He angles his hips lower ... even lower until his pelvis strokes my clit with each thrust.

My fingertips curl into his back, my teeth into his shoulder ...

Seventeen years of fantasizing about this moment that I thought would never happen.

Again, I orgasm a few seconds before a moan escapes him. He pumps into me harder than any man has done before him. Then he stills. A mass of rigid muscles and bones going limp over my body. The world's heaviest weighted blanket.

"Josephine," he whispers against my ear. It's a sigh. Or maybe something more reverent, more desperate.

Whatever the meaning, it gives me goose bumps.

It fills my eyes with tears.

There's no way I'm crying after sex.

Still, this doesn't feel real.

I'd sit up. Grab my clothes. And run to my bathroom to shore up the wall around my heart. But Colten's large frame has my body pinned to the floor.

With his chest pressed to mine, I feel his heart beating, compromising the strength of mine.

"I need you to go," I whisper past the lump in my throat. I suppose it's bad form to ask a guy to leave after sex while he's physically still inside you. It's all about survival, and sometimes survival mode isn't flattering.

"I'm not a guy you picked up off the internet. Sorry." He deposits soft kisses along my neck to my jaw … to my mouth. Then he relinquishes a grin. "I broke into your house. So just plan on being held hostage the rest of the night. Then I'll leave in the morning. After coffee."

"It's just sex."

Again, he chuckles. "Yeah, yeah … it's *just* sex. The way it was always *just* a kiss. *Just* my hand up your shirt. *Just* your fingertips slipping into the back pocket of my jeans. You've failed miserably at minimizing everything about us when it suited you." He lifts his head and rolls us so he's on his back.

I sit up, straddling him while I tuck my breasts back into my bra. "Just is *just* a word, no matter how I've ever used it." I stand, snagging my clothes from the ground, and make my way to the bathroom. "You minimized us to nothing when you left." I shut the door behind me.

After a good fifteen minutes, I open the door, ready to kick him out of my house. He's not here. "Colten?"

Nothing. Peeking out the front window, I don't see his vehicle. After a deep sigh, I head to bed. That's that. I had sex with Colten Mosley. Now I know.

I can check that box off some ridiculous list in the back of my head before I crawl into bed, curling into a ball, wrapping my arms around my midsection. With my eyes closed, I imagine my arms are his arms. I imagine what it would feel like to only feel the good things.

His touch.

The warmth of his smile.

The caress of his words at my ear.

He made me hate him. It's a poison that won't leave my body.

CHAPTER

Twenty-Two

"PLANS FOR THE WEEKEND?" Alicia asks Friday afternoon.

It's been four days since Colten left my house without a goodbye. His usual MO. Detective Rains visited yesterday, but Colten hasn't so much as sent a text to me.

"I'm driving to Des Moines early in the morning. My parents' neighbor died. She was like another grandma to me. She moved in right after my brother was born, and she was his babysitter for years. Vera made the best blackberry jam from her blackberry bushes."

"Sorry to hear about her death."

I shrug, stuffing my PPE in the trash. "Colon cancer. She was seventy-two."

"Well, have a safe trip."

I smile. "Thanks. See you Monday."

I ARRIVE in Des Moines a little before eleven Saturday morning. The funeral's at three, and I need a shower after leaving so early this morning.

"Hey, hon." Mom pulls me in for a hug after I set my overnight bag by the stairs. "How was the drive?"

"Fine."

She releases me. "Benji called this morning. His flight was canceled, so he won't make it."

I frown. "That's too bad. I was looking forward to seeing him."

"Well, now Colten can sleep in his room instead of on the sofa sleeper."

"What?" I nearly choke on my words.

Mom heads into the kitchen. "He should be here soon. I'm surprised you two didn't ride together. I can't believe you didn't tell me you two reconnected after he moved to Chicago. I had to hear it from Becca. She called me after visiting with you there. Gosh, I hadn't talked to her in ... well, too long. She sounded good."

I watch her cut potatoes for the grill. "He ... he's a homicide detective, so our paths occasionally cross. He said his mom was in town, so we had dinner one night. I'm not sure that's reconnecting. And uh ... why is he staying here?"

"He's coming for Vera's funeral, of course."

I shake my head slowly and mumble, "Wow. He

couldn't make it to his own father's funeral, but he'll come home for a neighbor's funeral."

"What's that, Josie?"

"Nothing. What I meant was, why is he staying *here?*"

"It's just for one night. Your dad and I thought it would be silly for him to get a hotel room. He's always felt like a son to us anyway." She glances up from the cutting board, stilling her hands. "Is everything good between you two now?" Her brow furrows. "I know that's probably a silly question. What's it been? Seventeen? Eighteen years? I hope you've both had a chance to laugh it off and move on."

"Laugh what off?"

"The whole fiasco of him choosing to enlist when you were heading off to college. You never said anything, but I knew you were upset that your friend was leaving to enlist. But look how everything turned out for the best?"

Friend?

"You know, there are a lot of affordable hotels around here. Benji's bed is a twin bed. Colten would probably be more comfortable in a hotel. I bet he only accepted your offer because he was afraid of hurting your feelings."

Before she can respond to my brilliant suggestion, there's three knocks at the door, and it creaks open behind me.

"There's my boy." Mom wipes her hands and takes quick steps past me to the front door.

"Hey, Savannah."

I roll my eyes at all of it.

My boy? Pfft ...

Slowly turning, I plaster on a fake smile as he releases my mom and grins at me.

"Hey, Josie. I got to thinking about it, and it's crazy that we didn't just ride together."

"Mmm ... well, I had no idea you were coming to Vera's funeral."

"It was a last-minute decision."

"As are most deaths."

Colten's smile swells a little more, but I'm not giving him the satisfaction of admitting that I'm in a snarky mood.

"Take your bags upstairs, you two, then let's get lunch ready." Mom heads back to the kitchen.

I grab my bag and head upstairs without giving Colten another glance.

"How's your back?" Colten asks from my bedroom doorway before I even get my bag deposited onto the bed.

"It's fine." I turn, crossing my arms over my chest.

Bruised. Heavily bruised.

"Have you already bitched to your mom about the unfairness of me coming to Vera's funeral but not my father's funeral?" he asks, moseying into my room, right to the window that faces his old house and his old bedroom window.

"No."

"Liar." He glances over his shoulder at me.

I avert my gaze to my feet. "It *is* rather insensitive."

He returns his attention to the window. "Yeah, well, so is fucking around on his family."

"Funerals are not for the dead; they're for the living."

"I know."

"Yet you didn't care enough about your mom and brother to show up."

"I grieved him before he ever died, and nobody planned a fancy gathering to offer their condolences to me. My mom and Chad made excuses. Excuses are lies. They lied. When I made the decision to not come to his funeral, I didn't lie. I was honest."

I scoff but don't follow it up with anything.

Colten turns, eyeing me with suspicion before simply eyeing me everywhere. All men have a signature expression that says they've seen you naked. It's sly and cocky. "I left because you asked me to leave. In case you were wondering."

"I wasn't," I say.

"Liar."

"Stop calling me a liar."

"Or what?" His wandering gaze snaps to my face. "Are you going to tell on me?"

I sit on the edge of the bed. "I'd like it if you could behave this weekend. My parents don't need to know that I ... slipped."

"Slipped?" He coughs a laugh. "Are you calling what happened at your house a slip? Like you're a sex addict and you slipped? Or like you physically slipped and landed on my dick?"

He's not going to bait me. Nope. I keep a neutral expression. Rewarding him with any sort of response will only feed his obnoxiously huge ego.

Our silent standoff leads him to me. Not what I want. He squats, lowering to his knees then sitting back on his heels in front of me, hands resting on his thighs. "I'm sorry, Josie. Even if I can't bring myself to regret the path my life has taken, I can promise you that I've lived with the pain of knowing that I hurt you."

I shake my head and start to stand, but he lifts onto his knees and grabs my wrists, guiding me to sit back down on the bed.

"There has to be a way to make things right."

"There's not."

"There must be a way to make things a little less wrong. On the floor in your entry, things felt a little less wrong." He tries to hide his grin, but a half one pulls at his lips.

This grudge is heavy. It's exhausting. It's sticky. I can't shake it. I don't want it, but I can't get past it. An uncrossable sea. I've never been able to let things go. Maybe this grudge-holding curse is in my DNA.

"Best sex of my life," he says.

"I don't doubt that, but it doesn't change anything."

There it is, that showstopping grin. "It's amazing you're still single, Josie. With your winning personality and humble spirit, it's really just ... baffling."

"I need to help my mom with lunch. I'm sure my dad is in the garage. He'll want to see you first since he likes you better than me."

"Because he sold me his car?"

"Because you have a penis."

"Josie, I don't think your dad has any use for my penis. I mean ... I owe him a debt of gratitude for not cutting it off when we were teenagers, but I don't think he thinks about my penis. But I hope you do. God ..." He bites his lip and closes his eyes while easing his head side to side. "I really hope you think about it. I hope you miss it because it sure does miss you." When he opens his eyes, he frowns. "And can we call it something less clinical than penis?"

"It's a penis."

"It's your best friend."

"This conversation is over." I shove his shoulders, and this time he lets me go.

"To Vera." My dad raises his beer bottle while we eat lunch on the three-season porch.

"To Vera," Mom, Colten, and I echo.

"Still not drinking, huh?" Dad eyes my water glass while he and Colten enjoy their beer and my mom sips a glass of wine.

"Still not drinking." I set my water glass on the table.

"Never? You've never taken a drink, Jo?" Dad continues to probe.

I don't know why he thinks I would lie about it. "No, Dad."

"Why do you think you've had such an aversion to alcohol?"

"I'm not sure it's an aversion. I simply have no desire to have it. Never have. I don't know why, but it's not exactly a bad habit to avoid."

"Are you dating, hon?" Mom asks.

"When I have time."

"Anyone special?" She passes me the bowl of cucumbers and onions in vinegar.

"You're not using dating apps, are you, Jo?" Dad asks. "Those are bad news. Nothing more than creeps looking for sex, right?"

I say "no" in the same breath that Colten says "yes."

Tossing a hard scowl in his direction, I clear my throat before shifting my attention back to my dad. "It's a mixed bag. It's also about the only way to meet people these days. I've met a handful of decent guys, but I haven't met anyone with big enough balls to handle my profession."

"My point exactly, Jo. You need to find a friend who can get you a date with a decent guy." Dad takes a bite of his burger.

My phone vibrates in my back pocket, and I retrieve it.

Detective Mosley: My balls are huge.

I glance up at him across the table. He dips his chin to his plate to hide his grin while setting his phone on the table facedown.

Josie: Not really. I've seen a lot of testicles, so I would know.

He glances at his phone and smirks.

"Colten, I was so glad your mom called me. She seemed overjoyed that she got to spend time with Reagan while your ex-wife went on her honeymoon."

"Not ex-wife," I say. "He didn't marry her. He just impregnated her." I stab a potato with my fork and bring it to my mouth, pausing it at my lips when I realize all eyes are on me. "What?" I shrug. "He did."

Colten clears his throat. "For what it's worth, which isn't much at this point, I did propose to Reagan's mom, but we both knew our relationship wasn't there. We had feelings for each other, but not the kind that two people should have when they get married. It was the right call."

"That's mature of you. Is there anyone special in your life now?" Mom asks.

Colten chews a bite of food and looks right at me as I sip my water. "As a matter of fact, I am seeing someone who I think is pretty special."

I choke on my water.

"She's a doctor. Incredibly confident. Sometimes she's stubborn to a fault, but I like her feisty side."

215

Dad belly laughs. "Sounds like Jo. You should introduce them. They'd be best friends."

I stare at my half-empty plate.

"She's a little commitment phobic, so we don't go out much. I know she's not ready to meet my friends. She got burned years ago, and she's having a hard time getting over it even though it's been nearly two decades."

"I don't know, Colten. She sounds unstable," Mom adds. "You might be too good for her."

"I doubt it," I mumble before shoving a bite of food into my mouth.

Colten seems to be the only one who hears me, and he nudges my foot under the table. I return his gesture with a hard kick to his shin. He grunts, drawing concerned looks from my parents.

"You okay?" Dad asks.

Colten nods, reaching down to rub his leg. "Cramp. Long car ride."

"How's Benji?" I ask, opting for a change in conversation.

AFTER LUNCH, we get dressed for the funeral and load up in my mom's Camry. I stare out my window, hands tightly folded on my lap as we make our way to the service. Colten leaves his hand on the middle seat between us like he used to do when we were younger. I'd set my hand next to him, letting our pinkie fingers touch without my mom or dad noticing. It used to feel intimate and a little forbidden.

Things have changed. We can't be trusted to let any parts of our bodies touch.

However, the second we join the line of people filing into the church, Colten rests his hand on my lower back. I try to squeeze between my parents as soon as we enter the church, hoping to claim a seat between them instead of next to wandering hands Colten. Sadly, my dad reaches for my mom's hand, blocking my attempt. When we slide into the pew, I nestle right up to my mom, so much so that she shoots me a funny look that I ignore.

Colten unbuttons his suit jacket and stretches his arm behind me, resting it on the polished wooden edge, his fingers lightly teasing my hair. It makes me shiver, and I scold my body for such a weak reaction while he half grins in victory.

Mom shows me the picture of Vera on the front of the funeral program. It's a photo that my mom took of Vera at the Pella Tulip Festival.

"Denise asked me if I had any photos from our trip to Pella because she talked about it all the time," Mom whispers.

I nod, smile, and try harder to ignore Colten's close proximity.

The service begins, and I watch her family in the front pew. She had three children: Denise, Abby, and Phillip. Abby died of a rare brain tumor after she had her first child—Vera's first grandchild. Shortly after, her husband, Jerry, took his own life because he couldn't deal with the grief. I've only seen Denise once before today. She visited from DC with her two children the summer before my sophomore year. And I've never met Phillip.

As the service continues, I think about anything but the words flowing from the podium. It's my funeral trick. If I don't listen to the speakers, I won't get emotional and leave a blubbering mess. Sometimes, I take the clinical approach and imagine doing the autopsy where they are a stranger to me. What was the cause of death and how I discovered it.

Colten's arm around me disappears, jolting me from my alternative thoughts. He stands and wedges his way out of the pew and then walks to the front of the church.

"What is he doing?" I whisper to my mom.

She points to the funeral program, and his name next to the song "Ave Maria."

They asked him to play the piano? I shouldn't be surprised because Vera had a grand piano, and Colten loved to play it instead of his keyboard. Still, how many years has it been since he's seen her? Did she have it in her will? Did my mom suggest it to her family? Did he offer on his own when he heard the news?

The adult version of Colten Mosley in a sharp black suit, playing the piano … it does things to me that should never happen at a funeral service.

"He has magical hands," Mom whispers, leaning closer to me.

I blush. God ... I hope she doesn't notice. I can't refute it. Colten's hands know what they're doing.

By the time he's finished, I think I'm the only one not crying. New funeral trick: imagine Colten doing magical things to me with his magical fingers.

When he returns to the pew, he eyes me with an expression I can't read. His arm returns to the back of the pew behind me while his lips touch my ear. "Hard-ass. Do forensic pathologists not cry at funerals?"

Before I can answer, Vera's son takes the podium. "That was beautiful. Thank you, Colten."

Colten gives him a tiny smile and an easy nod.

Phillip continues, "My mom moved to Des Moines years ago to be closer to her sister who was battling breast cancer. Denise and I were in college and our dad had ... passed on." He clears some emotion from his throat. "Denise and I were worried that she might feel lonely or overwhelmed with responsibility. But we quickly learned she had neighbors who adopted her as part of their family. And we heard so many stories about Colten and Josie." He laughs a little. "I'd never met them, but I felt like I knew them from all the stories Mom shared. She loved listening to Colten play the piano. And Josie ... are you here?"

A few people look around, and Mom nudges my arm.

I slowly raise my hand and smile.

Phillip gives me a nod. "Hi, Josie. Nice to finally meet you. My mom adored you. She said you were the most inquisitive child she had ever met. She said you devoured books like she did, and you questioned everything and everyone. And she just knew you would marry Colten. I guess she was right."

I stiffen.

My parents chuckle.

Colten plays it cool like ... WE'RE MARRIED.

Of course, Phillip thinks that because Colten has his arm behind me like I'm his property.

I return a constipated smile. Do I shake my head? Is it proper to correct a grieving son in the middle of his mother's funeral?

Phillip continues his gratitude for the people who graced Vera's life.

We make the slow drive to the burial. In my attempt to ignore Colten, I find myself listening to the minister say some final words about Vera.

I watch her kids console each other and her grandchildren.

Then I think back to my times with Vera.

"Colten has another girlfriend. Would it kill him to not have a girlfriend for ... two seconds?"

Vera laughed as we spread blackberry jam onto warm biscuits in her kitchen. Mom sent me over to return several mason jars, and Vera easily persuaded me to eat biscuits and jam with her.

"He's biding his time."

"What does that mean?" I asked.

"It means he's distracting himself with other girls until he can have the one he really wants."

"Who's that?"

She bopped my nose. "You, silly."

"Me?"

"Of course. He always has stars in his eyes when you're in the same room. I predict you will marry Colten Mosley someday. You'll be Josephine Mosley. No man will love you like Colten." She shrugged, swiping a finger through the jam on her biscuit. "That's just my prediction."

I didn't know Vera's track record with predictions, but I liked her, and I trusted her.

Colten hands me a folded tissue, bringing me back into the present. It takes me a few seconds of eyeing him suspiciously before I realize he's handing it to me because I have tears streaming down my cheeks. Only ... they're not because Vera died.

I'm crying because my dream ... my fate died.

CHAPTER
Twenty-Three

"She killed her family. Changed her name. And moved to the Midwest. She's the perfect serial killer. Sweet old lady who makes jam."

I didn't one hundred percent agree with Josie's assessment as we spied through the hedge bushes at Vera Hollinger crocheting in a wooden rocking chair on her front porch. Then again, at twelve, all we had to do on the weekend was make up stories about people, so I played along.

"I bet she has retractable claws."

Josie snorted.

"Are you two munchkins going to hang out in the bushes all day, or are you going to come here and offer me a proper introduction?" She didn't glance up for a second.

We froze, covering our mouths to hide our gasps.

After sharing several wide-eyed blinks, I let my hand slide from my face. "She might be nice," I whispered.

Josie's hand flopped to her side as disappointment stole her expression. "Fine," she mumbled, pushing through the bushes.

"Well, hello there. I'm Vera Hollinger. Who are you?"

Josie pushed me in front of her as we plodded through the yard to her porch steps.

"I'm Colten, and this is Josie. She lives there." I pointed to her house on the same side of the street. "And I live right across the street."

"It's a pleasure meeting you, Colten and Josie. Do your parents know where you are?"

"We're not babies. We can go wherever we want," Josie said. "My dad's the police chief."

A tiny grin wrinkled Vera's face. "I'm aware. I met your parents several days ago. They told me to expect two very inquisitive kids snooping around here."

"What are you making?" Josie nodded to the yellow ball of yarn on Vera's lap.

"I'm not sure yet. I think it might be a hat for my sister."

"It's summer," Josie stated the obvious.

"Indeed. But my sister has no hair, and she's often cold."

"What happened to her hair?" I asked.

"It probably fell out. Does she have cancer?" Josie decided to step in front of me like I was too stupid to ask the right questions, and I probably was.

Vera's gaze returned to the yard, then the crochet hook in her hands, and she nodded.

"Sorry," Josie and I said in unison.

"If she dies, Roland Tompkins will take good care of her."

"Josie," I gritted her name between my clenched teeth.

"I'm just saying ..." She shrugged.

"Who's Roland Tompkins?" Vera asked.

"He's the funeral home director. Josie has a weird obsession with death."

She elbowed me. "I do not. I just like to do things that are more interesting than hit a ball with a bat or play the piano."

Vera's hands paused, and she glanced up again. "I play the piano."

"Me too," I said.

"I don't. My dad thinks survival skills are the best hobbies to have," Josie said.

"Josie kills Bambi."

Again, she elbowed me. "I've never killed a deer, stupid."

"I'd love to hear you play the piano sometime. I have a beautiful piano that my husband bought me. I don't play it much anymore, but I can't bring myself to get rid of it either."

"I don't have a real piano, just a keyboard," I said.

"Oh ... then you'll love my piano. It's a shiny black Steinway & Sons. It was just tuned after I moved in. Would you like to see it?"

"Can't. I have to ask my mom," I said.

"I'll take a look," Josie said.

I rolled my eyes. She wasn't supposed to go into strangers' houses, and she knew it.

"Why don't you both check with your parents and we'll see it another time. I picked some of the blackberries from the bushes out back. Maybe you can come for biscuits and jam."

As all kids did at twelve, we lit up with excitement at the possibility of Vera making jam and biscuits for our next visit.

"We'd like that," Josie said. "Bye."

"See you later, munchkins."

We ran back to Josie's house, out back, and straight into the woods where we climbed our favorite tree.

"I should ask Vera to teach me how to crochet," Josie said.

"Why?"

"It's a useful skill, and I bet it's something that won't ..." She popped her lips several times. "What was the word my dad used ... oh! It won't *intimidate* boys like when I fish and hunt."

"What's that even mean?"

"Intimidate?"

I shook my head. "No. Why did he say it?"

"Because I don't have a lot of real friends besides you."

"Maybe it's the other girls who think you're weird."

"Who said anything about being weird?" She wrinkled her nose and squinted at me.

"I'm just saying—"

"You don't know what you're saying."

She wasn't wrong. It was possible other boys were intimidated by her because she sure intimidated me. As much as I jumped at opportunities to mock her or call her weird, I really wanted to live inside of her head. I'd never met anyone like her. Not another kid, not even an adult who looked at the world and life the way Josephine Watts did. Living in her world was like living in a movie.

A mystery.

An adventure.

Maybe even the beginning of a love story.

CHAPTER

Twenty-Four

THE SUN SETS while Mom and I do dishes, and Colten has a beer on the deck with my dad.

"Did your mom make your dad help with dishes?" I ask her. "Because my mom used to make my dad do the dishes. This feels a little 1950s to me."

She laughs. "Your dad's back has been bothering him lately. Standing in one place for too long aggravates it."

"What's Colten's excuse?"

She gives me a hip-check as we stand at the sink. "What's your deal with Colten? You don't act like adults together. You act like the same two kids who used to terrorize the neighborhood. If I didn't know better, I'd say you're holding a grudge."

"What do you mean, 'if you didn't know better?'"

"You're thirty-five. So accomplished. Independent.

Brilliant. I can't imagine a mother who is prouder of their daughter than I am of you. It's not the 1950s. And you are a shining example of what it means to be a woman right now. You've never depended on a man. I haven't given up hope that you will one day find someone who complements your life and whose life you will complement as well. I think growing up with Colten next door taught you so much about relationships ... and eventually about letting go. To this day, I'm in awe of how gracefully you two parted ways after graduation."

I dry the colander so long the stainless-steel shines like new. If I look at her, she'll see the lie. All that motherly pride will spiral down the drain with the dirty dish water. When Colten abandoned me, I did an Oscar-worthy job of hiding the pain.

I perfected the brave face.

I regurgitated the "I'm happy for Colten" speech.

I touted my accomplishments ... my college acceptance letters.

Loving Colten Mosley came with a hefty price. I had to let my heart break in complete silence. It felt like someone asked me to keep living without breathing. Everyone except his mom thought I was sad about my "friend" enlisting.

"I think I'm going to take a walk before bed." I drape the towel over the dishwasher handle.

"What time are you leaving in the morning?"

"Early. Maybe six. So I won't be long."

"Okay. I'll make sure the coffee's ready."

"Thanks." I slip on my tennis shoes and exit the front door, making my way to the back of the house, hoping Colten and my dad are too busy talking to notice me.

To my delight, my tree is still there. Not as much to my delight, it's a little harder for my thirty-five-year-old self to climb it. But I manage to get to the first big branch, letting my feet dangle as the crickets and frogs sing the song of summer with barely a sliver of sun left at the horizon.

"You were quiet at dinner," Colten breaks my peaceful train of thought.

I glance down at him.

"It's been an emotional day," he says with a little grunt while he jumps to grab my branch, pulling himself up easier than he ever did as a kid. Figures ... life just got easier for him. "Did you know that Vera thought we would get married?" He chuckles. "She never told me that."

I want to shove him out of the tree and pray that he breaks both legs and a sharp stick impales his penis like skewering a kabob. "Would it have made a difference?"

Again, he chuckles. It's an insecure laugh. "You didn't want to marry me."

"I love how everyone seemed to know what I did or didn't want at the time. I love how everyone knew better than I did what was best for my life. It was such a relief to not have to busy my brain with making decisions for myself. Whoa!" I start to fall off the branch like I did the time I broke my arm.

"Can't work with broken bones, Dr. Watts," Colten says with his arm hooked around my waist, steadying me again.

One of my hands grips the branch while my other hand grips his leg. I catch my breath. I used to be fearless. Even when I did fall from the tree, I wasn't scared. Just in pain.

"I'm going inside." I nod for him to move out of my way so I can climb down.

Colten hops out of the tree with little effort. I, on the other hand, make the dismount look incredibly difficult. Yes. Things have changed. I have a healthy fear of breaking something.

"I've got ya." He grabs my ass as I ease down the trunk.

"I've got it, handsy." When my feet hit the ground, I turn and take a step away from him.

"Listen, I should not have let it get so far at your place. The attraction mixed with so many years of not seeing you ... mixed with your emotional fragility. It just all—"

"Wait." I narrow my eyes. "My *emotional fragility*? Are you kidding me? There was nothing emotionally fragile about me that night or any other night for that matter."

Colten shrugs before sliding his hands into his back pockets as the wind starts to pick up, bringing in the forecasted storms. "I assumed I caught you having a weak moment. Why else would you have sex with someone who you, in your words, 'hate?'"

It's a good question, but the answer is not emotional fragility. That sounds weak. I'm not weak. I'm ... well, I'm not sure, but we're going to find a more accurate word than "fragile" to use.

"Maybe I just wanted to get laid. And you ran my date off, so ... slim pickings."

A grin confiscates his entire face. "You had sex with me because I was your only choice? You're going with that story?"

I cross my arms over my chest and lift my chin. "A *true* story."

"Stop scraping your teeth over your bottom lip if you don't want me to kiss you."

I freeze and release my lip from my teeth. "Asshole."

"Stubborn overthinker." He steps toward me, hands making a play to grab my face and kiss me. That's what has always followed "stubborn overthinker."

I bob and weave once before running as the clouds open up and drop buckets of rain on us.

"Ahh!" I squeal, squinting against the rain as my shoes fail to grip the wet ground.

Colten grabs my arm, keeping me on my feet just seconds before I nearly land ass first in the mud. His hand slides from my upper arm to my hand.

Our fingers interlace, and he runs toward the house with me a few steps behind him.

We slip into the side garage door, me in his arms,

his lips inches from mine until my dad clears his throat.

I jump right out of Colten's hold and wipe the water from my face. "Hey ... uh ... we got caught in the rain."

Dad wipes his hands on a towel. He should be in bed with Mom, not out in the garage cleaning his guns. His silence makes me feel like a child getting caught.

"Go get dried off while I have a word with Colten."

"A word?" I chuckle. "No. I'm not twelve or fifteen. I don't live here. And you don't tell me what to do. If you need to have a word with Colten, then you'll have it in front of me."

"Fine." Dad cocks his head and eyes Colten. "Are you screwing my daughter?"

Well, shit ...

"Yes."

"What?" I whip around, jaw unhinged while Colten keeps his steady gaze on my dad. Not so much as a flinch. "We are not..." I turn back toward my dad "...we are *not* in a relationship."

"I didn't ask if you're in a relationship. I asked if you were screwing," Dad says.

I say "no" again as Colten says "yes" again.

"Jesus ..." I shake my head. "First, my sex life is none of your business. I'm thirty-five. But since Colten is being such an asshole about it ... yes, we had sex once. And it will never happen again."

"Is that correct?" Dad has the nerve to ask Colten for confirmation.

I'm ready to kill them both.

Colten slides his gaze from my dad to me. Face straight and unreadable.

I pivot and stomp my feet toward my dad, hands on my hips. "What is wrong with you? Why are you questioning me? Why are you questioning us? Why can't you be a normal dad who sees something that wasn't for your eyes and slithers out of the room in embarrassment because his daughter is a grown woman who has sex with whomever she pleases whenever she pleases?"

Immediately, I realize how bad that sounded. Still, I own it. Whatever. If I'm having sex with a new guy every night—which I would not do—that's my business, not his.

Dad frowns.

I blow out a long breath, losing my will to let this be a big deal when it's not. I'm leaving in the morning. What's the point? "I had an itch. Colten scratched it. End of story."

His frown deepens.

"I never would have cheated on her," Colten says.

"W-what?" Did I hear him right?

This has become a private conversation between my dad and Colten. Neither one will look at me. It's like I'm not here.

"Doesn't change anything." Dad lifts a shoulder.

"I know. I just need you to know it. Even if you made me doubt it then, I know better now. I'm not my father."

"Thank god for that. Everything turned out for the best. The past is the past." Dad nods several times.

"Did you ..." I can barely say the words because my brain's struggling to put the pieces together. I take a step closer to my dad. "Did you know?"

My parents never knew, or so I thought. Colten's mom promised to not say a word. And I respected Colten's desire to have my dad's respect since his dad was simply ... a terrible husband and father. I thought it would all work its way out.

We would graduate.

We would be adults.

And we'd tell my parents that we were in love.

He blows a long breath out his nose. "I wasn't stupid. Or blind. Or deaf. Did you really think you could sneak around behind my back without me knowing?"

My head eases side to side. "Why didn't you say anything?" I ask, just above a whisper.

"I did. I said something to Colten."

This shouldn't hurt. It's been too long. But it does. Seventeen years ago, Colten carved the most jagged hole into my heart. And all this time, I had no idea that my dad handed him the knife.

"How could you?" I turn around, facing Colten. "How could *you*?"

"Josie ..." Anguish spreads across Colten's face.

"You chose my dad over me? Is this some cruel joke?"

"I chose you," he says.

My head shakes over and over again.

"Your future."

"No," I snap. "You chose *your* future, and it didn't include me."

"Jo, it was nearly twenty years ago," Dad interrupts. "A childhood crush. Look at you now."

Look at me now. I'm so tired of hearing that everyone around me saved me. Nobody saved me. I saved myself. They have no fucking clue ... not a single one of them.

"You had a scholarship, Josie. I didn't. And I didn't have the money for college. I didn't have a clue what I was going to do. And when you said you wanted to take a year or two to decide if medical school was what you wanted ... I knew it was because of me." Colten runs his hands through his hair, face still distorted with those lines of anguish and desperation.

"Well, aren't you an arrogant asshole for assuming that. And a liar for not just saying that. You joined the fucking Marines just to get away from me. Were you willing to die for your country because of your heroic patriotism or because you *so* desperately wanted to please my dad and go someplace you knew I would never follow you?"

"Jo, it was infatuation. Lack of a better choice for both of you. Not love."

I knew my dad always wanted me to be a boy, but I never noticed all the ways he subtly belittled me and my feelings. Starting with my name. And I let him because I wanted to be the apple of his eye. I wanted to prove that I was just as good as any son. And I was different, so fitting in, if only in my dad's eyes, mattered to me.

"Not love …" I echo. Colten used those same words when he ended us.

There is nothing left to say to either man, so I brush past my dad and head into the house. Instead of taking a shower, which I need, I set my phone's alarm, change into a nightshirt, and crawl into bed. I don't want to risk seeing Colten or my parents again before I leave early in the morning.

CHAPTER
Twenty-Five

JOSIE WATCHED ME SELF-DESTRUCT, and I knew she'd be part of the wreckage. Still I didn't have the nerve, or maybe a true incentive, to stop it. Misery loved company. And I was miserable.

By our senior year, I'd found the one thing more toxic than misery and hate ... spite.

Doing the opposite of my father's wishes became my life's mission, even if it was at my own demise. He told me not to drink or do drugs.

I got a fake ID, drank every weekend, and scored some pot from a kid named Tyler Vogt.

My dad told me baseball players didn't need to bulk up. It might limit my swinging ability. I lived in the weight room.

Lived on protein.

Lived to disappoint him ... to spite him.

I deserved the World's Greatest Fuckup Award by the end of the year. I got my first DUI. Got suspended from playing baseball my senior year. Lost my chance for a scholarship. And nearly didn't graduate after starting a fight with Andy Miller because he took Josie to the prom (I was suspended from that too) and told everyone she sucked his dick in the parking lot. Of course, I didn't believe it was true, but it didn't matter. Either way, I was going to beat the living shit out of him because Josie was mine.

Until ... the perfect storm.

Two weeks before graduation, on the heels of the prom fiasco, I was going to tell Josie's parents about us. Despite my bad behavior, her dad liked me. He blamed my behavior on my father's poor example. I had no fucking clue what I was going to do with my life, but it involved Josie.

I'd go wherever she decided to go to college. She had more than one scholarship offer. Josie was the smartest person I knew and the only person who brought any sort of peace to my life. If I had to get a job at a hardware store or bagging groceries, I was prepared to do it. Anything to be with Josie.

If I let her take off to college without me, some smart, put-together guy would steal her. Of that, I had no doubt.

Just as I sped down the stairs, on my way to talk to the chief, my dad came in the front door.

"Where are you going?" he asked.

"What do you care?"

He grabbed my arm to stop me. By then I was so much bigger than him; it wouldn't have taken much for me to have put him on his ass.

"Your mom told me you've been secretly pining for the chief's daughter."

My parents' reconciliation pissed me off. I couldn't believe my mom took him back. And apparently that meant she was sharing everything with him again.

I jerked out of his hold. "Well, it's not going to be a secret much longer."

"She's the smartest decision you've ever made. I'm amazed you haven't screwed that up too. Josie's going to make something of herself. Maybe her work ethic will rub off on you." His approval of her stifled my plans. It sucked all the oxygen from my lungs. I managed to shut the door behind me and trek over to her house, but I no longer knew what I was going to say to the chief.

Spite … so much spite.

"Colten." He gave me his manly nod before spraying foam on his Chevelle's tires. "What's up?"

I had no words, just thoughts that never made it out of my mouth.

I love your daughter. I have since the moment we first shared cookies and milk. I didn't know those feelings I had way back then were love … but they were. I'm going to follow her to college and take care of her. I have no clue what I'm going to do with my life other than do right by her. Do I have your blessing?

I cleared my throat, but I couldn't clear my head.

The echo of my dad's words wouldn't stop whispering in my ear, prodding my conscience, and igniting my natural instinct to spite him. "Um ... I was going to talk to you about Josie and me, but it's not uh ..."

Chief Watts stood tall and drew in a breath so deep I think he took all of the oxygen from the garage. When he let it out, his mouth tipped into a disapproving frown. "I'm not blind or stupid. I know you have a little crush on my daughter. And I think she probably has some sort of feelings for you too. But it's a little late to be having this conversation with me, don't ya think?"

Think? I had no idea what to think. What conversation did he think I was going to have with him? A confession? A mission statement? An apology?

"Josie's going to medical school. We're all very proud of her, aren't we?" he asked.

I nodded slowly.

"I think you're lost, son. I think you need something that will give you direction again. Discipline. Life skills. A clean slate."

I agreed. I needed Josie. Did that mean I was agreeing with my father?

"I was a lot like you. I had a shitty father. Chip on my shoulder. A mile-long list of bad decisions. Then I enlisted in the Marines. It changed my life. Mentally. Physically. Emotionally. Other than marrying Savannah, it was the best decision of my life. It made me the man she wanted to marry."

The military?

My parents were anti-war. My dad scoffed at the idea that any young person would voluntarily sign up to risk their life for their country in what he called "endless wars."

"You think I should enlist?"

He rested his hand on my shoulder, giving it a firm squeeze. "I do. I think you should let Josie live her life, the life she's been earning through hard work and dedication. Don't be the person who pulls her heartstrings and derails her future over infatuation or a lack of a better choice. It's not love. Let her go. Wish her well. Then pack a bag and get some real-life skills for yourself. If you decide on college, it will be free. Or you might choose law enforcement like I did. Whatever you choose, it will be the right decision for *you*. Okay?"

He read my mind ... only not really. I had too many voices in my head drowning out my own. Too many emotions. Love. Hate. The desire to please. The pressure to do the right thing.

The right thing ... I had no clue what that looked like.

Josie was going to be a brilliant doctor. She'd probably cure cancer or some other awful disease. And I'd ... what? Bag groceries? Stock shelves?

Or ... defend my country, acquire life skills, serve my community.

I thought we could wait for each other. We could be together after reaching our full potential. Was that fair? What if I died? What if she passed up opportunities to find love while waiting for me ... and then I died?

"Yeah," I said with my heart in my throat.

"Hey, I never got a chance to ask you. What did Andy Miller do to earn your fist in his face a dozen times?"

"He started a rumor about Josie that wasn't true." I didn't know if it was true. I hadn't talked with Josie since the incident. She wasn't happy with me. But I had to believe it was just a rumor. That was the only thing that kept me from killing Andy.

"Just between us, thank you. I've always felt better knowing you've been looking out for Josie's best interest. I know she can be a handful, and maybe that's why she's never had a lot of friends. You've been like a big brother. I won't ever forget it." He glanced over my shoulder and nodded. "Speaking of my awesome daughter ..."

I turned my head as Josie pulled into the driveway. She climbed out of her red Civic and pulled off her sunglasses. It wasn't anything new to see me hanging out with her dad, but the distrust on her face leaked her emotions without saying a word.

"What are you two doing?"

Her dad returned his attention to the Chevelle. "Solving the world's problems."

She scoffed. "I highly doubt that. I'm going for a run."

"I'll go with you."

Josie's right eyebrow slid up her forehead. "You

don't run. You lift weights and try to intimidate innocent people." She eyed her dad as if to make sure he wasn't focusing on us.

My lips twisted. "I do run. Let me change my shoes."

She blew her hair out of her face and rolled her eyes. "Whatever. If you're not back in five minutes, I'm leaving without you."

By the time she finished her warning, I was already to the street. "I learned how to tie my shoes a long time ago," I hollered. "I'll be back in less than two minutes because I need to grab socks."

Minutes later, I beat her to the end of the driveway, but not by much. She wanted to leave me behind. The second she saw me, she started a fast-paced jog. I sped to catch up.

"How's Andy's face?" I asked.

"How was being expelled from school for two weeks and nearly not graduating?"

I grinned. "It was good. I spent most of my time with Vera, eating biscuits and jam and playing the piano. Slept in. Caught up on laundry …"

"You're lucky Andy didn't press charges."

"He's lucky I didn't break his fucking nose."

When we reached the end of the street, she stopped, hands parked on her hips, black hair falling out of her ponytail. "I don't need you to defend my honor. If I decided to beat the shit out of every girl who talked about what you did or didn't do with her, I'd be in juvie."

"Should I be offended that you've never felt the need to defend my honor?"

"Pfft ... you're not defending my honor. You haven't even asked me if it's true." Josie's dark eyes narrowed, daring me to ask her.

It didn't matter. Okay, it mattered, but I wasn't going to confess that. Either way, Andy deserved everything he got and then some. I shrugged. "It's a moot point." I started jogging again.

"Why?" Her feet slapped the pavement behind me.

"Because it's none of my business at this point. And when you leave for college, it won't be any of his business either. He'll be here, working for his dad. It will be hard to suck his dick remotely."

"And where will you be?"

"Basic training."

"What?"

I raced past her because I wasn't ready to have that conversation with her. I wasn't even sure if that's what I was planning on doing. It came out, and I felt the need to commit.

Commit to a direction.

Commit to a purpose.

Commit to letting her go.

And it fucking hurt.

"Jesus, would you stop and look at me?" She grabbed the back of my shirt.

I sighed and turned. "What?"

"You can't enlist."

"Why not?"

Her lips parted while her head swiveled in denial. "B-because ... it makes no sense."

"It makes perfect sense. I fucked up my scholarship opportunities. I have no clue what I want to do with my life. My dad's an asshole, and my mom is pathetically gullible for taking him back. I have no reason to stay around here—"

"Me! You stay for me!" Panic infiltrated her words, and it took herculean strength to steady my emotions.

"You're not staying here. You're going off to college."

"Then you come with me. We talked about this so many times. I'm tired of our stupid hidden relationship. Part of me was relieved that time your mom caught us. I just wanted to have a normal relationship with you. This stupid facade is about to end. We tell my parents, and we don't give a fuck what they think. You don't need my dad's approval anymore. We don't need anyone's approval."

"It's not about approval, Josie. It's about our future. But *we* don't have a future right now. There's your future, and there's my future. One of us will have to sacrifice for the other, and that's ridiculous. We're too young to make rash decisions because of some..." I searched for the best word, but the only one that came to mind was her dad's word "...infatuation. Maybe we've felt a bond because of close proximity or simply lack of a better choice. That doesn't mean it's ..." I sighed and lowered my voice, choking back my emotions and calming my frustration. "That doesn't mean it's love."

245

Tears filled her eyes. I'd only seen Josie cry a handful of times, and it usually involved a physical pain like falling out of a tree or cutting open her knee. She bit her quivering lower lip and wiped her tears the second they fell to her red cheeks. "Y-you don't l-love me?"

Yes. God ... I loved her more than any other human being. I loved her more than myself. I loved her more than God even if that was a sin. I loved her *so* much that I had to let her go. And that meant I had to lie to her. That hurt more than any physical pain *I* had ever experienced. "I care about you. You're my best friend."

Josie stopped wiping her tears; there were too many. Instead, she took off running.

Let her go. Just ... let her go.

I couldn't let her go. Not like that. If I couldn't tell her *the* truth, I wanted to tell her *a* truth. I let her run for a while, keeping a safe distance behind her. With each step, I imagined one day we'd find each other again, and the timing would be right. She would be a doctor, saving lives. And I would be something infinitely better than I was in that moment. I would be a man who didn't need to please a police chief or wreck my life to spite my father.

The more distance we covered, the more those words solidified in my mind. I would let her go to be that better man. Just ... not yet.

When she reached the batting cages, she continued to run to the field where we used to race each other, the field where we believed bad people lived, waiting to kidnap us. Josie stopped, bent over, and rested her hands on her legs while she gasped for air. Her shoulders shook, and her deep breaths morphed into howling sobs while she dropped to her knees, her body folding onto itself.

I kneeled in front of her and pulled her to me.

"No!" Her arms flailed as she tried to keep me from holding her.

I hugged her arms to her body and all of her to me. She wriggled and wriggled while crying more than I had ever seen her cry ... more than I had ever seen anyone cry. After a while, she stopped fighting me, and her sobs subsided into tiny hiccups while her hands fisted my shirt.

"Don't leave me," she whispered.

Gritting my teeth, I swallowed hard. Tears burned my eyes, but I couldn't set a single one free.

"It-it's us, C-Colten. It's a-always been u-us ..."

I kissed the top of her head. Said nothing. Felt *everything.*

"Tell me you l-love me."

I love you.

Tightening her grip on my shirt, she pounded my chest and glanced up at me with sad, red eyes. "Tell me," she croaked out the words.

I gritted my teeth harder and refused to blink.

She released my shirt and grabbed my face, moving to her knees again and kissing me with a punishing intensity. I kissed her back, memorizing the taste of her mouth, the feel of her tongue against mine, her soft hands on my whiskery face, the rise and fall of her chest brushing mine.

Did she know how many times I wanted to leave the world? Leave the pressure of my dad's expectations, the embarrassing shadow of his indiscretions, the cloud of depression that hung over our house for years. Did she know she was the reason I kept going? The promise of *us*?

I lived wholly, eternally, unequivocally for Josephine Watts.

Why didn't I tell her when it mattered the most?

I never thought I'd let her go.

I never thought I'd miss my opportunity to say all the things I kept inside for so many years.

Yet, there I was ... suffocating in a miserable bubble of unshed tears and unspoken emotions. My heart clogged my airway, throbbing, burning like my eyes. I wasn't sure I could live without her, but I had to try.

She pushed me away and stood, taking my hand and tugging it until I stood and followed her into the woods. We didn't make it far before she grabbed my shirt again and pulled me to her as she rested her back against a tree trunk. Sticks and winter's compost crushed beneath our feet as I pressed my body to hers.

Her fingers teased my abs beneath my shirt before she worked it up my torso. I broke our kiss and discarded my shirt as she did the same to hers.

Again we kissed. Never feeling her hands on my body again felt like its own torture. Would I die for my country? I didn't know yet. But I would have died for

Josephine Watts. I would have died in that moment had it meant I never had to let her go.

"I love you, Colten. I love you more than anything or anyone," she whispered as I kissed my way down her neck.

That lump in my throat doubled. It stung and pulsed. A monster of grief with a chokehold on me. I could barely breathe.

Her fingers teased the waistband of my jogging shorts. I moaned into her mouth. When her warm hand slid into my briefs, my hips jerked, and I broke the kiss, moaned louder, a growl of sorts, while my forehead rested on hers. "Josie ..." I whispered.

"I want this," she whispered while her hand tormented me. "I want this with *you*."

Pulling her hand from my cock, I took both of her hands and held them to my chest. And we remained idle, sharing each breath, saying everything without saying anything.

Again, her body vibrated with emotions, stifling new sobs while my nose rubbed against hers, while my lips ghosted along her face, while I pressed one last kiss to her lips.

Josie wasn't some girl in my life; she *was* my life. The sun. The air. Gravity. My whole world and reason for existing.

Did she feel it? Really *feel* it in her soul?

"Good luck, Josie. You're going to be a huge success."

When I took a step back, she squeezed her eyes

shut and covered her face with her hands, trembling with emotion. I grabbed my shirt, turned toward home, and didn't look back.

But I heard the two words she whispered, and they hit me so hard, my steps faltered under the weight of their real possibility.

"Don't die ..."

I had what I needed to get my diploma, so I did not go back to school. I skipped my graduation (another solid "fuck you" to Coach Mosley), and I never saw Josie Watts again, until seventeen years later.

Life never went as planned.

CHAPTER

Twenty-Six

I'VE NEVER HAD huge aspirations. No plans to cure cancer. No intentions of being the best at anything. I went to medical school because everyone thought I'd be a good doctor. And ... Colten Mosley left me half naked in the woods after rejecting me, after not saying those three words to me.

Here we are, seventeen years later, and he's once again following me.

"Are you really leaving without saying goodbye to your parents?" Colten asks as I get into my car a little after five in the morning.

He tosses his bag into the back of his vehicle and shuts the door.

"When did you become an early riser?" I mumble, sparing a tiny glance in his direction.

"Marines. Four a.m. every morning. We really

should have ridden together." He has the nerve to act like nothing happened last night, like I didn't discover the truth behind his cowardliness.

"No. We should never do anything together again."

"Never is a long time."

I grunt. "Tell me about it."

Before he can respond, I climb into my car and shut the door. For six hours, he follows me home, stopping once for gas and to use the restroom. He doesn't say anything; he hangs back like a cop tailing a suspect. A few miles before my exit, he goes right toward his house, and I take my first full breath in six hours.

An hour later, my phone rings and "Detective Mosley" illuminates my screen. I hop off my stationary bike and take a sip of water, thinking hard about not answering it. I've had enough of him for a few lifetimes.

"What is it?" I answer as clipped as possible.

"You're breathing hard. Are you having sex?"

I click *End* and toss my phone on the chair. Again, he calls me. I ignore it this time. Then it chimes with a text.

Detective Mosley: I've taken a bullet twice. I've been resuscitated once. Stitches more times than I can count. And none of that hurt like it did when I left you in the woods seventeen years ago. Just thought you should know.

I stare at his text and sip more water.

Another chime of a text.

Detective Mosley: Don't blame your dad. He made a suggestion, but it was my choice.

Grabbing my foot, I stretch my quads while rereading his texts.

Detective Mosley: I should have said it, but it wouldn't have changed what I did, so it felt cruel to say it.

I switch legs, feeling his words deeper than I want to feel them.

Detective Mosley: But I felt it, Josie. God … I felt it in my fucking soul.

"TEENAGER DROPPED off at the ER entrance. They didn't even stop the car." Dr. Cornwell waggles his eyebrows.

I shrug, feeling a little melancholy this morning which means I'll take whatever he gives me. After he assigns two more cases to me, I don my PPE and head to the autopsy suite.

"Morning." Detective Mosley smiles before masking as I brush past him, heading to the cold room.

The abandoned body is my first case this morning, and I assume, the reason Colten's here.

253

"Morning," several students say as I grab the microphone to dictate the external exam.

Ignoring Colten, I talk my way through the exam, occasionally quizzing the eager students.

"She's good," Colten murmurs to one of the students as I make my first cut.

The young woman nods several times. "She's the best ... but don't tell Dr. Cornwell I said that."

I grin without looking away from the decedent, thankful that I'm masked and behind a face shield.

Twenty minutes later, when I'm solidly in my zone, Colten breaks his silence, but not with a question about the decedent. "What are you whistling?"

"I think it's 'Knocking on Heaven's Door,'" one of the young observers says.

"Do you always whistle?" Colten asks.

More than one of the students answers in unison, "Yes."

Colten chuckles. "You used to whistle when we'd do our homework together."

"You went to school with Dr. Watts?" The young woman who called me "the best" asks Colten.

"I did. She was my first love."

My hands pause and Alicia lets out an audible gasp that only I can hear. I hope only I hear her.

"For real?" the young woman asks.

"The realest," Colten says.

When I glance up at him, he winks.

"What happened?" she asks him.

"She became a brilliant doctor, and I joined the Marines."

"Are you married? Dr. Watts is single."

Who is this girl? Do I know her name? And how the hell does she know my marital status?

He chuckles.

Two hours later ... I've got nothing, and that frustrates me to no end.

"Nothing?" Colten asks.

I shrug. "We need to wait for toxicology."

"Did you miss something?"

I exit the suite to use the restroom. "Unlikely."

"Did you get my texts?"

I pause at the locker room door. "Yes." I push through it and use the restroom before donning new PPE. When I exit, my shadow awaits me.

"Have dinner with me tonight."

I breeze past him. "No."

He grabs the back of my gown where it's tied and tugs it to stop me. I sigh. Colten's never been so relentless—that was always my role. We have a silent standoff. I don't turn toward him, and he doesn't let me go. We've had more silent standoffs than I care to remember.

After a few seconds, he releases me, and I get back to work.

SUNDAY, I grab pho on my way home from errands and settle onto my sofa with the warm bowl of broth and noodles and a good book. While I slurp the last of it, there's a tap at my window facing the front yard. I make my way toward the noise, contemplating grabbing my gun, but then I see a white piece of paper pressed against it with black Sharpie writing.

I'M SORRY

I shake my head and return to the kitchen.

Tap. Tap. Tap.

Blowing out a long breath, I peek around the corner again.

I SHOULD

HAVE

SAID

IT

It takes time for his words to penetrate the scar tissue around my heart. Time for me to convince my feet to carry me to the front door. Time ... Has seventeen years been enough time for an eternal grudge?

"Let me say it, Josie," Colten says from the other side of the door. "Let me say it when I don't have to walk away. Let me say it when it doesn't have to be a consolation. A really shitty goodbye."

If I open the door, my heart wins, and my pride and conscience will never fully recover.

"I was just too fucking stupid to figure it out. I was too angry at my dad. I was too persuaded by your dad. I was lost. I was weak. And you deserved more, Josie. So much more."

I rest my palms and the side of my face on the door.

"And I remember thinking ... what if some day we find each other again and everything is just right? The time. The place. Just everything. And here we are, Josie. It's not fucking coincidence."

There's another pause, and I wonder if he's given up. I hope so because I can't take much more.

"You. I would have chosen you."

I narrow my eyes, the side of my face still pressed to the door.

"When we went to the batting cages and talked about being kidnapped, and we discussed who we'd choose if only one of us could live ... I would have chosen you to live because for so very long, you've been the only purpose to my life."

"Jesus ..." I whisper, blinking back the tears.

I wait. And wait. I wait until I hear nothing. I wait until my legs are tired of standing in one place. I wait until his confession no longer seems real. Then, I crack open the door, and he's still there.

"I'm not going anywhere because I. Love. You. Josephine Watts."

My lower lip gives me away with its uncontrolled trembling before I can curl my lips together to hide it.

Colten lets the white sheets of paper fall to the ground and takes one step toward me, hands on my face, fingers in my hair, lips claiming mine. I grip his arms to steady myself.

I let myself fall a little into him. I let myself fall a little for him.

257

I let myself feel something less than hatred. All that hatred because he made his mark on a nine-year-old girl's heart, and she ... *I* have never been the same.

I've always been his.

He kicks the door shut behind us and walks me backward, clueless to where he's guiding me, reckless as we nearly trip. Am I too old to be clueless and reckless with Colten Mosley? I hope not.

"Do you know where you're going?" I giggle while he kisses my neck, hands palming my ass.

"I'm a detective, Watts ... I'll figure it out." He does.

He finds my bedroom after we leave a trail of clothes in the hallway. When the back of my knees hit the bed, his hands ghost along my skin to unhook my bra. It slides down my arms, and my hard nipples brush his bare chest while his lips feather over mine, teasing me.

My breath morphs into a soft panting with every excruciatingly slow move he makes. His middle finger slides under the crotch of my panties, teasing my clit.

"J-jesus ... what are you doing to m-me?" My voice trembles when I press my lips to his sternum.

"I'm trying to make you weak in the knees."

When said knees start to buckle, I release a nervous chuckle. "Done." In the next blink, I suck in a sharp breath while he thrusts his middle finger inside of me, his other hand sliding into the back of my panties. He squeezes my ass, pulling me flush to his chest.

"Yeah?" He grins, millimeters from our lips touching.

I really, *really* like adult Colten Mosley. His confidence doesn't waver for a second. He could make me orgasm with nothing more than that look in his eyes. He eases his finger out of me and uses it to trace my bottom lip. The tiny grin on his face swells a fraction before he licks my lower lip, a slow swipe of his tongue. He bites it with a low growl vibrating his chest. Then he sucks on my lip like I'm the best thing he's ever tasted.

"I need more," he says between kisses while his grip on my ass stings, making me feel like a meal to a starving man.

It's a heady feeling as I close my eyes and whisper, "More what?"

He cups my breast for a breath before his hand dives down the front of my panties. "More of this."

An unfamiliar ring tone interrupts us. It's his phone.

"Fuck!" He sighs, removing his hand from my panties.

I bite my lips together and take a deep breath.

He traces his steps back to the hallway to find his jeans next to one of his sneakers. I inspect his perfect ass in those tight black briefs while I ease my ass onto the side of the bed.

"Mosley," he snaps.

I think I like grumpy Colten Mosley. I definitely like grumpy Colten Mosley half naked in my house.

"Yeah. Uh-huh ..." He turns toward me, and his brow knits together when his gaze lands between my spread legs like he's confused. "Okay," he says in a clipped tone, taking slow steps back to me while his eyes flit up my body to meet my gaze.

It's only then that I realize my hand has drifted down the front of my panties while gawking at him.

"I'll be right there." He tosses his phone onto the bed next to me. "Watts, what the fuck are you doing?"

"Are you leaving?" I inch my hand out of my panties. Maybe he didn't really notice. Maybe he thinks I had an itch.

Well, I do have an itch of sorts.

"Yes, I must go. I'm sorry." He kneels in front of me and drags my panties down my legs.

"What are you doing?"

He doesn't look at me.

"C-Colten!" I suck in a harsh breath when his face plants between my legs. I fall back onto one elbow while my other hand grips his hair.

"I'm saying goodbye," he mumbles.

"Col ... just ..." My head spins with each slurred word that fights past my lips. "God ... yesss ..." Just before I orgasm, I think I might lose consciousness. My knees squeeze inward, trapping his head when my pelvis jerks.

"I have to go," he says, wedging his head out from between my legs. I completely collapse back onto the bed.

On a satisfied sigh, I lift back onto my elbows and watch him get dressed. "I feel bad."

"About what?" he murmurs, zipping his jeans before tugging on his shirt.

"I'm rather satisfied at the moment, and you're leaving, well ... *not* satisfied. So I feel a little bad for you."

He shoves his feet into his sneakers and takes several long strides to get back to me.

I sit up, and he cups the back of my head and kisses me. Pulling back an inch, a half grin tugs at his lips, and he whispers, "I highly fucking doubt it."

I don't want to grin. I'm not sure I'm ready for him to fully know how ridiculously happy I am, but I can't help it.

"I'll see you later." He kisses my forehead before heading toward the front door.

He's gruff.

He's sexy as hell.

He's intimate and tender.

And I think he's finally ... mine.

CHAPTER
Twenty-Seven

By NINE O'CLOCK, I jump onto my stationary bike and sweat until close to ten. Then I shower for bed and give up on seeing Colten again tonight or even getting a text or phone call.

I arrive at work on Monday by seven.

Dr. Cornwell eyes me over his glasses. "Am I distracting you with work?"

"I have court this afternoon, and I'm meeting with a family in an hour. It wasn't an unusually slow night. You and Glasby can handle two cases. If it were me, I'd split it and each take one."

He rolls his eyes at me just as Glasby strolls into the conference room.

"What?" Glasby says.

"Nothing. Just a big day for you and Cornwell.

Good luck." I sip my coffee to hide my smirk while I head to my office.

As I review my notes in preparation to meet with the Harvey family about their daughter who committed suicide by running her car into a train, I keep a close eye on my phone. This is ridiculous.

I should call him or text him. I'm a grown woman. My days of stalking Colten Mosley are over. Yet I can't help myself. I'm on a physical high.

It's the sex.

I know what I've been missing for seventeen years, and now I'm pissed off at every woman who has had Colten's hands, mouth, or any other body part on them.

Eventually, I'll come down from the sex high and have to deal with the emotional reality that I'm still mad at him. I still have so many questions that he needs to answer.

By the time I get to court, I'm ready to crush my phone like it's my phone's fault that Colten has been ghosting me. I give in. I hate it, but I do it anyway.

Josie: Hi.

Yep. That's it. One word. Like "tag, you're it." A knock on his door. A nudge to see if he's paying attention.

I have to relinquish my phone to get through security at the courthouse. As I make my way to the courtroom, Dylan Paine, the most cutthroat attorney in town, calls my name. When I glance over at her, I see him, Mr. "He Hasn't Responded To My Text" Mosley.

"I've called your office at least a hundred times. I need the Kaylee Robinson report," Dylan says like she thinks I'm in charge of getting a report to her that I didn't write for an autopsy I didn't perform. She's always given me the impression she doesn't believe I'm a real doctor or part of the justice system.

I ignore her for obvious reasons.

"Oh ..." She leans into Colten and playfully nudges his arm. "Have you met Detective Mosley? Surely, you've run into each other by now."

Colten's grin grows in tiny increments. "We're actually old friends."

Friends. Is that what we are now?

"Oh? That's crazy. Small world. Aren't you originally from Iowa, Josephine?" She's never called me Dr. Watts, except when questioning me on the stand, and even then, she says it like it leaves a bad taste in her mouth.

"I am. So is Colten."

Dylan lifts her eyebrows. "Colten, huh?"

Yes, Dylan ... I'm on a first name basis with the detective because I orgasmed in his mouth yesterday, and I showed him my breasts before I even really had anything to show him.

"Well, I'm meeting with a client. Tell your office to call me back."

I give her a tight smile. I won't be telling "my office" anything.

"Call me sometime, Detective."

Last I knew, she was married. But her "call me" sounded personal, not professional.

"Should I tell her, or do you want to tell her that you don't call people?" I ask the second she saunters off toward the exit.

"New phone." He pulls said phone out of his pocket. "I haven't downloaded anything from the cloud yet, so I didn't have your number."

"And you forgot where I lived?"

He slips his phone back into the pocket of his suit jacket. Then he loosens his tie and unbuttons the top two buttons to his shirt. "I had a little trip to the ER last night." He shows me the bandaged area on his neck. "Seven stitches. Missed my artery. I brought a gun to a knife fight, but I was outnumbered."

I stare at his neck without saying anything.

"Don't gasp like that, Josie. I'm good. I'll be fine. Really, no need to overreact." He feigns when I *don't* react.

I smirk and lift my gaze to his. "You weren't on my table this morning, so I wasn't worried. Maybe I should teach you how to use your gun properly."

"Maybe I should put something in your mouth to shut you up."

Again, I let my amusement free with a small grin. "Small things are choking hazards."

"Fuck you," he says on a laugh.

"I thought you would, but you tried to get yourself killed instead."

265

Complete satisfaction lights up his face. I haven't forgotten how to verbally spar with him.

"I have a stack of paperwork. There's a slim chance that I get more than two hours of sleep tonight. But I want to take you to dinner this week."

I step closer to him, picking at the corner of his bandage and pulling it back just enough to see his stitches. Yes, whoever cut him missed his carotid, but just barely. After I replace the bandage, I button his shirt, basking in our little bubble as he watches me. I fix his tie and glance up at him, my hands still on his tie.

"Do you love me, Josephine Watts?"

My lips twist as I lift a shoulder, not ready to declare a single emotion because they're all so blurred. "I *something* you."

He returns an easy nod. "I have to get back to the station."

My gaze returns to his tie as I nod several times. "I figured. I have to get to court."

His hands take mine, pulling them away from his tie and interlacing our fingers while guiding our hands behind my back, forcing me to look up at him again. "Go set the record straight."

"I will."

My confidence pleases him. I can see it in his eyes. Can he also see that he's the weakest part of me?

I'm too busy looking at him to see anyone else, but I feel people's gazes as they pass us. Maybe people I know; maybe people he knows. They're wondering what we're doing, our intimacy on public display.

I don't care. I'm done hiding, and I think he is too.

"Are you going to—"

He doesn't let me finish before bending down. "Yeah, I am." He kisses me. It's soft and quick, too quick. "Bye," he whispers over my lips before releasing my hands and adjusting his tie.

I get one last smile from him and a sexy wink.

THAT EVENING, while making dinner, I get a call from him.

"Did you find my number in the cloud?"

He chuckles. It's deep and slow. "Not yet. I haven't had time to mess with the cloud, and by mess with the cloud, I mean have the IT dude do it for me. I got your number the old-fashioned way."

"By asking me and writing it down on a napkin or the back of a junk mail envelope? Because I don't recall that."

Again, he gives me that chuckle, and it reaches through the phone and touches me in a way that makes me miss him despite having seen him earlier today. "No, I pulled it from the internal database."

"Did you get a warrant?"

"I did. It was Sunday afternoon, which I know how hard it is to get a warrant on a Sunday, but I did. It was at your house. I had to get on my knees to do it, and it required some very particular lip service. Eventually, I was granted a solid 'yessss,' which I interpreted as permission to gather information on you in any way I deem necessary." He sighs. "I'm drowning in paper-work. I'm so fucking tired. My wound itches. And I just want to know what your bed feels like because I can't seem to make it there despite two solid attempts. How are you?"

I don't answer right away. Instead, I let his voice and his words echo in my head. He's the old Colten, using me as his safe place to let go of his day's frustra-tions. And he's the new Colten with different frustra-tions. But one thing hasn't changed ... not being with me still brings him down.

"I'm playing baseball twenty-four-seven. It sucks. I haven't seen you for more than two seconds while passing you in the hall at school. Just meet me outside for a few minutes."

I waved from my bedroom window. "Look. You're seeing me."

He grumbled. "Not the same."

"I was grounded all last week. I can't risk sneaking out at ten-thirty on a school night. Sorry."

"I'm good. Filleting fish. Want me to bring you dinner?"

I can hear the riffling of papers in the background. He has me on speaker, and he's working as we speak.

"I want *you*, Watts. I already had dinner."

"Takeout?"

"Food truck."

I laugh. "Same thing."

"Filleting fish, huh? You know you can buy fish already filleted. Don't you ever get tired of dissecting shit?"

"I usually find the cause and manner of death before I have to dissect too much shit. But to answer your question, no. I don't get tired of dissecting things. Are you having an affair with Dylan Paine?"

He coughs. "S-she's married."

"Hence the word *affair*."

"Do I come across as the guy who sleeps with another man's wife?"

"I'm getting to know the new Colten Mosley, so I'm not ready to make a judgment on that."

"I'm the Colten you knew seventeen years ago, just with more hair, more scars, and more—"

"Experience."

He hums. "I hope so."

"Who was your first?"

"My first what?"

"Sexual encounter."

"You, Josie."

"We didn't have sex."

"No, but we were sexual."

"Intercourse. Who was your first penetration?"

He coughs another laugh. "Jesus, Watts ... you're so clinical."

"I'm a doctor."

"Mindy."

"Mindy who?"

"I don't know," he says. "I met her at a bar the week before basic training. I was drunk. She was drunk. And we fucked. At least, I think there was penetration. The details are sketchy. It was in the back seat of her Chevy Malibu while we waited for her friend to come drive us home."

"Sounds romantic."

"It was. I thought about proposing, but not knowing her last name or literally anything else about her made finding her again difficult. Who was your first?"

Before I answer, I hear him whispering something to someone else.

"Are we talking about our first sexual encounters with an audience?"

"No," he says. "Rose just dropped another stack of files on my desk. She's gone. You were saying?"

"I'm going to let you get back to work." I toss my fillets into a bowl of marinade.

"You're not off the hook. You owe me the story of your first time."

"You owe me a lot more than that, but we'll save that for another conversation."

"Good night, Josie."

"Night."

CHAPTER
Twenty-Eight

THERE'S a mass shooting at a nightclub the following night which means Colten will live at work, especially since the shooter is still at large. I stay plenty busy with the bodies of the gunshot victims and my own reports to type up.

By Friday, they have the suspect in custody, and the community in mourning gets a tiny sigh of relief and hope for justice.

I leave work just before six and decide to visit Colten at the station.

"Hey, Dr. Watts. What's up?" Detective Rains glances up from his desk behind stacks of paperwork.

"I'm looking for Colten, uh ... Detective Mosley."

"I sent his tired ass home. I'm sure he'll be here again early in the morning, but he was running on fumes. Anything I can help you with?"

I shake my head and smile. "Nope. Have a good weekend. You should probably get some rest too."

He barks a laugh. "I have three kids at home, all under the age of ten. Work is my idea of rest."

"Fair enough. Good night."

"Good night, Dr. Watts."

I don't give it much thought before I steer my car in the direction of Colten's house. There doesn't appear to be a light on anywhere in his house. My finger moves toward his doorbell, but I stop just before pressing it.

With my foot, I nudge a planter to the side.

"No ..." I shake my head and laugh out loud. "You do not have a house key under your planter, *Detective Mosley*." He's probably the make-my-day kind of guy who dares anyone to break into his house.

While I unlock his front door, I try to remember if I saw a security alarm. The door opens in silence, so I think I'm in the clear. I tiptoe upstairs to his bedroom. He's asleep on his back, arm cocked over his head. Removing my clothes down to my panties and bra, I slide into the other side of his bed. Opting to let him sleep, I keep my distance, staring at him until I fall asleep.

Early in the morning, a large, calloused hand splays along my belly, hooking me and turning me to face him. Our legs scissor, and I realize he sleeps in the nude.

He brushes some hair away from my face. "Did you break into my house?"

I grin. "I have a warrant."

"I'm going to need to see it."

I hold up my hand and wiggle my fingers.

He narrows his eyes.

My grin swells while said hand slides beneath the sheets and grips his erection, slowly stroking him.

He groans, eyes drifting shut, lips parting for a few breaths. "You're right. That definitely warrants breaking into my house."

I grin while kissing his bare chest. His hands tangle in my hair softly before clenching it and tipping my head back to kiss me with vigor.

It's a good kiss. Hard but slow like every move we make. We're a tight band of need yet controlled. Unhurried.

Colten releases my hair to unhook my bra. Then he pulls me on top of him, flinging my bra to the side while I kiss my way up his neck. He fists the backside of my panties and gruffly peels them from my body.

Everything is new but familiar.

He rocks his hips and pushes into me sitting astride him. His hands grip my hips to guide me at his pace.

"Touch yourself, Josie."

I open my eyes to his intense gaze and cup my breasts. He rocks his pelvis harder into me. The muscles in his jaw flex for a moment. His right hand releases my hip, clutching my wrist to pull my hand from my breast to his mouth. Like a lion savoring its prey, he licks my fingers several times. Then he guides my hand to my clit.

I touch myself for him. Desire builds in his eyes

while his tongue makes a slow swipe along his lips, and his gaze affixes to my hand.

"You're the most exquisite human I have ever known," he rasps.

We spend the early morning hours lost in the sheets. I haven't been looking for *a* warm body; I've been looking for *his* warm body.

Spooning naked with tangled legs and woven arms while he hugs me to him, he kisses the back of my shoulder. "Tell me about your first time."

I giggle. "I'm not telling you about my first time while we're like this."

"Fine. Tell me about your second time. Was it me a few weeks ago?"

"Mosley, you do realize I'm an expert in death. I know ten different ways to kill you that would look like an accident or suicide."

He squeezes my breast that's been cupped in his hand like a security blanket since we assumed this position. "I'm just going to stick with my original belief."

"And what was that?"

"That you kept your virginity for me."

"Sure. That's why you saw a guy leaving my place in the morning when you surprised me by bringing your mom for a visit. What do you think I did with that guy all night?"

"He looked like the loser kind who has a foot fetish. I assumed you slept, and he snuck photos of your feet.

They're probably all over the internet, and now hundreds of thousands of guys jerk off to your feet."

I wriggle my body around to face him, giving him the hairy eyeball.

His breast hand becomes an ass-squeezing hand as he pulls me closer. "I'm good to go again." He grins while his erection slides along my belly.

"Tough luck, Mr. Duck. I'm hungry."

His grin doubles. "That works too."

"Solid food." I roll my eyes.

"It's pretty solid."

"Colten."

"Josie," he mimics in a high-pitched voice.

We're nine years old all over again.

"Donuts?" he asks.

"Tell me you work in law enforcement without actually telling me you work in law enforcement." I laugh.

Colten rubs his lips together to hide his grin for a few seconds. He's irresistibly sexy with his dark, whiskery face and messy hair this morning. "The donuts are for you."

"You don't eat donuts?"

He moves his shoulders in a weird shrug. "I was planning on eating you while you eat a donut."

Damn, he's good.

I don't even try to hide my grin. "Donuts work for me."

CHAPTER
Twenty-Nine

SEVENTEEN YEARS.

I honestly started to think I'd never see Josephine Watts again. Here she is, back in my life, making a mess of her cinnamon and sugar donut while I sit across from her at a round table, sipping coffee.

It really is a goddamn miracle.

She licks her lips, glancing at another couple coming into the donut shop. I could stare at Josephine Watts all day. I still can't believe she's back in my life.

"I think you're the biggest disappointment of my life," she says as whimsically as one might say while suggesting a movie.

I study her for a second from behind my cup of coffee, waiting for her to elaborate.

She doesn't.

"That's not exactly something a guy likes to hear

after he drops seven dollars and fifty cents on coffee and a donut for a girl."

Josie blows the steam from her coffee and grins. "Let me elaborate."

"Please. I'd love to know where this is going."

"I've always been logical. Curious. Scientifically minded. I operate on facts. I easily detach from things, which is why I'm so good at my job."

"Wow, don't be so modest."

She chuckles. "I didn't say I'm the best, but I'm good at it. I imagine you're good at your job too. You've never done anything half-assed that I can remember."

I nod several times. "Carry on."

"You've been this unsolved mystery in my life. People in my line of work don't like checking that 'undetermined' box. It's frustrating. What did I miss? How did I miss it? Are there more questions to ask the family? To ask the investigators? I like things neat and tidy. Go through the process. Make a determination. Move on. But with you, I haven't been able to move on. It's easy to blame you for how we ended, but I, and I alone, have been the one in control of my reaction to what happened to us. And frankly ... I'm disappointed in myself for moving on all these years without really letting go. I'm disappointed in myself for carrying around this chip on my shoulder. I deserved better."

I let her words sink in; then I reach across the table and take her hand, turning it to expose her forearm and the tattoos on it. Leaves and vines like her other forearm. My thumb traces one of the vines. "I don't think you have these tattoos to cover track marks."

Josie's eyes narrow a fraction, studying her arm and the tattoos as if she hasn't seen them before, as if they're not hers. "Cutting. I did it before it was really popular." She grunts. "Maybe I was a trendsetter. It got me through my first year at college. Eventually, I got tired of wearing long-sleeve shirts all the time. I got tired of guys seeing them and thinking I was unstable. It just …" Her sad gaze lifts to mine. "It took away the pain. Pain numbing pain."

My thumb continues to trace the scars underneath the black lines of ink. "Was I that pain?" I whisper.

She sits back, pulling her arm from my hand. "I didn't tell my parents about us. I didn't tell them how crushed I was the day you left me in the woods." She shakes her head and whispers, "I didn't tell anyone. Now, I realize my dad suspected something … but he didn't know the depth of my feelings. Your mom knew, but I never let her see the extent of my pain."

"Was I the pain?" I repeat.

Josie keeps her gaze on her mug of coffee and nods.

"Josie …"

She holds out her arms. "I let another human crawl under my skin, like the sharp tip of a scalpel. That's disappointing. I should have known better. I should have done better." When she wraps her hands around her mug, her eyes blink up, giving me her attention and a hint of her beautiful smile. "I know why you left me. It took seventeen years, but I know. It might take seventeen more to fully understand why I didn't let go, why I let the ghost of our past drag me through so much pain and resentment for nearly two decades. It's ... disappointing."

"Life is really fucking hard."

Josie nods.

"Well, here we are for whatever reason. I say we seize the moment. We should move in together or ..."

Her eyes widen.

I shrug. "Or ... get married. You know ... something like that."

She's frozen in place except for intermittent slow blinks.

Scooting my chair forward, I reach beneath the table and grab her bare legs, giving them a squeeze. "Seventeen. Years. We've spent too much time apart. Let's just do it. Let's be together."

Josie shakes her head, lips parted. "N-no ... I'm not marrying you or moving in with you. I don't even know if I want to be married at this point in my life. And I like my living arrangements."

"I like you in my bed," I say.

"I was in your bed last night, and it didn't require a certificate of marriage or a change of address."

"You're as stubborn and as difficult as the day we met." I release her legs and lean back in my chair.

"For the record, Mosley, you had your chance to have all of me. I would have married you the day after graduation. But things have changed."

"What's changed?"

Her fingernails tap the side of her coffee mug. "I discovered my true self-worth. I realized I don't need you."

"Still here you are, the morning after spending the night with me."

She grins. "I said I don't need you. Doesn't mean I don't want you."

"What if I'm an all-or-nothing? A packaged deal? What if I don't want to be your boy toy?"

"You've been my boy toy since the day we met."

She's not wrong.

"What if I want a wife?"

She pushes back in her chair and stands, clutching her purse. "Then you should have married your daughter's mother."

I follow her to the door, digging my key fob out of my pocket. "Can we swap house keys?"

"Why do I need your house key when I found your top-secret location in less than ten seconds?"

I open the passenger door for her because I'm a gentleman (sorta). Before she gets in the vehicle, I pull her into my arms, forcing her to look up at me. "I love you, Josie."

She smiles, but damn my unlucky life to hell, if she doesn't reciprocate the sentiment.

"You used to love me," I say, but it sounds more like a growl.

"I did. Silly me."

"Love me again."

"I'll think about it."

"Like you're going to think about moving in with me? Like you're going to think about marrying me?"

"Disclaimer: I'm not going to marry you. But let's say you had the slightest chance of marrying me." She curls two fingers into quotes and lowers her voice like mine. "I say we seize the moment. We should move in together or get married. You know … something like that." She ends her quote and gives me a tight smile. "That's not the way to go about it. In fact, it might be the worst proposal in the history of proposals. So now I'm starting to really question your side of the story regarding Katy and the proposal. Did she say no to your proposal because you didn't love her? Or did you give her a multiple-choice question with marriage as one of the possible answers?"

I don't give a shit that she's busting my balls at every turn. She's in my life, in my arms. Last night she was in my bed. If she made this easy for me, I'd be shocked. Josephine Watts has always been a marathon of mind-games and emotions. I'd be disappointed if she didn't make me work for it.

I grin. "Do you want to A: go back into the donut shop so I can bend you over the bathroom sink and fuck you before we grab a few more donuts for later? B: stop by the grocery store with me on the way back to my place because I'm out of food? C: marry me? D: move in with me?"

After a few seconds of no reaction, she twists her lips. It thrills me that she's playing along. We're going to the grocery store. That's fine. I don't expect a miracle today. Then ... she gives me a miracle. Just ... uh ... not at all the one I expect.

Wriggling out of my arms, she sashays back to the donut shop. "Listen, Mosley, if we get arrested for public indecency, you'd better be ready to call in a favor."

CHAPTER

I CAN'T HELP but wonder what my life would have been like had Colten not ended us. Would we have gotten married? Would he have gone into law enforcement? Would I be dissecting bodies? Would we even still be together?

"You're glowing today, Dr. Watts," Colten says as we stroll through the aisles of the grocery store. "Pink cheeks. Swollen lips. Ruffled hair."

"Two decades ago, you knew better than to gloat," I say, tossing food into the cart that's not for my kitchen. "I liked that Colten better."

"Nonsense. That pimple-faced kid tripped over his words and fumbled his dick." He grabs the box of salt-free crackers from my hand and returns it to the shelf before I get it into the cart.

"He was endearing."

"Embarrassing," Colten grumbles.

"When do you see Reagan again?"

He tosses a bag of potato chips into the cart. "Hopefully for her birthday in two weeks. It's a party. You should come with me."

"Hmm ... I'll check my schedule. I might have a date that weekend."

"Speaking of that pimple-faced, dick-fumbling kid," he says, "the one who sat idle while you dated other guys? Yeah, I'm not him. I'm much closer to the version you knew right before we graduated ... the one who beat the shit out of what's his face who took you to prom."

"Andy?"

"Sure whatever." Just the mention of Andy's name seems to irritate Colten. It's kind of cute.

"I think you're too mature for that."

"Try me."

I grin, finding a unique satisfaction in this conversation.

"Did you?" he asks.

"Did I what?"

"Suck his dick?"

An elderly lady passes us, and from her scowl, I'd say her hearing is pretty good, and she's not a fan of sucking dick.

"Is it a little sadistic that it brings me joy knowing that question has sat unanswered in the corner of your mind all these years?"

"I wouldn't call it unanswered. More like unconfirmed. I'm pretty sure I already know the answer."

"I did it."

Colten doesn't say anything, but his body stiffens, and he takes a hard swallow, teeth clenched.

"I didn't want to start college with so little experience."

I'm fairly certain he just flinched, but he won't look at me. He picks up the pace and throws items in the cart that I'm not sure he even wants.

In the checkout lane, he ignores me. When I reach for one of the bags, he grabs it first, carrying all the bags while taking long strides toward his car.

His poor bread takes the brunt of his anger before he slams the back door and climbs into the driver's seat. I can barely keep a straight face while my ego gobbles up his brooding attitude. Just as he reaches for his seat belt, I lean across the center console. He cocks his arm, giving me his elbow to stop my motions.

I cup his chin, forcing him to look at me while I grin. "I asked you to take my virginity. You passed on that opportunity. Why did I owe you my mouth around your dick?"

It's too perfect. I'm not sure anything can make up for what he did to me, but I deserve every little morsel I can steal.

"I didn't suck Andy's cock," I whisper before sucking on his lower lip and teasing it with my teeth while my other hand tugs on the button to his jeans.

"But I'm going to suck yours." I release him from his briefs.

"Josie ..." My name falls from his lips with a little anguish. He's conflicted.

A little mad.

A lot turned-on.

Which one will win?

His hands gather my hair while he lets out a groan as my answer.

We've managed to channel our inner horny teenaged selves where every look and every conversation leads to something sexual. My dad isn't here to ground me. My mom isn't here to tell me how playing hard to get is the smart choice.

I'm not ready to share an address with Colten or marry him. But this orgasm high we've been on ... always chasing the next one ... well, it's pretty spectacular.

"Jo-s-sie ... fuck ... you."

I release him from my mouth and turn my head, glancing up at him with raised eyebrows.

He grips my hair tighter and bites back his grin. "If you stop, I will fucking die."

I lick it. "Oh, Andy ..."

"Josie ..." he growls my name and grips the side of his seat, his hips making a tiny thrust toward my mouth.

I giggle, collecting more of those morsels of torture. Then I finish the job because that's what detailed oriented people do.

"F-fuuuck ..."

I sit up and grin, licking the corner of my mouth just as the old lady from the store walks past the front of his car. He blows out a long breath while his body slumps like his spine evaporated with his orgasm. His hands work to tuck, zip, and button.

I fasten my seat belt and reach down by my feet, retrieving the small box from the floor. After pulling out a donut, I take a bite and grin. "Palate cleanser," I mumble.

If a look for the love child of adoration and mystification exists, it's residing on Colten Mosley's face. "I knew you loved me." He smirks, starting the car and shifting it into drive.

I snort, slowly shaking my head. Blow job equals love through the eyes of a man. Figures.

Before we get his groceries put away, his phone rings. He listens, frowns, nods, and says three words. "On my way."

"Call me later?"

Colten shrugs. "You could come with me. I know a guy with a badge. Ever seen a real crime scene?" He slips his phone into his pocket and pushes me up against the counter.

I rest my hands on the edge of the counter and chuckle. "I have my own badge."

Pressing his lips to my neck, he grins before kissing me. "Might as well come get a preview of your work for tomorrow."

"Who died?"

He lifts his head and takes my hand. "That's what we're going to find out."

The second we get out of the car, Colten flashes his badge, and I dig through my purse for mine. By the time I get it, he's twenty yards ahead of me, huddled with the crime scene unit near the end of the pier.

He's no longer Colten, my reunited childhood crush; he's a detective and I am a forensic pathologist. Richard Claiborne, the medicolegal investigator, gives me an extended glance when he looks up from the body on the pier.

I answer his unspoken question. "I was in the area."

He nods.

I meet with the coroner who pronounced the time of death.

Scene briefing.

Walk through.

Preliminary examination.

The decedent's abdomen has been mutilated.

"Look what we have here." In the sand a few feet from the body, there's a tied latex glove finger. "He's a mule," the officer says.

I walk farther down the pier toward the other body. A shock wave of whip-like snaps drowns out all other noise.

Gunfire.

I start to turn, then ...

CHAPTER
Thirty-One

IT's an unnerving sonic boom of deadly projectiles moving through the air. Guns are drawn. Chaos ensues.

I immediately search for Josie, but I can't move. There's too much gunfire. Too many bodies falling to the ground. The crime scene turns into a war zone.

Josie. Josie. Josie ...

I fire at the armed insurgents clad in black vests, a circle of them firing at us while several others grab the bodies. They're robbing our fucking crime scene, but I don't care. Take the bodies. Where is Josie?

For some reason, Beethoven's *Moonlight Sonata* plays in my head. It's what I played when life felt out of control as a teenager. It's what soothed me during my time in the war zone. Today, it's a preamble to death.

Josie. Josie. Josie ...

As quickly as they appeared, the armed men fire their way toward a moving van, load the bodies, and speed off as my team, those who aren't wounded, climb into squad cars in pursuit of them.

I hear my name, but it's a mere echo. Beethoven's too loud, drowning out everything while I run toward the pier—the last place I saw Josie.

Her bag's near the edge, halfway between the location of the two missing bodies. I follow the blood. Her blood? I don't know, but it leads me to the side of the pier. Diving into the water, I frantically search the cloudy abyss for any sign of her.

Josie!

I swim toward her body, seemingly suspended in the water. Her shirt's caught on a piece of scrap metal lodged in the sand and rock. Blood swirls in the water around her. As my lungs begin to burn, I free her and drag her to the surface.

"Help!" I yell on a gasp. "HELP!" I swim toward the shore, but no one's running to help us because *everyone* needs help. They took two bodies and left a smattering of new ones.

Just as I get her out of the water, an officer and a paramedic help me, taking over.

She's gone.

I've seen enough bodies to know ... she's gone. Still, I listen to Beethoven and remain unmoving as they work on her. She's been shot. And she's not breathing.

"She's gone," I whisper, but no one is listening to me.

I shouldn't have left her. Seventeen years ago, I shouldn't have left her. I should have followed my fucking heart. It might have changed the course of our lives forever. Maybe she wouldn't have been a medical examiner, and maybe I wouldn't have gone into law enforcement.

We'd be married with two unruly kids she never imagined wanting. But finding *the one* changes everything. Our house would be small, but our hearts would be full ... and beating.

Josie's heart is not beating, and mine feels incredibly purposeless. I think about Reagan's exuberant smile and the way she squeals "Daddy," and it's the most beautiful sound in the world. The sonata's tempo picks up. Reagan needs me. I have to keep breathing, keep living. I made it seventeen years without Josephine Watts in my life. What's eternity?

I didn't deserve her anyway, and we both knew it.

The paramedics transport her to the ambulance. My feet trudge through the sand under the weight of my drenched clothes and the gruesome cloud of gravity.

Bodies ... there are bodies everywhere with one less medical examiner to autopsy the ones that won't make it.

I shoulder my way past the paramedics, grabbing her hand as they try to push me away. "I should have said it." The words rip from my chest as I hold her limp hand. "Josie ... fuck ..." I can barely breathe past the pain gripping my throat like a noose. "I should have ...

said it." I lose her hand when she's lifted into the ambulance. My fingers thread through my hair as my eyes burn and my head inches side to side. "I love you ... I love you."

The back doors to the ambulance slam shut, lights flashing, people swarming all around me. And Beethoven fades along with the ambulance lights. I hate that I know I can't follow her body. I'm hardwired to step over dead bodies to save the living. Bravery doesn't take time to mourn until the battle is over.

Josie's killers are on the run. The battle is not over.

BY THE TIME I catch up to the rest of my team, they're calling for air assistance as the shooters fly off in a helicopter.

"FUCK!" I slam my car door and kick the toe of my black boot through the dirt.

"We'll get 'em." Rains holsters his weapon before resting his hand on my shoulder. "Where were you?"

I shake my head, finding it nearly impossible to speak. Gritting my teeth, I clear my throat. "Josie ... Jos ... Dr. Watts ... she ..."

Rains wrinkles his face. "Oh fuck."

I nod and glance up at the sky.

"I'll meet you back at the station," he says.

"I have a stop to make first."

When I arrive at the hospital, it feels like the bones in my legs are splintering, refusing to carry me toward her body. I have to see her to know ... for it to feel real because reality evaporated hours ago, replaced with hell on earth.

What will I tell her parents?

"Where's Josephine Watts?" I ask the nurse and shake my head. "Dr. Watts. She was brought in several hours ago."

The nurse checks her computer.

"Has next of kin been notified?" I ask.

"I'll check." She shakes her head. "Dr. Watts is still in surgery."

"What?" She's mistaken.

"Are you family?"

I pull out my badge.

"You can wait in the waiting room, or I can call you when she's out of surgery."

She's alive ...

For nearly three hours ... I've thought she was dead. My heart pounds, aching from the brutal fists of reality striking it over and over today. Even this new sliver of hope cuts into all four chambers because she still might not make it. Sometimes hope is the evilest bearer of bad news.

I sit in the waiting room when I know I should be writing up reports or checking with Rains to see if they caught the shooters. After a rancid cup of coffee, I call her parents, but it will take them a while to get here. Will she wait for them, or will they show up just to wait for some other medical examiner to complete the autopsy and release the body to them for the funeral?

JEWEL E. ANN

She should have stayed at my place or gone home to pack her shit and move in with me. Literally anything that would have kept her far away from the evils of humanity. This is on me. I invited her. I was selfish for wanting more time with her.

Hours later, Josie's out of surgery and in the ICU in critical condition.

"If she makes it through the night, then she has a good chance of waking up," the doctor says.

I nod. Then I sit and wait some more.

CHAPTER
Thirty-Two

Mom.

She smiles, but I don't trust it. My dreams have been too vivid.

Dad.

He's in my dream too, but they're not doing anything except staring at me. Mom has tears in her eyes.

My gaze circumnavigates the room. It's not my bedroom. It's a hospital room. Great ... one of these dreams again. In a few more blinks, I'll be autopsying myself. This is a crazy, reoccurring dream that I have at least once a month. Last time I found cancer; the time before that, it was asphyxiation.

"Josephine, I'm Dr. Panchak. Can you hear me?"

"Yes," I rasp. Jesus, my throat hurts. The pain in this dream is more vivid than others have been.

I squint when he shines a light in my eyes. I jump when he presses a stethoscope to my chest.

He chuckles. "Sorry, it's a little cold."

This is *so* real.

Dad brings his phone to his ear, but I can't make out what he's saying as he slides his gaze to me every few seconds.

"You had a gunshot wound," Dr. Panchak says. "Do you remember that?"

"No," I whisper.

This doesn't feel real. Is it real?

"Do you know the year?"

"Twenty-twenty-two." I reach for my throat as the words cut like razor blades.

"Good. Do you know the two people standing behind me?"

"My parents."

"Excellent. You were pulled from the water, resuscitated, and we removed the bullet from your small bowel and repaired it. We're keeping you for a few days, but I expect a full recovery. You were very lucky someone pulled you out of the water when they did."

"Did they find him?" I whisper.

"The shooters? I'm not sure. We can check on that for you."

"N-no ... there was no gun," I say.

My parents give the doctors a look. I've seen that look before. It's the look you give someone when you're in the presence of a crazy person. But I'm not crazy.

"Josie ..." My mom grabs my hand when the doctor

steps aside, tapping his tablet while my dad sidles next to me, opposite my mom. "Colten pulled you from the water. Your dad just called him. He'll be here soon. He's been here for days. We told him to go home and shower."

"There were two. They were about five and eight."

"Two what?" Dad asks, his brows furrowed.

"Two girls. He buried their bodies in the cemetery."

Mom squeezes my hand. "You need to rest. We're so glad you're going to be okay. I'm sure things are a little confusing now. You've been unconscious for two days. I think you need to give your brain a chance to recoup and catch up. We'll talk about what happened later. Okay?"

Later? What about the families? Have they notified the families? They're going to be equal parts devastated and relieved. Closure is incredibly bittersweet. I'll ask Colten when he gets here.

Within the hour, Colten arrives. He rests his hand on mine and clenches his teeth while swallowing. "Hey," he says as if he's the one with a sore throat.

"Hey. Did they get him?"

He shakes his head. "You mean them? And no. They crossed the Mexican border and took out several border patrol officers in the process."

"What are you talking about?" I cough and point toward the glass and pitcher of water the nurse brought in for me.

Colten pours me some water and holds it to my mouth so I can sip it from the straw.

"I'm talking about the remains of the two girls at the cemetery. You know, the long hair tied to the oak tree branches at the church?" The sicko shaved their heads.

Colten's nose scrunches, eyes squinted. "Josie, you've been unconscious for two days. They're going to run some more tests before you're discharged, but I think you're a little confused right now. Maybe you're recalling autopsies you've performed."

"The church was in Nashville."

"We're going to grab something from the cafeteria," Mom says.

Colten glances back at her and nods once before offering me a sympathetic smile. "I'll look into those bodies and get back to you."

I start to protest. This is urgent. But I can see from the look on his face that my pleas will not be expedited. "Thanks."

When my parents exit the room, he brings my hand to his mouth and presses his lips to it while closing his eyes. "Fuck, Josie ... I thought you died. You weren't breathing." He opens his eyes, and that one look is filled with so much anguish it makes my heart ache.

"I heard you saved me. Thank you."

His Adam's apple bobs, and he nods. There's a storm of emotion in his eyes. I don't know what to say. I never get to say something was "a little touch and go," but a family's loved one will be okay. They'll pull through. Nope. Never. That's not part of my job.

Josephine Watts died of hypovolemia due to major vessel injuries from an abdominal GSW.

Or maybe I'm not out of the woods yet. Maybe my ending could change.

Josephine Watts died of septicemia following an abdominal GSW.

"Now can you see if they found the girls' bodies?" I ask.

Colten offers me a tiny headshake. "Josie, you're confused right now. I don't know what girls you're talking about."

"Then why did you say you'd check on it?" It's so vivid in my head. Is it a dream? Who dreams of something so morbid? My fascination with death has never led me down the road of imagining such horrid homicides.

"Because you need a chance to physically and mentally heal. And I didn't want to upset you. Can you give it a few days, and then we'll revisit what's bothering you if it's still bothering you?"

"I suppose," I whisper. "What happened to me?"

"I was called to investigate a double homicide at the pier, and we were ambushed because the bodies were mules and they wanted their drugs. You were on the pier, fell into the water after you were shot. And I pulled you out." His voice shakes with those last five words. "I'm ... so fucking sorry. You shouldn't have been there."

He thought I was dead.

I'd say this is karma for what he did to me right

before graduation because there were many days I wondered if he was alive. But I don't believe in karma, so this is nothing more than a tragedy. A close call that no human deserves to experience.

I WAKE up in the middle of the night, and I can't breathe. My mom calls for a nurse.

"There's m-more."

"Shh ..." Mom tries to soothe me by stroking my hair. "It's just a dream."

My abdomen screams with pain, and the nurse gives me something for it ... something that knocks me out until morning.

The next day, I see a neurologist. The exam and all the scans come back normal. Then I see a psychiatrist. They think I'm mentally unwell. If I don't shut up, they'll have me on the kinds of medications that will leave me with very little pain and barely coherent. So I shut up about the girls. For now ...

"What's going on between you and Colten?" Mom asks while I take tiny bites of mashed potatoes.

I'm hoping to go home today.

Dad doesn't move from the chair by the window. He's on his second nap of the day. I'd nap, but when I close my eyes, I see things. Things that make me mentally unstable according to everyone else. So I don't sleep without heavy drugs that shut off my mind.

"We're ... something." Just as I say those words, I

have a flashback of us in a car doing something that's frowned upon in public. It makes me smile, the kind that warms my cheeks.

"What's that look about?" Mom asks. "Is it something romantic?"

It's something sexual. I think. At this point, I don't trust my thoughts. Reality is blurred. Maybe I dreamed it. Lord knows I've had a plethora of inappropriate dreams in my lifetime about Colten Mosley.

"Maybe. It's new."

Mom nods slowly, rubbing her lips together. "I see. I always wondered if you two would end up together."

Speaking of …

Colten pops his head in the room, doing his usual late day check-in.

"Hey, beautiful." His smile makes me feel beautiful, but only for a few seconds. I've caught a glimpse of my knotted hair in the bathroom mirror. It's not beautiful.

Dad stirs, peeling open his eyes and stretching his arms over his head on a big yawn. "Looks like our shift is up for now."

Mom rolls her eyes before kissing my head. "I'm not sure what your 'shift' is aside from watching TV and napping. But yes, we can go to dinner now. We'll see you later, sweetie."

"They're discharging me," I say.

She gives me a frown as Colten sits on the edge of my bed. "I fear it won't be until tomorrow now."

I shake my head. "I'm leaving today."

My parents try to appease me with fake smiles before exiting the room.

"Missed you today," Colten says, leaning in for a kiss.

"Have I given you a blow job lately?"

He stops an inch before my lips, blinks several times, and clears his throat before releasing a soft chuckle. "Why do you ask?" He pecks my mouth and sits up straight, loosening his tie.

"Because it popped into my head. We were in your car."

He fails at suppressing his grin. "The day of the shooting. We uh ... did a lot that day."

My memories around that day are sketchy at best. "A lot?"

"Let's just say it was a good day ... until it wasn't."

"My mom asked about us. Have you not said anything to them?"

"It hasn't come up. It's hard to fit 'I'm in love with your daughter' into conversations about drugs, mass shootings, and a GSW to their daughter's abdomen that caused her to nearly drown."

"Was it a good blow job?"

"Jesus Christ ..." Colten rubs his face, trying to wipe off that grin.

It was a good blow job. I figured. Blow jobs make me less crazy than talking about dead girls and the whereabouts of their bodies. I really need out of here. I need my computer and some time alone.

"When we do disclose our relationship status to your parents, let's not start with the blow job. Okay?"

"What is our relationship status?"

Colten opens his mouth to speak then pauses for a few seconds. "We're getting married."

My face scrunches. "What?"

"Yeah. It's probably part of that day's events that you don't remember. I proposed over donuts and coffee. You said yes. Then we went grocery shopping and home to discuss ... wedding plans." His grin doubles. "And then I was called to the pier, and you came with me."

I really need my memory of that day to come back. "You proposed without asking my dad first? He's awfully old-fashioned. I don't know how he's going to feel about it. And I'm surprised I said yes."

"Oh? Why is that?" He cants his head to the side.

"Because I can't imagine wanting to get married."

Gazing out the window for a few breaths, he twists his lips. "You didn't say yes. You said no. And then I asked you to move in with me, and you shot me down again." He cringes, returning his attention to me. "Sorry, bad choice of words."

I grin. "That sounds more accurate."

"But now that you've danced with death, I'm sure your outlook on life has shifted." He kisses the inside of my forearm over my tattoos that cover another great shift in my life.

"Rains? Is he okay?"

Colten nods. His drooping expression squeezes my heart. "But we lost two others, and three were injured."

"Are you okay?" I cup his cheek, and he leans into my touch.

"I didn't get shot."

The pad of my thumb tracks his lower lip. "Are you okay?"

His gaze makes a slow assent to mine.

"I didn't die," I whisper.

He nods and takes a hard swallow before wedging his large body in bed with me, burying his face in my neck on a long exhale. "I think a part of *me* did," he mutters.

The gravity of all the things I can't remember from that day settles on my chest, leaving a dull ache. I wish I remembered. I wish I could take away Colten's pain.

I wish I knew why I can't stop thinking about these girls.

CHAPTER
Thirty-Three

"I'M in love with your daughter, but she won't marry me or even move in with me," Colten spews out his confession over dinner—his belated birthday dinner— a week after I'm released from the hospital. He doesn't even glance up from his plate.

My mom smirks. Yeah, she knew.

Dad? Not so much. He's waking up from his igno-rance-is-bliss state. And now he looks sorely hungover with the news.

"And since you're leaving tomorrow..." Colten blots his mouth with a napkin and risks a glance in my parents' direction "...Josie's going to move in with me so I can take care of her."

"I'm not," I blurt.

He clears his throat and smiles, but not at me. It's like I'm not here. It's reminiscent of the hospital when everyone talked about me while my eyes were closed, but I could still hear them.

"What I meant to say is I'm going to stay with her at her place ... because she's comfortable there ... until she gets better, which realistically could take several months if not longer. So you both can feel rest assured that she'll have all of her needs met."

This is a coup. I'm being ambushed again!

I think Mom's going to cry.

Dad? Nope. No tears in his eyes. He clears his throat and eases his fork onto his plate. "Colten, I'm sure you have good intentions, but ..."

"I love her. I've loved her nearly my whole life. And I'm sorry that you're just now finding out, but it doesn't change the fact that ..." He shrugs. "I love her."

Mom wipes a tear. I don't know how to react. I'm mad. And touched. And ... something.

Dad eyes me for confirmation. I don't know what to say, so I say the obvious. "He loves me."

"And do you love him?"

Damn you, Dad!

The room shrinks with all eyes on me, a tiny specimen under a microscope. I give my attention to Colten, the perpetrator.

I'm not marrying you. I'm not moving in with you. I will not be manipulated. I will not give you anymore blow jobs. I'm mad as hell right now!

"Yes. I love him."

It's a lottery-winning smile that engulfs Colten's handsome face. I'm sure it feels amazing to have someone say those three words when you need them the most. He didn't show me the same consideration seventeen years ago, but ... whatever. I have to let that shit go.

Dad torments Colten with his silence and unreadable expression. But this man who loves me reaches under the table and squeezes my leg as if to let me know my dad's feelings about us no longer matter. Where was this Colten when I felt the need to cut my skin?

Dad stands. All eyes shift to him and his stony expression. "I can't think of a better man for my daughter. You have my blessing." He slaps Colten's shoulder and squeezes it.

His blessing?

No. No blessing required. This isn't a marriage. It's not even cohabitation. It's temporary in-home nursing.

I'm fine. I can walk to the end of the street and back. I can walk upstairs, albeit rather slowly. And despite Dr. Cornwell's insistence that I take a minimum of twelve weeks off work, I'm going back in two ... maybe three.

"You're restricted from lifting more than ten pounds for eight weeks. How are you going to lift and reposition dead bodies?"

AFTER MY PARENTS leave the following day, and I'm no longer being monitored twenty-four-seven, I grab my computer. I have four to five hours before Colten will be off work and here with his things, a changing of the guard.

Hair hanging from trees at churches.

Remains of girls' bodies buried in cemeteries.

My fingers furiously type in different searches, but they all come up with the same results.

Winston Jeffries. 1892 to 1901 reign of terror.

Long hair tied to tree branches in Nashville, Tennessee, churchyards.

Young girls. Shaved heads.

Nearly a decade of kidnappings.

The bodies were never found.

NEVER. FOUND.

Jeffries was convicted of thirty-seven counts of first-degree murder and hanged in Owensboro, Kentucky, on February 10, 1902.

I search for Winston Jeffries copycats.

I search for literally everything I can think of that might make sense of what's in my head. Before I realize it, the day passes. I've not taken my required walks. I've not eaten. And I've not touched my pain meds.

"Honey, I'm home," Colten announces as he traipses into my living room, depositing a big duffle bag in the hallway first.

Shutting my laptop, I smile. "Hi."

His forehead wrinkles. "What are you doing?"

"Nothing. Why?"

"Because you look guilty."

I shake my head. "No. Guilty of what?"

"What were you looking at on your computer?"

"Nothing much."

"Porn?"

I hesitate for a few seconds.

"Seriously? Are you seriously watching porn?"

I give him a tight smile and lift a shoulder.

The priceless look on his face is exactly what I need after a long day of not figuring out a damn thing.

"Bullshit," he says, kneeling on the floor in front of me, wedging his body between my legs and nuzzling my neck. "I missed your lying ass today."

I giggle when he bites my neck. Then I hiss because laughing doesn't feel good after surgery.

He sits back, a cringe stealing his face. "Sorry."

I have to quell the urge to ask him to look into the missing girls for me. I need peace of mind. I can't focus on anything else, yet I can't keep pushing this subject when no one takes me seriously. They say it's confusion since the accident, but it's not.

"What do you want me to heat up for dinner?"

I grin. "My mom really went overboard. We have meals and cookies for weeks."

He sighs. "I'm good with that." Bending forward, he rests his head on my lap.

I slide my fingers through his hair.

He hums like a cat, purring with each stroke. When we're like this, I don't feel those missing seventeen years. I just feel him.

My best friend.

My lover.

My Colten.

"Long day?"

Again, he hums. "So long. I have a pile of paper-work on my desk, but I left it for tomorrow because I needed this."

"Your hair stroked?"

"You."

Feeling needed in this kind of way is indescribable.

"I should take a walk. Want to go with me? Then we can warm up dinner. Shower. And eat cookies in bed while watching a show. I love my parents, but I was also so happy to see them go home this morning. Is that terrible?"

"No," he murmurs like he's half asleep already.

"We can skip the walk. You're too tired."

"Nope." He sits up and scrubs his hands over his face. "Rehab. Rehab. Rehab. You need to walk. And I'm your guy."

My guy ...

Colten stands and offers me his hand to help me to my feet even though I can do it by myself, even if I'm still a little slow. His arms snake around my waist. "The shower part ... was that an invite to shower with you? I mean, I need a shower. And you know ... global warming and lakes drying up ..."

Of course, I want him to shower with me, but I don't give it away without making him squirm a bit.

"No funny business. I promise."

I laugh. "Does anyone call it 'funny business' anymore?"

"Somewhere, I'm sure." He kisses me.

I grab his shirt, keeping his lips to mine. When we kiss, I don't think about the bodies of girls with shaved heads. When we kiss, I don't think about the pain.

He pulls away and shakes his head while licking his lips. "Not fair. I just declared no funny business, and you kiss me like that?"

"Like what?"

"Like you want me to have a fucking hard-on all night." He adjusts himself.

"Or that I missed you today."

He grumbles. "That was more than a missing me kiss. Let's go for that walk."

"STOP!" I scream, jackknifing to sitting. "Ouch! Fuck ..." My hand goes to my incision while Colten sits up and wraps me in his arms.

"I've got you," he whispers. "It was just a bad dream. Just a bad dream ..." He hugs me with a gentle rocking motion.

Tears make hot tracks down my face. I don't know if I'm crying because of the dream or because my body did something it was not ready to do.

"Josie ..." he kisses my face, claiming all of my tears. "Was it about that day?"

It was about a day, but not the day he's implying. The same thing happened ... only the girls were different girls. A different church. Different tree. It was so real. I tried to stop him, but I couldn't because I couldn't see him. I've never seen him. Just the girls.

"Yeah," I say in a shaky voice. I want to tell him more. I *need* to tell him … tell someone before this gets worse.

"Did you take your pain meds?"

I shake my head.

"Why not?" His fingers ghost along my arms.

I shudder. "Because I don't like how they make me feel."

"Isn't that the point? To *not* feel?"

"Hand me the pills," I say just before swallowing back a little bile. I don't have a weak stomach, but this is different. It's not what I see in my dreams. It's what I feel.

Colten hands me a pill and a glass of water from the nightstand. "It won't last forever. You need to sleep. You've been restless for hours."

I nod and hand the glass back to him.

With my heart still racing, he spoons me. I wish I could find his arms in my dreams … my nightmares.

"I've got you. Just rest." He kisses my head.

I try to focus on the warmth of his body against mine. His skin pressed to mine like a shield. His arms an impenetrable armor. Still, I'm afraid to close my eyes.

CHAPTER
Thirty-Four

THE PROBLEM with having an unforgivable asshole for a father was the embarrassment that came with people finding out about his indiscretions. Yes, plural.

"Is it true your dad grazed Holly Gill's breast during study hall?" Anne Perez asked at a party a week before the end of our junior year.

For the record, his first affair was with a woman who cut his hair. Thankfully, and I used that word lightly, she was of legal age. The school had no real grounds to fire him. However, Holly was seventeen, days shy of her eighteenth birthday, and a senior when my dad was filling in for the study hall supervisor and allegedly grazed her breast with his nose.

Yep, his fucking nose.

She was walking through the cafeteria during study hall, running late to her next class, and my dad stopped her because she had both of her shoes untied. She also had a jammed finger from volleyball and said she couldn't tie her shoes because her fingers were buddy taped.

Good ole Coach Mosley helped her out. Tied both shoes and *allegedly* slowly stood via his nose touching her breast. There were rumors that he did, in fact, inhale, but he denied it. Apparently, he went to stand, lost his balance, and fell into her. Nose to breast. And the alleged inhale was a gasp on his part.

Shock and embarrassment.

After years of reconciliation, my dad betrayed my mom's newly earned trust.

"I think it's true that Holly Gill manages to shove her tits in everyone's face. And most guys have been a victim of her being a slut," I yelled over the music, taking a long swig of my fourth or fifth beer.

"I heard he could be fired." Anne took my beer and helped herself to a sip.

"She's not even the one who filed the complaint." I tried to roll my inebriated eyes.

Some other kid in study hall made the anonymous complaint. When asked about it, Holly shrugged it off and said she didn't remember, which was not an actual denial that it didn't happen. My dad flat-out denied it.

"Didn't your dad cheat on your mom?" Anne continued to feed my desire to drink more beer.

"I don't know, Anne. Did your mom try to suck my dad's dick?"

She gasped as I tipped back my beer again, a little

unstable on my feet and unaware of my surroundings, mainly, the staircase right behind me.

Thunk. Clunk. Thunk. Clunk.

I ate it with one step backward.

No one called an ambulance because we were all underaged kids drinking at Tanner Collier's house while his parents were out of town. I could have died all in the name of keeping everyone else out of trouble. Tammy, one of the not-so-drunk girls at the party, called my "emergency contact," aka Josephine Watts. She knew Josie was my friend of sorts and figured she'd know a way to make sure I didn't die and everyone else didn't get in trouble since her dad was the police chief, and he liked me.

Everything blurred from that moment on until I cracked open my eyes, completely clueless as to my whereabouts or how I got there. A warm body was pressed to my back, and gentle fingers caressed my hair.

"I'm gonna be sick," I said before rolling out of bed to the floor. That was when I realized I was in my bedroom. I did something like a half walk, half crawl to the toilet and vomited over and over.

Josie was there, rubbing my back.

Josie was there with a glass of water.

Josie was there with her kind eyes.

Josie didn't say a word ... she was simply there.

As I sat on the cold linoleum floor, sipping the water, my other hand wiped the sweat from my forehead, only ... it wasn't sweat.

"You cut your forehead when you fell down the stairs," Josie said. "I couldn't find any bandages, and I didn't want to leave you alone to run to my house for them because I'm worried you might be dying of a brain bleed, and I don't want you to die alone." She was kidding.

I thought. Actually, I didn't know. After all, it was Josephine Watts. I could usually read her, but I was too drunk that night.

"Chad's asleep. Your dad's not home. And I think your mom took some sleeping pills and passed out on the sofa. Don't worry. It's not an overdose; I counted them."

My dad was probably off accidentally boning Holly Gill. One of those freak accidents where he tripped, and his dick landed inside of her. No wonder my mom needed pills to sleep, and I wouldn't have blamed her had she taken the whole damn bottle.

I handed Josie the glass of water and slumped to the side. Dying of a concussion felt like a welcomed opportunity compared to the pain. "I fucking hurt everywhere," I groaned.

"You fell down a flight of stairs." She chuckled, positioned herself behind me again, and again, held me to her, caressing me, while whispering, "I've got you," in my ear.

The next morning, we were back in my bed. I had no recollection of going from the bathroom floor to my bed, but I must have at least crawled because there was no way little Josie carried me.

"My mouth tastes like ass," I rasped while opening my eyes.

Oh my fucking head ...

It pounded.

Josie was tucked under my arm on her side, hugging my torso. I didn't want to move, but I had to take a leak before I sprang a leak in the bed.

"Your dad's going to kill me, gut me like one of his trophies, when he finds out where you are."

She nuzzled my neck. I didn't want her nuzzling my neck. Well, I did, but not when I smelled like vomit and ... ass.

"My dad thinks I'm at a friend's house. And your mom is on her morning walk."

I peeled her arm from my torso and groaned while shifting to sitting. "I'm going to shower. Thanks for ... everything."

After I made it two steps toward my bedroom door, Josie cleared her throat. "Need help?"

I glanced over my shoulder, eyes squinted.

She chewed on her lower lip, struggling to maintain eye contact with me. God, I loved her so fucking much. It was then I realized she wasn't wearing anything but a T-shirt of mine and striped cotton panties in shades of pink. Her dark hair hung over her shoulders and fell partway over her face, hiding some of her nervousness.

Did I want Josie to help me shower? The answer was as simple as the question: did I have a dick?

But ... where was Chad? When would my mom be

home from her walk? What if Chief Watts discovered Josie was at my house instead of at a friend's house? Since I managed to survive near alcohol poisoning and a tumble down a flight of stairs, I decided to call it while I was still ahead.

"I can manage."

She averted her gaze and nodded.

I was a stupid fuck. I was just too stupid and young to see it.

"Wait for me?" I asked.

She nodded again, picking at a string hanging from the hem of my T-shirt.

After I showered, brushed my teeth, and gargled twice to get rid of the ass taste, I peeked my head out of the bathroom and listened for my mom or Chad.

Nothing.

With a towel around my waist, I took two long strides to my room and closed the door behind me. When I turned toward Josie, her eyes were huge. She tucked her knees toward her chest under my tee and leaned against the wall at the head of my bed. Her unblinking eyes drifted south to my towel and back up my body.

"F-feel better?" she croaked before clearing her throat.

"Yeah." I felt marginally better. Cleaner. But my whole body ached, especially my head. It was hard to say if the ache in my head was from the alcohol or the fall.

"I uh ... see you found a bandage?"

I nodded, touching my head.

Her gaze roved along my torso. "You're bruised."

Glancing down, I tried to see where her eyes had landed.

"There." She motioned with her head.

I inspected my ribs and abs while she crawled off the bed and padded her bare feet to me.

"Here." She feathered her fingertips along the red area on my hipbone just above the towel.

I shuddered from her touch, and that made her glance up at me. We stood idle and silent for several seconds. I needed to get dressed, but she was in my room. I should've taken my clothes into the bathroom with me, but I wasn't thinking straight. Instead, I had a growing erection behind my towel because Josie touched a bruise on my hip.

And she was in my T-shirt.

And I'd gotten a glimpse of her panties before I showered.

And I'd considered rubbing one off in the shower while thinking of her in her pink panties, but I didn't because I didn't want to take the extra time.

I should have taken the extra time.

Instead, there I was, adjusting my towel and tucking my abs, anything to hide it from her.

"Kiss me, Colten," she whispered, taking a step closer.

Jesus ... don't get any closer!

"Um ..." I tried to speak past the thick desire clog-

319

ging my throat and stifling all coherent words. I took a step backward, my back hitting the door.

Josie lifted onto her toes, slid her hands behind my neck, and pulled me to her mouth. It was a slow kiss.

I clutched the front of my towel, holding on for dear life. Her warm tongue teased the seam of my mouth, and I opened for her. Our tongues touched, tentative at first, like we'd done so many times before; then our mouths fused with more need, also like we'd done in the past.

This time was different. I didn't have underwear and pants with a zipper and button keeping my dick under control.

She hummed, and I swore I was going to spew just from the kiss and the graze of the towel over the head of my erection. I told my other hand to remain fisted at my side.

Don't touch her!

It didn't listen.

It went straight to the hem of her shirt (my shirt) and worked its way up to her bare breast. Had God really existed, she would have been wearing a bra, a barrier that might have tripped my thoughts long enough to come to my senses.

No bra.

No God.

Her nipple was so fucking hard, hard like my erection. I cupped her breast and she moaned, making her tongue reach deeper into my mouth. When the pad of my thumb rubbed her nipple, our kiss faltered. Her chin dropped a fraction, and her lips pressed to my neck. I backed her to my bed. My towel hand started to weaken, but I kept it fisted.

Josie's overly curious fingers tugged at my towel.

"Uh-uh ..." I held strong. Sorta strong. My resistance weakened; and to be honest, it was downright flimsy at that point.

The only person in the world, who I gave more than two fucks about, wanted me in a way that made me feel like I didn't need the alcohol. Like my loser dad didn't exist. Like I had a purpose. And my purpose in that moment was to touch Josephine Watts.

Ever since the piano bench incident, the tension between us had been high. Either she hated me, or she was torturing me. Really, one and the same.

And when she wasn't firsthand torturing me, she was kissing some other guy which made me see every shade of red.

With one hand, I couldn't do everything I wanted to do to her, so ... I had to let the towel go.

She paused, taking a long breath to eye my erection bouncing between us. I grabbed her face and kissed her again. She started to lose her balance, so I guided her onto the bed and covered her body with mine as we kissed.

Her hands tentatively teased my bare back, easing their way down to my ass while spreading her legs to accommodate my torso. I didn't have a condom, not that we were going to have sex. We weren't. I was ... ninety percent sure of that. All I had to do to keep from going all the way with her was think of her dad killing me.

Unfortunately, that thought wasn't enough to make me completely stop.

"Colten ... don't stop."

And that right there was the reason I reserved that ten percent chance of having sex with her. Josephine was the worst temptation. She would have given me her virginity on so many occasions. I was a fucking saint.

Kinda ...

I shoved the T-shirt up her torso, and she grabbed it, taking it over her head. That was not what I was going for. Without the shirt, the only thing keeping us from doing something incredibly stupid, something that could get her pregnant and me killed, was her cotton panties. I might as well have wrapped a one-ply tissue around my dick and said a prayer to a god I knew wasn't going to do me any favors at that point.

"Do..." she panted "...you have ... a condom?"

I sucked her nipples and cupped her perky tits with my hands. "No," I murmured. "I'm ... not going ... to go ... that far."

Her fingers found their favorite place in my hair as she continued to writhe beneath me. Arching her back then planting her feet and lifting her pelvis toward me.

She wanted it.

I wanted it.

Why did *it* have to be so wrong?

Why did *it* come with so many possible consequences?

Damn ... why did working up to *it* feel so good?

"How far are you going to go?" she asked on a harsh breath.

Good question. I had no clue. And I certainly didn't want to stop.

I just knew that every time she lifted her hips, rubbing herself against my abs, I drove my cock into the mattress a few inches below her spread legs.

"You feel so ... g-good." She found her rhythm against me, and I kept telling myself I'd stop after a few more seconds.

And a few more.

More.

More.

More ...

I was well on my way to drilling a hole in the mattress.

"Colten? Are you awake?" Mom called from what sounded like a partial ascent up the stairs.

Major boner-killer.

Josie shoved my chest.

"Getting dressed, Mom. Be down in a bit."

Flying off the bed, Josie searched the floor for her clothes, putting them on in a matter of seconds.

I dressed a little slower, watching her to see if she was watching me.

She was.

"Oh my god ..." Josie whispered when we made eye contact.

"It's fine. She knows nothing." I rubbed my temples. Without Josie's naked body distracting me from my hangover, my head started to throb again. I think the erection and near ejaculation drew the blood and pain away from my head.

"You go downstairs and distract her while I sneak out," she said, shoving her feet into her shoes.

"Why'd you come?" I had to ask.

She stood up straight, cheeks red. "I didn't. I was close, though."

I shook my head. "I mean, why did you come get me from the party last night?"

Josie blinked. "You're my best friend. Wouldn't you have done the same thing for me?"

Stupid question.

There was nothing I wouldn't have done for Josie. I just wasn't sure she felt the same since I'd taken to drinking so much and being a dick at times because of the hatred I had toward my dad. I took out my frustration on too many people.

My mom.

My brother.

And sometimes Josie.

"I don't deserve your friendship, Josie."

She gave me a sad smile that I couldn't quite figure out.

"I'll go distract my mom."

She nodded.

324

I headed to my door.

"Colten?"

"Yeah?" I turned.

"I wanted you to ..." She pressed her lips together for several seconds. "I wanted you to go all the way with me."

Me. Fucking. Too.

I didn't respond with more than a tiny nod because I wasn't sure how I felt knowing that it was all up to me to keep us from going too far.

CHAPTER
Thirty-Five

"WHAT ARE YOU DOING HERE, JOSEPHINE?" Dr. Cornwell asks the second I enter the autopsy suite.

It's been four weeks. I'm in full PPE, so he shouldn't complain, but he's going to anyway. I can tell by the disapproving tone of his voice.

"No *Dr. Watts* today?"

He chuckles. "Dr. Watts is on medical leave. *Josephine* has decided to make rounds today for some unknown reason."

"I missed you," I say.

He makes a gruff grunting sound as do several other ME's. "You're supposed to be home healing. My guess is you're not supposed to be driving yet."

"I didn't. I took a cab."

"You took a cab here because you missed me?" he asked, using pruning shears to clip the decedent's ribs before lifting the breastplate to expose the pleural cavities and pericardium.

"Green fluid. Probably pneumonia," I say.

He shoots me a look.

I grin behind my mask.

When he returns his attention to the pericardial sac, carefully opening it with his scalpel, I get to my real reason for my visit. "Have you heard of Winston Jeffries?"

"Do I look *that* old?"

"So yes. You've heard of him."

He chuckles. "He was a bit before my time, but yes, I've heard of him. He preyed on little girls with long hair, abducted them, shaved off their hair, and hung the locks from churchyard trees."

One of the students observing him gasps.

"Do you know of any copycats since him?"

"No. But I haven't watched the news in a day or two. Should I be preparing for hairless girls to flood my schedule tomorrow?"

"I hope not. Just ... curious."

"You paid for a cab because of a sudden curiosity about a man who was executed over a century ago. Exactly what pain meds did they give you?"

"I can't find anything that says for sure if the bodies were ever found. I don't think they were. Everything I've read says they weren't."

"Have you tried Wordle? I hear it's all the rage. Really, Josephine, what are you up to?"

I need to tell someone. And I think I could tell Dr.

327

Cornwell if he weren't surrounded by students, and if there weren't two other bodies being autopsied by my colleagues who would jump at the chance to accuse me of losing my fucking mind.

"Wordle, huh?" I ask.

"Or Netflix. I'd go for a rom-com. A chick flick. No medical shows. No horror movies."

I nod. "Got it. Well, thanks for your help." I head toward the door.

"Did I help?"

"No. Not really."

While I exit the building, my phone rings. It's Colten.

"Hi," I answer.

"Hey. I was in the neighborhood, and I decided to check in on you, but you're not here."

"See? That's why you're such a brilliant detective." I put him on speaker to order a ride.

"Where are you?"

"I brought some cookies to work." It's not a lie. I did intend on bringing cookies, but I forgot to grab them from the freezer last night to thaw out.

"And how did you get to work?"

I roll my eyes. "I take back my comment. You're not a very good detective. It's called a cab, Detective Mosley. Uber and Lyft were solid options too. And before you try to scold me for leaving the house, it's been four weeks, and I'm feeling better."

My wound is feeling better. Beyond that, I'm either sleep deprived if I skip my meds or walking around in a fog that makes it impossible to focus if I do take them to sleep.

"You didn't sleep well again last night. You should be napping."

I didn't sleep well because I had another dream. More girls with shaved heads. More bodies buried in a cemetery just above bodies that were buried earlier in the day.

"You are more than welcome to start sleeping at your own place so my restlessness doesn't rouse you from your beauty sleep."

"What place? I sold my house when we decided to move in together."

I smirk as the car pulls up to the curb. "Nice try."

"You'd miss me if I weren't there."

"I wouldn't."

I would. I'd miss him terribly because I've grown accustomed to the sound of him coming home (*home* ...) and collapsing on the sofa before resting his head on my lap while releasing a long day's sigh, like being with me is his first real breath of the day.

"I love you too," Colten says.

I grin and shake my head. "Gotta go. See ya later." I end the call and give the driver my next stop. Dr. Terrance Byrd.

Terrance went to medical school with me, and we saw each other about six months ago at the court-house. He's a psychiatrist.

"Can I help you?" his receptionist asks when I close the office door behind me.

"I'm here to see Dr. Byrd. I don't have an appointment, but I was hoping he could squeeze me in for a few minutes between appointments. I'm Dr. Watts from the medical examiner's office." That has nothing to do with my visit, but I know it's her job to screen all visitors who are not on his schedule for the day.

"He'll be occupied for another forty-five minutes with his current appointment. I can take your number and have him call you if you don't want to wait."

I take a seat, gingerly bending my torso, and smile stiffly. "I've got time."

Right on the nose, Terrance emerges from his office after his patient exits. He smiles. "Josie. How are you?" Giving me a slow once-over, he frowns. "I was sorry to hear about your accident. Thank God for miracles."

I grin. "Miracle indeed. I'm healing quite well. Do you happen to have a few minutes I can steal?"

He glances over at his receptionist. "Can you move my one o'clock to one-thirty?"

She nods.

"Come on in." He gestures with a snap of his head.

It's a dinky office but calming and neutral with wood wall art and deco planters full of succulents.

"Have a seat wherever you're comfortable. Can I get you something to drink? A snack?"

"I'm good. Thanks." I take a seat in a chair by the window.

He grabs an apple and sits on the leather sofa. I think I took his chair.

"So what brings you by?" He takes a bite of his apple, probably his lunch.

"Have you ever had anyone have a near-death experience who then had visions or dreams of things that are not related to the near-death experience or anything in real life at all? *But* they feel real. And each dream builds on the other dream, becomes more real, more detailed."

He chews a big bite for several seconds. "Not in those exact words. But I wouldn't say any two near-death experiences are exactly alike. What did you see?"

I thought I was ready to have this conversation with someone, but now that I have the opportunity to share it with someone who is trained to deal with this, I find it really hard to say the words. It's not like I saw Colten's dad or my grandparents.

"Josephine?"

I drag my gaze away from the narrow succulent garden on the windowsill behind him. "I saw long locks of hair from little girls' shaved heads tied to tree branches in a churchyard. Then I saw where the bodies were buried, but I didn't see who did it."

I'll hand it to Dr. Terrance Byrd. He's perfected controlling his reaction. And I thought I was an expert at suppressing emotional responses.

"Where are the bodies buried?"

"In a cemetery. They were buried on top of caskets that were recently buried so that no one would get suspicious and look there for the bodies."

"How do you know that?"

"Know what?"

He stares at his apple for a few seconds. "How do you know that's why they were supposedly buried there?"

I shrug. "It's the most logical explanation."

Terrance nods slowly. "Have you recently had a girl with a shaved head on your table?"

"No."

"Read books about shaved heads?"

"Not recently."

"This started after your heart stopped?"

"Yes. I have dreams … well, nightmares, but only if I don't take medication for the pain or to help me sleep. Sometimes I wake up screaming. It's so real. And I remember every little detail from the nightmare. And they're not all the same. Each time they are different girls, and their hair is tied to different trees in different churchyards. So I looked it up, thinking maybe it's an actual thing that has recently happened. But I can't find anything except a serial killer who did this exact same thing in the late 1800s, early 1900s."

Terrance takes another bite of his apple, studying me or maybe just absorbing my words. "Had you read or heard about this killer before your accident?"

"No."

His eyebrows draw together while he stares at his half-eaten apple again. "Your scans came back normal?"

"Yes."

"Did you have a concussion?"

"No."

"How long were you out? No pulse?"

"I don't know."

"Have you had any dreams like this before? Or even just lucid dreams?"

"No."

He sighs slowly. "What's your inclination? What's your gut tell you that you should do about it?"

I laugh. "My gut's telling me to go to Tennessee."

"What do you expect to find in Tennessee?"

"I don't know. Maybe an old cemetery that matches one from my dreams. Maybe ..." I twist my lips. "Is it possible that my near-death experience didn't put these visions in my head? What if it took away other memories that would give the images context? What if I studied Winston Jeffries when I was a child, and those are the memories I lost?"

"What are the chances that, as a child, you would have studied a late nineteenth century serial killer?"

My nose scrunches into a guilty expression. "I sorta had a thing with death. So if I'm being honest, it's not wildly impossible or even all that unlikely. Dahmer. Bundy. DeAngelo. I was curious."

"Well, trauma can cause selective memory loss. And you're right, losing parts of our memory can make it difficult to understand some of the memories that do exist. Context is everything."

Chewing on the inside of my lip, I flit my attention back to him. "We took a trip to Nashville when I was eleven or twelve. I don't remember everything we saw, but I wouldn't be surprised if we walked through a few cemeteries."

He shrugs. "When you're feeling better, check it out. See what you find. It might help put your mind at ease. Maybe something will trigger other memories and put everything into context."

I nod slowly. "Maybe."

"Don't do anything extreme like dig up graves."

With a tight grin, I roll my eyes. It's a preposterous idea ... if it were anyone else but me.

"Let me know what you find out. Now you've piqued my curiosity."

I hum. "Mine too."

CHAPTER

Thirty-Six

"I THINK YOU SHOULD SEE SOMEONE," Colten says, waltzing down the hallway Saturday morning in a pair of shorts, no shirt.

"Congratulations," I say, pouring him a cup of coffee instead of entertaining his topic of conversation which has to do with my nightmares. "I heard you caught your killer. Did you find the saw? I have to know ... was the cord six feet? When did you get home last night?"

"Slow down ..." He chuckles. "After two in the morning. And we have our *alleged* killer. We don't actually know yet. And if you must know, we have a saw and the cord is indeed six feet, but the handle is not red."

I nod slowly. "Interesting. Tell me what you've got on him. I'll tell you if you're going to get a conviction."

He takes the coffee and kisses me. "Good morning. Let's not get off topic. About last night …"

"I'll take the sleeping pills. Or you can sleep in the guest room. Or go home. You need your sleep."

"Josie, it's not about my sleep." He sips his coffee before taking a seat at the counter and pulling a cinnamon raisin bagel from the bag. "It's about your nightmares. Were you having them before the accident? You didn't the night before the accident when you stayed at my place."

"We were having sex all night. I'm not sure I had the chance to dream. But no. I wasn't having these particular nightmares."

He sighs, setting his mug on the counter with one hand while rubbing the back of his neck with his other hand. His palpable frustration makes the air between us thick with unspoken words. "Is this about the shooting or are you still thinking about the girls or hair or … whatever?"

I know he thinks my mental status is on shaky ground, and he doesn't want to hear it. "It's uh …" I stare into my coffee mug. "The girls."

Colten sighs. "Tell me about the nightmares."

I glance up, hesitating with my response until I know he's really ready to listen. "It's always a church-yard. Always long hair tied to the branches. Sometimes I see the girls with their shaved heads. They look terrified one minute and dead the next. But it's so magnified in my mind's eye that I can't make out a location. I'd say their ages are anywhere from eight to eleven.

All white. The bodies are always buried in cemeteries in recently excavated plots. It might have something to do with Winston Jeffries."

"Who is Winston Jeffries?"

"An infamous serial killer who did this in the late 1800s."

He nods slowly. "I'll look into it. See if there's been any recent copycats."

I pause my coffee mug at my lips. "You will?"

Colten takes a bite of his bagel. "You're a dog with a bone. You always have been. If looking into this helps you let it go, then I'll do whatever it takes. I don't want to spend our entire married life dealing with your dreams."

I sip my coffee and mosey in his direction. "You won't."

Turning to the side, he widens his knees on the stool and pulls me into his body, hands resting on my ass as if it was made for that very reason.

"We're not getting married, so there is a zero percent chance of you spending time *dealing with my dreams* because there is a zero percent chance of me marrying you."

His lips twist as his mind searches for the perfect comeback. "Is it just me? Would you marry some other guy?"

"Tell me why you want to marry me."

"To make it hard for you to get away," he replies without a second's hesitation.

I hug my belly with one hand as I chuckle. It's a lot better, but laughter still gives me a little zing.

Colten takes my coffee from my other hand and sets it next to his before helping me (unnecessarily) onto the stool next to him so that our legs are scissored. I love that he likes to be close, always a part of his body touching mine. And now it makes more sense if he's afraid I'm going to "get away."

"Women have typically received the unfair label of 'ball and chain.' Colten Mosley ... are you saying that you want to be my ball and chain?"

"You've always been a little slippery." He takes another bite of bagel, but it doesn't completely hide his smirk.

"Slippery?"

He nods while swallowing. "One day I was your boyfriend. The next day I wasn't. The second I got another girlfriend, you stalked me, tempted me, pissed off every other girlfriend I attempted to have. You said jump. I asked how high?"

"I never said jump."

His hands slide along my bare legs, just under my nightie, thumbs teasing my inner thighs. "It was a look you gave me. I think it was even the very *first* look you gave me. It said jump, and I was a goner. Did you not see the way *I* looked at you? Every fucking look asked 'how high?' It still does. I don't think it's physically possible for me to walk this earth without gravitating toward you."

Seventeen years ... and not a day's passed that I

haven't thought about Colten, not a day that my thoughts haven't gravitated to my memories of him.

That smile, the one hijacking his lips and gleaming in his eyes … it's everything. He leans in a few inches from my lips. "Every woman who has asked me if I loved her has received an extended pause for an answer. As long as there is a Josephine Watts walking this earth, I am incapable of loving another woman." He tips his chin and rests his forehead on my collarbone. "You're it. Always have been. Always will be."

"I'll marry you," I whisper.

Colten lifts his head slowly, confusion etched into his face. "What?"

I shrug a shoulder. "I'll marry you, *if* … you take me to Tennessee."

The confusion deepens. "What's in Tennessee?"

"Sightseeing."

He searches my eyes for a few breaths before grinning. "I'll take you anywhere."

I can't help but mirror his smile. I've loved this boy nearly my whole life.

Colten's lips press to mine. It's slow—lazy Saturday slow. I know he needs to go into work, but he doesn't seem to be in a rush.

Did I really just agree to marry him?

His words have always played me with the ease his fingers drift along ivory keys. He effortlessly makes me want him … need him.

Ghosting his lips from my mouth to my ear, eliciting a flurry of goose bumps along my skin, he whispers, "How are you feeling this morning?"

"G-good ..." My fingers tease the nape of his neck while my tongue fumbles my words. My heart works a little harder to accommodate all the sensations Colten elicits.

"Want to feel even better?" He sucks the skin below my ear, his hand inching between my legs.

No panties.

Nothing to slow him down.

His finger makes an easy swipe, stopping at my clit, circling, torturing.

I swallow the pooling saliva in my mouth before I end up drooling all over him. My legs spread another inch. He grins just before kissing me again.

The soft satin of my nighty teases my hard nipples, and all I want is to feel his naked body pressed to mine.

He slips two fingers inside of me, fucking me with his hand between my legs and his tongue in my mouth.

My fingers dig into his back as he stands, hunched over me.

Kissing me.

Fingering me.

Rubbing the heel of his hand against my clit while his other hand cups the back of my head, deepening the kiss.

A tiny tug grips my abdominal muscles, but I can't register any discomfort because all I feel is the build up to my orgasm.

Col-colten ... Colten ... oh god ...

He stills his hand and slows the kiss while my body stiffens for a few seconds before melting into a limp state. It pulls a grin from him against my mouth. Of course, he's proud. In a matter of minutes, he's expertly manipulated my mind and my body. Josephine Watts's puppeteer.

Now who's the one asking how high without saying the actual words?

But just to make sure, I frame his face with my hands. "Do you love me, Colten?" I selfishly want one last confirmation. I want what he couldn't give any other woman.

"Yes," he says without hesitation. A wide grin acting as an exclamation point.

I tingle from the aftereffects of the orgasm *and* reality sinking into my conscience. Emotions burn my eyes, but I keep them in check. "I love you too," I whisper, dragging the pad of my thumb over his lip before kissing him again.

CHAPTER
Thirty-Seven

COLTEN GOES into work for a few hours while I do more research. I suppose I should call a bunch of people to tell them I'm engaged, but I really don't care if I'm married to Colten. It's for him, not me.

I won't take his last name.

I won't give him more babies.

I won't do his laundry.

He gets a piece of paper that says I'm legally his wife.

And I get to go to Tennessee with him.

It's a fair exchange.

I do more research on Winston Jeffries, but I can't find anywhere that says the bodies were found.

They're in the cemeteries.

Frustrated, I move on to near-death experiences and get lost in vlogs and YouTube videos. Just when

I'm ready to call it quits for the day, I find a vlog on the fourth search page. No one goes to the fourth search page unless they feel desperate.

Hello. My name is Desperate.

It's a simple vlog about a woman's near-death experience, not at all like mine. She struggled to deal with voices in her head. I don't have voices, just visions. At the end of her vlog, she has a link: *For More Help.*

I click the link.

It takes me to a webpage that's all black except for a tiny light in the middle of the screen and an email in the upper right corner. Clicking on the email link, I send a message:

Hello,

I came across your information while searching online for near-death experiences. I recently had an experience that has left me with visions that I don't understand. Would we be able to chat sometime?

Regards,

Josephine Watts

"There's my fiancée," Colten says, loosening his tie as he rounds the corner to the living room.

"We're not using those terms." I shoot him a quick look before closing my browser and my computer.

"No?" He scratches his stubbly chin, cocking his head to the side.

"No." I reach for my glass of water on the coffee table, gulping it down until I emerge out of breath.

"Girlfriend?"

My nose wrinkles while I shake my head, returning the glass to the coffee table. "Sounds a little immature."

"Lover?"

"Not a word I'd want you using in public."

"My woman?"

"Caveman."

"Sex toy?"

I snort.

Colten smirks. "Bingo. Sex toy it is. I can't wait to introduce my new sex toy to my friends. Do you, Colten Mosley, take Josephine Watts to be your sex toy for better or worse in sickness and in health until death do you part? Why yes ... yes I do."

I stand, grabbing his loosened tie and pulling him to me. "Last chance to get it right."

His face explodes into amusement while he feathers his knuckles along my cheeks. "You're my Artemis."

He remembers.

My lips twitch, even if I want to act like I don't know what he's talking about.

"She was fiercely protective of those who were considered weak. Reclusive but passionately defensive. A champion of purity ... the virgin kind. I have it on good authority that you are no longer a virgin, but I think the rest still applies. Oh ... and we must not forget her lack of mercy and an overabundance of pride."

"I've caved to your ridiculous need to be my husband, so clearly I've lost a little pride."

"Ouch ..." He stumbles back a step, but I don't let go of his tie. "You wound me, Artemis."

"Stop." I giggle. "Artemis is not going to work. Let's stick with Josie or Dr. Watts."

"I knew you before your titties filled out a bra. And I know they didn't fill out a bra because you showed them to me before you wore a bra. So I don't think I can call you Dr. Watts and keep a straight face."

"Do women still show you their tits for half a Twix? Or now that you're all grown up, do you have to work a little harder for a sneak peek?"

"The question is ... what on earth do your dating app pricks get for a six-course meal if you flashed me for half a Twix?"

"Why are they pricks?"

"Because you're mine."

I shorten my grip on his tie, forcing him a little closer to me. "I wasn't yours when I dated them."

His lips corkscrew, eyes narrowed. "Hmm ... you sure about that?" He's so damn playful. "Do you think it's possible..." his head ducks, relieving the tension on his tie, coming inches from my lips "...that the reason I'm single and so are you is because I've always been yours and you've always been mine?"

I slowly shake my head. "What are you doing?"

His gaze sweeps over my face, the way someone takes in a breathtaking view. I feel it everywhere.

Lifting on to my toes, I rub my nose against his. "I already said yes. You don't have to chase me anymore."

"You deserve to be chased. Pursued. I fell in love with the girl I knew I could never contain. Let me chase you forever because I love that moment when you look back at me and grin. That moment when I know you love knowing that I always have your back."

Jesus ...

I think he broke my heart so easily seventeen years ago because I knew I would never meet another Colten Mosley. He's my once-in-a-lifetime.

"Tell me about Tennessee. What are we doing in Tennessee? You threw that into the conversation this morning like asking me for my wallet while undressing."

I release his tie and head to the kitchen to browse the fridge for dinner options.

"Have a seat. I'll start something," he says.

"I'm fine." I open the fridge and pull out a few bowls of leftovers.

"What's in Tennessee?"

I set the bowls on the counter and turn toward him. It's not that I'm afraid to tell him ... okay, I'm a little afraid. "It's where Winston Jeffries killed all those girls in the late 1800s."

Colten covers his face with one hand, hiding his frustration behind it before letting it fall to his side. "Josie—"

"You said you'd take me anywhere if I agreed to marry you. No stipulations. If you're going to try to talk me out of going, then I'm going to renege on saying yes to your proposal."

The muscles in his jaw flex. He can gnash his teeth all he wants. It won't change anything. He pinches the bridge of his nose. "And what are we going to do there? Get permission to exhume the dead bodies so you can study them?"

"We can't get permission to exhume bodies that haven't been found."

"You said they were buried in a cemetery."

"Yes, but to my knowledge, no one else knows that."

"Jesus, Josie ..." He shakes his head. "Do you hear yourself?"

"You didn't experience what I did."

Colten eyes me with a mix of pain and frustration. "Are we going to every cemetery we can find? Most that probably weren't there in the early 1900s? Are we going to churchyards that weren't churchyards when this Winston guy killed these girls? Are we going to—"

"I don't know!" I turn, feeling the same level of regret that's on Colten's face for pushing me this far. "I don't know," I whisper.

He sighs. "I just don't want to feed your ..."

"My? My what? My craziness? My insanity?"

He glances at the ceiling for a few seconds. "I want you to get better, not worse. I feel like ..." Returning his gaze to me, he frowns. "I feel like you're chasing the boogieman. A year ago, Reagan was so afraid of the boogieman. Well, I think she just called it a monster. So when I had her with me, I promised to stay up all night, standing guard at the end of her bed. After she fell asleep, I went to bed. I woke early the next morning to return to the end of her bed before she woke up. But she was three. You're thirty-five."

I'm hurt that he doesn't believe me. At the same time, I don't know what I expect him to believe because I don't know what's happening to me. "What if during my near-death experience, I was shown a ... vision. A premonition. What if this is not something that has already happened, but is about to happen? Some people have very accurately predicted events in the future. What if I can stop something terrible from happening?"

Colten curls his lips between his teeth while drawing in a long breath. "Do you know how many anonymous tips we get about premonitions? Do you know how many of them come to fruition?"

"How many of them come from people who have had a near-death experience?"

"Josie ..."

I hate the sympathetic expression on his face. It's pure pity.

"For the record, I saw a psychiatrist, and he suggested I go to Tennessee. So even if you think I'm insane, going to Tennessee is not the insane part."

"The psychiatrist you saw right after the accident?"

"No. I saw one the afternoon you called looking for me. The day I took cookies into work."

"Why didn't you tell me?"

"I just did."

He frowns. "Josie ..."

"I didn't tell you that day for the same reason I'm already regretting telling you now. I hate that look on your face."

"Listen, there are several other people I know from the day of the shooting who weren't physically injured, but they're struggling with some PTSD. Not all PTSD is the same. The mind can do weird things after something so stressful. And if you keep having visions in your sleep, maybe you should see a sleep specialist."

"Wow, Dr. Mosley. Did they teach you that in medical school? If only I would have gone to medical school, then I would be smart like you. And an expert on the human brain."

"Josie, don't do this."

I pull a plate from the microwave and hand it to him. "I'll go by myself."

"You're not going to Tennessee by yourself."

I put the other plate in the microwave. "I think we established my age and the ridiculousness of unnecessary fear. Let's stay with that theme and not get overprotective about me going to Tennessee by myself. Believe it or not, before you came back into my life, I did a lot of things by myself, including live by myself."

Colten glances over at me while he fills a glass from the fridge's water dispenser. "You want me to leave?"

"I don't care."

"Well, try. Try to care, Josie. I'm done with the games. They were fun for a while, but I'm not really going to let you pity marry me. If you don't want to marry me, we won't get married. If you don't want me living here, I'll leave." He sets the glass on the counter next to his plate and sits on the barstool.

"By all means, Colten. Whatever you want ... whatever you need. I'll try to care, like you cared the day you obliterated my heart seventeen years ago." I hold out my wrists. "I cared then. I care now. So back the fuck up and tell me who doesn't care?"

Colten stares at my arms.

I drop them to my sides. "I don't blame you," I whisper.

"I do," he whispers back to me.

I blink back my tears. "I've wanted one thing since I was a nine-year-old girl trying to win my dad's heart, trying to make friends, trying to find my place in this world."

Colten's gaze lifts to mine. "What?"

Swallowing past the lump of vulnerability in my throat, I ease my head side to side. How can he not know? "You." My hand quickly bats away a tear. "I've hated you so much for so long. Do you have any idea how hard it is to hate someone for that long?"

His Adam's apple bobs as his gaze shifts again, unable to keep it locked to mine.

"It takes *so* much love, the kind of love that relentlessly aches, eating away at your soul. And here we are. You want to live with me, marry me, do all the things that other people do. But I've never been 'other people.' I want you, Colten. Any way I can get you. However, I feel like you want me the way ... you want me. I've never been normal. If something really fucked-up is going to happen to someone after a near-death experience, it's going to be me. If that's too much for the adult version of Colten Mosley, then you can have a pass. No hard feelings."

He flinches, shaking his head.

I measure my next words carefully. "The reason my job exists is because not everything in life is what it seems. So even when you show up to a crime scene and find a body that has a bullet hole in the head, you can't definitively say the person died from that gunshot wound. Maybe they died of a drug overdose first, and someone shot them in the head anyway. *I* am the person who goes through the proper steps to make that determination. I deal with facts in my job. I don't write death certificates based on speculation. There is a process. So I'm going to Tennessee because I think it's part of the process. And you can stay here and wait for the chance to say, 'See, I told you it was the bullet to the head.' But I won't care if you're right. It's not about ego. It's about following a process. Facts matter. Sometimes being right is just dumb fucking luck."

Colten blinks a few times and murmurs, "I don't want a pass. Not ever. I'll go with you to Tennessee. You lead. I follow. That's just what we do."

CHAPTER
Thirty-Eight

THIRTEEN.

Officially teenagers.

I didn't feel a new level of confidence, nor did turning thirteen prompt my parents to give me more freedom.

The very day Josie turned thirteen, she was ready to demand full adulthood freedom. Chief Watts chose that very day to tighten the reins on her.

"Oh my god! My parents gave me a curfew. I mean ... they've always given me a time to be home, but it's not the same time. It's always been dependent on the situation. But now I have to be home by nine on school nights and ten on the weekends. It's ridiculous!" She nearly fell out of the tree from her animated ranting.

"Did you ask them why?"

Josie huffed, blowing the hair away from her eyes.

"They said I'm at the age where I'm more likely to get into trouble or be influenced by other kids. As if I'd do something stupid because someone else told me to do it."

I had a mile-long list of stupid things I had done because someone else told me to do them, and by someone else ... it was Josie.

"You don't have a curfew. I have one because I'm a girl. That's not fair. If my dad is going to call me 'Jo' and dress me in camouflage on the weekends to go hunting, then he needs to give me a boy curfew."

"What's a boy curfew?" I asked, swinging my legs to the same rhythm as hers.

"It's *no* curfew. Gah! Haven't you been listening?"

Listening? Sure, I was listening. I just wasn't focusing on everything. Josie had the best rants. You could tell she was well-read because her vocabulary and ability to build a strong case for her demands far exceeded my abilities or anyone else's who was our age.

"Listen, I heard a group of kids are going to sneak out and spend the night at the cemetery. I think we should go," she said.

"I don't think it's a good idea."

"You don't think anything is a good idea if it involves risk."

"I don't think something is a good idea if the risk involves your dad killing me for not stopping you."

"Fine, I'll go by myself. You stay home and have your mommy read you a bedtime story."

She never played fairly. I always felt coerced by her questioning my bravery. Later, I realized it was a challenge to my masculinity. How masculine did she expect me to be at thirteen? I had like ... four hairs in my armpits and maybe double that in pubic hairs. Nothing on my chest. Nothing on my face.

I sighed and grumbled. "What time are we sneaking out?"

Josie nudged my arm. "I knew you'd come around. My parents should be asleep by eleven. Let's meet out front at eleven-thirty just to play it safe."

She led ... I followed. That was us.

That weekend, I learned a lot about Josephine Watts. Mainly, what I learned was I had underestimated her creepy side.

While kids several years older than us jumped at every sound, freaked out, and ran home early, Josie didn't flinch. She moseyed from headstone to headstone making up stories for what killed each person.

"Beatrice died of a broken heart after her beloved Henry died a year earlier." She traced each name with her finger. "Calvin died when his wife found out he was cheating on her. She murdered him in his sleep, took their two kids, and fled to Canada."

I sat with my back against Beatrice's headstone, her story seemed less haunting. "You've scared everyone off."

Josie shrugged. "The zombie apocalypse isn't real. I don't know why everyone is afraid of dead people. I mean ... they're dead. Just empty bodies."

"Do you believe in Heaven?"

"No. But don't tell my parents. It's funny ... they thought it was okay for me to believe in Santa Claus and the Easter Bunny because they thought it was fun and cute. But them believing in God is even more ridiculous because they're adults. They should know better than to believe in something you can't prove. Right?"

She was asking the wrong person. I believed in God. There had to be a god and a Heaven so that there could be the devil and a Hell. My dad was going to Hell for cheating on my mom, the way Calvin's soul was probably in Hell for cheating on his wife in Josie's made-up world.

"Can you imagine being buried alive?" I asked.

"That doesn't happen very often. Instead of putting bells on the corpse's toes like they used to do, they use machines to see if the heart is working. That's what Roland Tompkins told us. Don't you remember? You were there too."

I spaced off during Josie's long conversations with the undertaker. Mostly, I thought about my next meal, but occasionally I'd imagine what songs would be played on the organ. Probably Schubert's *Ave Maria* or Handel's one about feeding his flock.

"When I die, I'm going to donate my body to science. After, of course, I donate my organs. Well, I suppose it will be my family donating my organs, if I have a family. My parents might be dead by then. I'm not getting married or having kids, so I won't have them to make that decision. Maybe Benji will do it for me. What do you want done with your body, Colten?"

"I want to be buried in a cemetery so my family can visit me."

"That's selfish. You should save lives by donating your organs. And help medical students by donating the remains of your body to science. When they're done with your body, your family will get the ashes. I don't know ... maybe they can bury the ashes, and you can still have a headstone. We'll ask Roland when we see him again."

"Why are you not getting married? Who's going to love you when your parents are dead?"

"Benji."

"What if your parents got in a car accident with Benji, and they all died, leaving you with no family except grandparents who will probably die before you? Then what?"

Josie traced the name on another headstone. I couldn't see it; we were too far away, and the closest streetlight flickered off. "Then you'll have to love me. That's what friends do, right?"

"No. Friends like each other; they don't love each other."

She scoffed. "You can love a friend without it being ... you know ... more than friends. And we've kissed, so we're sometimes more than friends."

"Well, I'm going to get married. I bet you do too. My mom always tells me the future is unpredictable.

Whatever I'm thinking now probably won't be what actually happens to me."

"BOO!"

I nearly pooped my pants when Josie sneaked up behind Beatrice's headstone.

"Ha! Scared you." She plopped down beside me.

"D-did not," I insisted despite my hammering heart and stuttered words.

She rested her head on my shoulder. "Colten?"

"Hmm?"

"If nobody else wants my ashes, will you take them?"

I had no idea what I was going to do with them, but she seemed sincere, so I nodded. "Sure."

CHAPTER

Thirty-Nine

A WEEK before our scheduled trip to Tennessee, Colten makes arrangements for Reagan to come for the weekend. I use it as an excuse to send him home for a bit. I know I'm keeping him awake at night. It's undeniable in his tired eyes and incessant yawning.

Since our argument two weeks ago, we haven't discussed the marriage. He didn't want a pity marriage, and I didn't say anything to correct him. Now, it's awkward. I really don't know where we stand. It's like the fight didn't happen, but it's also like he didn't propose, and I didn't say yes. I've been too preoccupied with my nonstop research to focus on where we stand.

After taking Reagan out for pizza Friday night, we watch a movie at his place. Reagan makes herself comfy in the big recliner with at least three blankets while Colten and I take the sofa.

I feel his eyes on me more than the TV, and I suppress the urge to ask him why he's doing it.

"Bedtime, Button," he says to Reagan as soon as the movie ends.

"Will you read me a story?"

He folds her three blankets. "Of course."

"Will Josie read one too?"

I smile. "Uh ... sure."

"Why don't you head upstairs with Josie. Get your teeth brushed and pick out a story. I'm going to do a few things in the kitchen, and then I'll be up."

Reagan heads upstairs as I stand from the sofa.

"Coming, Josie?" she yells from the top of the stairs.

Colten grins. "She adores you."

I roll my eyes. She hasn't known me long enough to adore me. "I'm coming."

While Reagan brushes her teeth, I wait in her bedroom. It's an explosion of pink paint, a mural of a white cat, and a dozen or so stuffed animals covering the single bed. I remove the stuffed animals and flip through the books on the shelf by her bed.

"Ready!" Reagan flies into the bedroom and leaps onto the bed. "Oh, my ponytail." She tugs at the elastic, and it gets tangled. "Help, please."

I work her hair out of the knot, freeing the elastic. Then I slowly run my fingers through her long hair. Winston Jeffries would have loved Reagan's hair. As soon as that awful thought enters my head, I pull my hand away from her head. "So ... what story are we reading tonight?"

"That one. *Magic Treehouse.*" She points to a book on the top shelf. "Chapter four."

"You remember what chapter you were on?" I laugh, grabbing the book.

"Yep." Reagan settles under the covers after grabbing a stuffed penguin from the floor and hugging it.

"That's a cool cat on your wall. I wonder who painted it."

"My daddy."

I chuckle, but Reagan is dead serious.

"Wow ... I had no idea your dad could paint."

"Grandma Mosley said Daddy can do everything."

I don't doubt that.

By the time I'm done reading a chapter, she's asleep. I put the bookmark in the book, slide it back on the shelf, and take a minute to stare at her in a peaceful slumber. Her dark hair framing her face. Her long eyelashes resting on her pink cheeks. Her flawless skin. I imagine she's what an angel would look like.

This little girl is part of Colten. He willingly (even if unknowingly) gave a piece of himself to another woman, and they created a life together. I think Reagan is special. Delightful. All the things an innocent child should be. So why don't I wish she was mine? Why don't I wish it was me who made a life with Colten?

The lack of those feelings makes me feel broken inside as a human. There are many people in the world who have no desire to procreate. I'm sure they don't feel broken. Maybe they made that decision later in life, as adults. They assessed their life, their careers, and their aspirations, and they decided parenthood wasn't for them.

Not me. I've *never* wanted children. I never played with stuffed animals or baby dolls and pretended to be their mommy. I have no maternal feelings. No ticking biological clock.

After shutting off the light, I gently pull her door partially closed just as Colten climbs the stairs.

"She asleep?" he whispers.

I nod.

"Thanks for reading to her." He stops on his way to her room, takes my face in his hands, and gives me a soft kiss, ending with a smile. "Be right back. I need to kiss her goodnight."

Of course, he's kissing her goodnight. That's what he does. He pulls dying women from the water. Kisses his daughter goodnight. And paints murals of cats. He's a normal human with normal instincts and feelings.

"You're leaving?" he asks on his way down the stairs.

I slide my feet into my sandals. "I am."

"You're allowed to stay here." He pulls me into his arms, my back to his chest.

I grin when he buries his face in the crook of my neck. "You paint, Colten? You painted that cat?"

"She asked. I said I'd give it a go."

"Give it a go ..." I laugh. "Are you bad at anything?"

"Apparently, I'm bad at convincing you to stay the night. I think I've been bad at convincing you to do anything ... ever. You always leave me guessing where I stand in your life."

I turn in his arms, sliding my hands into his back pockets. "I said I'd marry you. What more do you want?"

"I want you to *want* to marry me." He gathers my hair and pulls it off my shoulders, giving it a playful tug.

Lifting onto my toes, I press a soft kiss to the corner of his mouth. Taking several steps backward toward the front door, I shake my head and turn the handle. "Colten Mosley, you should know me better by now." I turn and head toward my car without shutting the front door. "I would never do anything I didn't want to do."

Just as I unlock my car, he calls, "So you *want* to marry me?"

"So it would seem."

"Fine. Stop begging. I'll marry you, Josephine Watts."

Hours later, I wake in a sweat, heart ready to burst from my chest and a clawing panic eating me alive. Something is so very wrong with me. For the first time, I question if I was supposed to live. Maybe Colten made a mistake by saving me. These are not dreams. They are fragments of reality. Whose reality? I don't know.

Is this a warning? Has the future been given to me? My mind doesn't work this way. I thrive on reason and explanation. Science. Testing. Solid data.

There are so many girls. So many bodies.

Grabbing my computer from my nightstand, I open it and start searching for answers. Two unsuccessful hours later, a new email chimes, and I open it.

It's from the parapsychologist I messaged in desperation a while back.

> *Namaste, Josephine.*
>
> *I have a feeling you've come to the right place. I can see you on the 14th.*
>
> *3:00 p.m.*
> *Athelinda*

She left her address—in Berkeley, California.

I'm not flying to California. Even thinking about it makes me want to commit myself to a mental institution. I might have considered a day drive, but there's no way I can justify airfare to meet with a person I found from a fourth page internet search.

> *Dear Athelinda,*
>
> *Thank you for replying to my message. However, I live in Illinois. I will continue to look for help closer to me.*
>
> *Regards,*
> *Josephine*

I stare at the time on my computer. 3:25 a.m.

Again, my email chimes. It's Athelinda. I realize she's on West Coast time, but it's still the middle of the night there.

Josephine,

It's two weeks out. If you're experiencing what I feel you're experiencing, it will not get better. It will get more intense. I'll save the date and time for you.

Athelinda

What she "feels" I'm experiencing? I've sent her two brief emails. How can she possibly have any sort of feeling about me or my situation?

I don't respond. It would seem like I'm arguing with her. There's no sense in engaging her anymore. I'm not going.

Sighing, I close my computer and rub my eyes before nestling back under the covers. My hand stretches across the bed to the empty spot.

I miss him.

I've missed him for seventeen years.

Colten wants to know where he stands in my life? In the middle. He's always in the middle of my thoughts with every other thought tripping over him.

Do I want to get married? No.

Do I want to be a wife? No.

Those are basic facts. Always have been.

Do I want to marry Colten? Do I want to be his wife?

Those are different questions. He's the exception to everything. He's always been the exception.

I've never liked carrot cake, but I love his mom's carrot cake. It's the exception. I don't know why. Is there a secret ingredient?

What's Colten's secret ingredient? I don't think I'll ever know. It's just *something*.

CHAPTER

Forty

Colten has a busy week preparing to be away from work for a few days for our trip to Nashville, so I don't see him.

I fall into the black hole of the internet. Every time I get lost there, I emerge with two possible conclusions: I either have a legitimate mental illness, or I have a brain tumor that the neurologist missed.

Reading someone else's mind is a distant third, but I don't like that one because I don't believe that's possible, and therefore it makes me feel mentally ill. Also, it imparts a responsibility to figure out whose mind I'm reading before they follow through with these murders.

On Thursday, Alicia stops by with tacos and a sinful chocolate cake.

"You look so good. Are you feeling as good as you

look?" she asks when I take the cake from her and close the front door.

"Mentally or physically?"

"Uh ..." She chuckles. "Both."

"Physically, I'm doing really well. I'm ready for work."

"Are you lifting heavy stuff?"

"Not yet." I grab plates while she pulls the containers of tacos from the sack.

"There's no way Cornwell will let you come back to work before you can lift heavy things. Last week, we had a four-hundred-pound man whom we nearly flipped onto the floor while trying to turn him."

"I'll lift with my legs."

"Pfft." Alicia rolls her eyes as we take a seat on the sofa with our plates of tacos. "How are you doing mentally? Any PTSD?"

"That's a really complicated question." I lean forward, biting into the soft shell fish taco.

"How so?"

I press a paper napkin to my lips and swallow. "I see things."

"Vision issues? Floaters?"

"No. I saw something; I had a vision, when I was unconscious or when my heart stopped."

"What did you see?" she mumbles over a mouthful of food.

I stare at her while she stares at her next bite of taco. Is she ready for this? "I saw long locks of hair hanging from trees in churchyards. I saw young girls having their heads shaved. I saw their bodies being buried on top of other dead bodies in cemeteries."

Alicia's taco drops from her hand back to her plate, eyes unblinking, lips parted with a little sauce smudged on the side of her mouth. After a few seconds, she swallows hard and licks the sauce. "That's uh ... weird. I mean ... probably not unheard of for people in our line of work. Is it related to a case you worked on? Is it the serial killer you were asking Cornwell about?"

"Maybe. I'm not sure anymore. If it would have been just once, I would not be thinking about it. I see disturbing things all the time. I don't have an issue letting them go. But I keep seeing things. The hair. The girls. The graves. I see them when I sleep, but the visions are equally as clear when I'm awake. So tomorrow, I'm going to Tennessee because I feel this clawing need to go there since the only thing I can find online that matches my visions is Jeffries. He was a serial killer who was executed in the early 1900s. He shaved the girls' heads. Tied their hair to churchyard trees. And buried the bodies in cemeteries over preexisting bodies. And since I can't find anywhere that says the bodies were ever found ... well, I just need to know." My words come out in a long trail, building momentum and leaving me breathless.

Alicia waits to respond. What's there to say? I'm mentally struggling. It's not a side she's seen of me because it didn't exist before now.

"I don't think it's a good idea for you to go to Tennessee by yourself."

"I'm not." I take a bite of my food. Then another bite. And another bite.

Alicia waits.

I chew, avoiding eye contact with her.

"So ... who's going with you?"

"Colten," I mumble.

"Detective Mosley?"

I nod.

"Are you on good terms with him again? I thought you held some animosity from the past. Are you friends again?"

"I think we're getting married."

"WHAT?"

Glancing over at her, I give her a sheepish grin. It's all I have to offer.

"Why?" she asks.

It's a valid question.

"I think the love part of our love-hate relationship might be more powerful than the hate."

She coughs a laugh. "Oh my gosh ... you're serious?"

"I think so. Right now, I have bigger things occupying my mind, so—"

"Where's the ring?"

"What?" I ask before taking a drink.

"The engagement ring. He didn't propose without a ring, did he?"

I stare at my left hand for a split second. "Oh, no ring. It wasn't that kind of proposal."

"Um ... what does that mean? I didn't know there were different kinds of proposals."

I wave my hand as though I can brush off the skepticism in her words. "It was spontaneous. Which is really more romantic, right? And I wasn't keen on the idea since I've never wanted to get married. But Colten has been the exception in my life for just about everything. Then, one day, he said some incredibly nice and heartfelt things to me, and I realized being married to him wouldn't be the worst thing ever. So I agreed to marry him."

Then he fingered me until I nearly fell off the kitchen stool. And they lived happily ever after. The end.

"That's ..." She grapples for words.

I point to the last bite of my taco. "These are the best tacos. Why haven't we had these before?"

"You see dead people and you're marrying Detective Mosley. And you want to talk about the tacos?"

"They're *really* good."

Alicia shakes her head a half dozen times. "When's the wedding? Did you tell Cornwell? Have you told your parents? What are you going to do in Tennessee? Dig up graves?" She sets her plate onto the coffee table and runs her hands through her hair. "Shit ... what are you going to do if you find the bodies? They'll arrest you. Quarantine you. Torture you with tests and experiments and then dissect your brain."

"That's a little extreme." I roll my eyes. If I'm honest, I've thought of all of that, even worse.

"Colten. Fucking. Mosley." She shakes her head and grins.

I chuckle. "Yep. I've said those three words just like that so many times."

"Is your family excited? They have to be. What about his family?"

My lips corkscrew. I haven't told anyone besides Alicia. And I assume Colten hasn't either, but I'm not sure. "We haven't shared the news. And maybe you should keep it to yourself until we do. Okay?"

Alicia's grin swells. "Aw ... I feel so special."

"That was my goal." I give her a toothy grin.

She laughs.

CHAPTER
Forty-One

COLTEN and I don't converse much on the flight to Nashville. It's not a romantic weekend getaway. We're not visiting family. It's not even a funeral.

"Where to first?" Colten asks when we get into our rental car.

"Just ... drive," I say, feeling a little off. The visions in my head becoming clearer.

"Okey dokey." He drives.

I scan the area for a few miles. "Turn right up here."

Colten gives me a quick sidelong glance then turns on his turning signal. A mile or so down that road, I whisper, "Next right."

He turns.

We take a left and one more right outside of the city.

"Stop!"

Colten slows and pulls onto the shoulder. I don't wait for him to completely stop before I jump out and jog toward a house on some acreage.

"Josie!" Colten chases after me.

The property has a wood fence corralling several horses in a lush pasture that leads to a barn and a sprawling house. A mansion, really.

"Jesus, Josie ... you're trespassing. And running. You're not supposed to be running." He grabs my arm.

I rip it from his hold and continue running in the same direction, stopping under a large oak tree.

Breathless.

A little scared.

And tingly all over.

"This is the tree. The first tree I saw," I say between labored breaths. "The day of the shooting."

"How do you know? How can you possibly know this?"

"I just ... do."

I see the hair flowing in the wind, all tied to the same branch. Two shades of brown and the longest locks in a nearly white blond. The barn stands where the church used to be. A tiny brick church with a steeple-covered bell.

I run my fingers along the rough bark. "This tree has been here for generations," I whisper. "Like every body that ends up on my table ... it has a story to tell."

"What's the story?"

I ease my head side to side. "I'm not sure, but I feel it. I'm going to know."

Colten walks around the tree, glancing up at the branches and flickering leaves. "When will you know?"

I close my eyes, letting my fingers slide down the trunk. "Soon."

"Josie, we need to go."

I open my eyes, following the sound of gravel crunching beneath tires. A white extended-cab truck rolls to a stop. A bearded man in jeans and a black button-down climbs out. He reaches behind the seat and retrieves a rifle.

Colten steps in front of me, putting himself between me and the man.

"This is private property," the man says in a gruff voice while taking slow but long strides toward us, gripping the gun with both hands across his body.

"Our apologies. We were just leav—"

I shoulder my way past Colten. "Is this the tree?"

"I said it's private property. It's not open to sightseeing." His grip tightens on the gun as the distance between us fades.

"Did Winston Jeffries tie young girls' hair to this tree?"

The man slowly peels off his sunglasses, revealing his dark squinted eyes and leathery crow's feet.

"Josie, let's go." Colten's hand cuffs my wrist.

"Who wants to know?" the man asks.

"I do," I say.

"Why?" He stops eight feet from us.

"Peace of mind."

He chuckles, coughing several times. A smoker's cough, wheezing and cackling. "Why on earth would knowing such a thing give you peace of mind?"

"Because I died eight weeks ago, and before they resuscitated me, I saw this exact tree."

He slides his sunglasses back onto his stony face. "I'll give you ten seconds to get the hell off my property, you crazy bitch."

"Thank you for your time. We are leaving right now." Colten grips both of my arms and guides me toward the fence and our rental car. "I think you've had your gunshot wound quota met for the year or, for that matter, this lifetime. Wouldn't you agree?"

"It's the tree. He all but said it. Did you catch that? It's the tree, Colten." I knew I was right from the second I saw it. I knew how to get to the tree without knowing where it lived. I feel vindicated and completely terrified.

Colten helps me over the fence and opens the car door. He doesn't say a word on the way to our hotel. He stops by a burger joint and orders food, but he doesn't ask me what I want. Maybe he thinks not talking about it will make it go away. I wish that were true.

I sip my drink without touching my food while he eats, occasionally glancing out the hotel room window. We each sit on our respective beds for nearly an hour, backs parked against the headboard, legs stretched out long.

"Josie," he exhales, breaking the droning rhythm in

my ears of the air conditioner, "how do you know that? Did you see it online? I know you've researched this ad nauseam. You must have seen images. Videos. Something. It's the *only* explanation. I know it. And if you really think about it, you know it too."

If I really think about it.

I've thought of nothing else.

"What if the bodies are there?" I whisper.

"Where?"

Sliding my legs off the side of the bed, I tip my chin and stare at my bare feet. "The place we're going tonight."

"THIS IS a class C felony punishable by up to ten years in prison and up to a ten thousand dollar fine," Colten says as I choose my shovel in the aisle of the home improvement store.

"Then we'll just get one shovel, and you'll wait in the car. Isn't being an accessory to a crime a little more forgivable in the eyes of the law?"

"I'll lose my badge."

Satisfied with the yellow shovel with a black handle, I head toward the checkout. "Then I'll take you back to the hotel first."

He mumbles something I can't quite decipher. When I get to the checkout and set down my shovel, a second shovel slides in next to mine along with two pairs of leather gloves Colten grabs from a checkout display. I meet his gaze, and he shrugs.

When she gives us our total, I reach for my credit card, but Colten hands her cash and gives me a look.

Okay. No tracking this purchase.

As we maneuver the shovels into the back of the vehicle, I ask, "Why?"

He shuts the hatchback and shrugs. "You give a new meaning to doggedly chasing your dreams. And I'm your ..." He sighs, sliding his hands along my face, fingers into my hair.

"You're my ride-or-die?"

He nods slowly.

Swallowing past the lump in my throat, I pull away and climb into the vehicle.

"Where are we going?" he asks, fastening his seat belt.

"Just drive."

Again, without further questions, he drives. I give him directions. I don't know where they came from, but they're in my head. Every right and left come out of my mouth on instinct until we stop at an old cemetery.

I'm eerily calm given the fact that I could be in jail by the end of the night. Colten follows my lead as we carry our shovels through the graveyard to the far corner, using the lights on our phones to guide our way. It's a magnetic feeling. The closer we get to the spot, the stronger the feeling gets.

I drop my phone and the shovel, squeezing my eyes

shut and pressing the heels of my hands to my eyes. "N-no ... No. No. No."

"Josie." Colten drops his shovel and pulls me into his arms. "What is it?"

Panic slices through my nerves, acid in my throat, a hundred pounds on my chest. I'm not asleep, but I can see it so clearly.

Elizabeth Allen

"They're close ... so close." I crack, choking on a sob as I see two girls, one halfway covering the other. Both facedown. Both with their heads shaven.

Dead.

"The dirt is ... f-freshly tilled." I grip Colten's shirt. I don't want to take a step closer, but I can't force myself to go backward either.

"Josie, tell me what to do. We can go home. Let's just go home." He alternates between stroking my hair and kissing my head.

"I ... can't." I want to. I so badly want to turn around and go home, but I can't run from what's in my head. It won't let me hide.

Taking a step back, I wipe my face. "Look for Elizabeth Allen," I whisper.

Colten picks up my phone and hands it to me. With the light of it between us, I see the horror on his face. He's not afraid of what we're about to find because he doesn't believe there's anything to find. That look is heartbreak. He loves a woman who is no longer the woman he remembers. Colten thinks he's slowly losing me. I think I'm slowly losing me too.

"Elizabeth Allen," I repeat taking back my phone.

He nods once, turning left while I go right because I'm being pulled right, each move no longer mine. Every decision is made before my consciousness has a chance to give it a second thought.

The rays of light from my phone drift from one headstone to the next until landing on Elizabeth Allen. Covering my mouth with my free hand, I stifle another sob. I've *never* wanted to be so wrong as what I want to be right now.

Why am I right?

Why do I know this?

How do I know this?

"Jesus ..." Colten whispers at my back. "How ... how did you know that name?"

I don't answer because I don't have the answer. I only have these terrible visions and the growing pain that comes with them. He's inches from me, yet ... I've never felt so incredibly alone. "Where's my shovel?" I mumble.

"You shouldn't be shoveling. You're not healed." He stabs his shovel into the ground. It brings a new round of tears to my eyes. He's risking everything for me.

I hold the light while he unearths the vision that's been haunting me for nearly two months. He's unearthing every night of stolen sleep. He's unearthing the unimaginable.

The dirt piles up next to me, the hole hollowing by the second. It's starting to feel as hollow as my soul.

"Stop," I whisper.

He doesn't hear me.

"Stop!"

Colten wipes his sweaty brow. I feel his questioning gaze on me, but I can't tear my eyes off the hole he dug. He climbs out of the hole.

"Josie!"

I jump into the hole. Falling to my knees, I claw at the cold dirt until my fingertips graze the brittle remains. Feeling tortured into submission, my mind stretches past its limits, grasping for truth, for reason. An explanation.

Pulling the last layer of dirt toward me, the human remains come into view.

"Josie, get out of the hole."

I start to cry again, but this time, I can't stifle it.

"Josie, don't touch anything else. Get out of the hole." When Colten's hand slides around my arm, pulling me to my feet, I try to find my legs, but I can't. He drags my limp body out of the hole like I imagine he pulled me out of the water after I died.

"I have to call this in. Josie, do you hear me?"

"C-Colten ..."

He cradles my tear drenched face while my lower lip quivers.

My gaze makes a painful ascent to his as my mind finds that explanation that's been just beyond reach until now. "I'm still in that hole."

"What are you talking about?" His face scrunches into confusion, his breathing as labored as mine.

"I think I was one of those girls Winston Jeffries murdered." My gaze averts to the grave again before quickly returning to Colten. "I found ... myself."

After a few breaths, he takes a step back and brings his phone to his ear.

CHAPTER

Forty-Two

THIS TRIP to Nashville was supposed to be closure, the end to Josie's wandering thoughts. This trip was supposed to give her mind a sense of relief so she could sleep.

Heal.

Work.

Marry me.

As suspicious and downright eerie as the journey to the oak tree felt, the owner gave us nothing definitive, and that allowed me to keep things in perspective, even if it only fed Josie's obsession.

Purchasing shovels? Fine. It wasn't a crime ... yet.

Letting her guide me to the cemetery? Suspicious, but possible. After all, she's done so much online research.

Even as I felt my career crumbling with each shovelful of dirt, I clung to a hope for closure. If I dug long enough, I would reach Elizabeth Allen's casket. I knew it in my gut.

Now, while officials arrive at the scene, while I watch them tape off the area, call in more experts, do all the things I've done so many times ... reality finds its way into my head. A brain worm infesting every inch of space.

"Tell the truth, Josie. No matter what they ask you, tell *your* truth. Tell them about your accident. The visions. The sleepless nights. The tree. Tell them about the unrelenting need to come here. Because if those remains belong to girls who were murdered well over a century ago, then you're not the killer. Tell them the truth, and let them deal with the rest."

She says nothing.

We reach the road, and they escort us to the back of a police cruiser. They have questions to ask, and we'll give them answers, even if they aren't going to like said answers. They will despise Josie's explanation, but they won't be able to formulate a better one. The unexplainable, sometimes "other-worldly" explanation for an event is something that haunts every investigator. We can't solve crimes without tangible proof, an eyewitness, or a confession that matches the crime.

On the way to the station, I reach for her hand and squeeze it, but she doesn't squeeze mine back. When we're questioned, she tells her truth, void of all emotion, and I tell mine. We're looked upon with skepticism because, after all, I'm a homicide detective from

Chicago, and she's a medical examiner. We came a long way to dig up the unsolved mystery from a crime that was committed way before anyone alive today was even born.

"Josie, you're going to have to talk to me," I say when we reach the hotel after being told to not leave town until they can question us more tomorrow.

She shuffles her feet into the room and stands at the window, staring out into the night. "What do you want to talk about?"

I don't know.

I have all the same questions as the police asked us tonight. I have all the same questions that they'll ask us tomorrow. She's not insane ... I mean, she found remains of bodies that were not in a casket. I don't know if they'll be able to identify the bodies, but they need to find an explanation better than Josie's for why the remains were there if we're not to believe her.

"I don't think you're mentally ill, insane, crazy ... whatever fucking word you want to use. I think this situation is what's crazy. It doesn't make sense in a way that my brain can comprehend."

"I know," she whispers.

I take a few more steps, standing behind her for several breaths before wrapping my arms around her, dipping my head to bring my lips close to her ear. "I love you, Josephine Watts."

With those words, she sucks in a breath and lets it out in a shaky exhale while wiping a few tears.

"Why do you think you were one of those girls? Does it feel like the only explanation?"

She eases her head side to side. "Because I felt it."

"Felt what?"

"The straight blade along my scalp. And ... the fear."

To be continued ...

ALSO BY
Jewel E. Ann

Standalone Novels

Idle Bloom

Undeniably You

Naked Love

Only Trick

Perfectly Adequate

Look The Part

When Life Happened

A Place Without You

Jersey Six

Scarlet Stone

Not What I Expected

For Lucy

What Lovers Do

ABOUT THE
Author

Jewel is a free-spirited romance junkie with a quirky sense of humor.

With 10 years of flossing lectures under her belt, she took early retirement from her dental hygiene career to stay home with her three awesome boys and manage the family business.

After her best friend of nearly 30 years suggested a few books from the Contemporary Romance genre, Jewel was hooked. Devouring two and three books a week but still craving more, she decided to practice sustainable reading, AKA writing.

When she's not donning her cape and saving the planet one tree at a time, she enjoys yoga with friends, good food with family, rock climbing with her kids, watching How I Met Your Mother reruns, and of course...heart-wrenching, tear-jerking, panty-scorching novels.

www.jeweleann.com

Made in the USA
Monee, IL
23 September 2022

14311009R00219